The River Rider

Also by Judy McGonagill

The River Rider

HEARTS OF TEXAS
BOOK TWO

JUDY MCGONAGILL

RISE UP
PUBLICATIONS

Book design by eBook Prep
www.ebookprep.com

March 2023
ISBN: 978-1-64457-599-4

Rise UP Publications
644 Shrewsbury Commons Ave
Ste 249
Shrewsbury PA 17361
United States of America

www.riseUPpublications.com
Phone: 866-846-5123

Chapter One

THE YEAR 1916, TEXAS

Her once pretty mass of reddish-blonde hair stuck together in sweaty strands matted about her pale, drawn face. Only a few years ago she had been youthful and pretty. Now with wrinkled skin and dark circles around her sunken eyes, no one would have guessed Hanna O'Donnelly was only thirty-six years old. Life had not been kind.

She labored to draw one more breath as she looked at her children gathered around her. She and most of her children realized it was for the last time. She studied their forlorn faces. How would they manage? Matthew was nineteen, a man now, and in the army. Matthew and Luke favored their father with the same black hair and emerald green eyes. He had been a handsome man, tall, and muscular for his slim frame. Ruth, Rachel, and Naomi took after her with their strawberry-blonde hair and aqua-blue eyes.

Ruth, now seventeen and a bride of three months, would have to step into her shoes as a mother to Rachel, now fourteen, Luke age twelve, and ten-year-old Naomi. That was an unfair burden to put on a new bride, but it was not one of her choosing. It was John Martin, Ruth's husband, that worried her. He was a decent sort, but she had witnessed his temper.

Hanna felt her life ebbing away, and try as she might, she could not hold back the end. She smiled and looked from one child to another. She hoped to etch in her memory every detail of her five remaining children to carry with her throughout eternity until they met again in Heaven. Then she closed her eyes to pray and slipped away.

The next day she was laid to rest in the paupers' section of the local cemetery, not near any loved ones that had gone before her but beside strangers. Her husband was buried two hundred miles north along with their nameless baby girl. Little Mark, only eight months old when he took a fever, lay in another cemetery some sixty miles away, also in a pauper's grave. None had headstones to mark their graves, and neither would Hanna Jones O'Donnelly. There was no money for such frivolous things. There had been so little money for living, and there was no money for death.

TWO YEARS LATER, 1918

Luke felt the lash of the horsewhip across his back. It bit into his flesh, which was only covered with a thin shirt. He bit back a wince.

"You should have had this barn clean by now," he heard his brother-in-law, John Martin, snarl as he drew back the whip to deliver another lash.

Fourteen-year-old Luke knew this would be the last lashing he would ever take from John Martin or any man. He was taller than John now and lots stronger from the endless days of grueling, hard work he was forced to endure for his vile, deplorable brother-in-law.

Anger and hatred boiled within his soul, threatening to overflow and choke him, as memories of the lustful glances John gave young

Rachel when he thought no one was looking flooded his mind. Luke grabbed the pitchfork leaning against a stall, whirled, and let out a roar, charging John like a raging bull, intent on impelling him against the wall of the old barn. Then he would watch with pleasure while John Martin's life ebbed away and his soul stepped into everlasting Hell.

John lunged sideways to avoid the strike, but not before Luke adjusted his aim, plunging the fork's prongs into John's upper thigh.

The man hit the dirt, yelling in agony as Luke yanked the pitchfork free and raised it to deliver the final blow.

Dislike had turned to distrust and then to hate. The loathing he felt for John had been building for two long years. Every lustful glance at his sisters, each lash of his whip, each kick of his boot, every curse shone bright in his mind's eye. Now it would be ended. Luke fully intended to kill John.

"No! Please, No!" John yelled. "Please, boy don't do it, don't kill me!"

Blood gushed around John's hand clamped around his thigh to pool in the dirt. But Luke could only see John eyeing little Naomi with that same lustful leer.

John knew he had worked the boy relentlessly because he could. He also knew he had taken advantage of Luke and his sisters because they were at his mercy. Now he was likely about to pay the ultimate price for what he had done.

If the law ever caught him for this, he would never be tried for murder. Too many people had witnessed John's abuse over the years. All he would have to do was plead self-defense.

The bastard slithered backward like the snake he was.

"I, I'll never strike you again, I promise!"

Luke trailed him, ready to strike the final blow.

"Luke, Luke, think of your sister. What will poor Ruth do with two babies and no husband? Surely you don't want to make her a widow with two babies to provide for."

The man's back hit the barn wall.

"I'll do anything you say, give you anything you want," John pleaded in a quaking voice.

Luke still held the pitchfork firmly, ready to thrust the final blow at any moment. When he heard John's last plea, he paused. Perhaps there was another way to rid himself and Naomi of the loathsome man.

"Give me three of your best horses, provisions for a week, and five hundred dollars." Luke had thought of asking for John's fine new automobile but knew it would be too easy for John to find them. Besides, with horses, they could cut through the countryside, making it much harder for him to send someone after them if he were so foolish.

"I'll take Naomi with me, and you can burn in Hell!" Luke snarled. "If you ever cross my path again, there will be no bargaining for your life. If I ever hear of you mistreating Ruth or those children, you will be shown no mercy. You will be begging me to use this pitchfork to end your sorry life before I'm through with you," Luke vowed as he glared at the piteous man lying in the dirt at his feet, now at his mercy.

"It's yours, it's yours," John breathed a deep sigh of relief, realizing his life had been spared. For an instant, he had no doubt his life hung in great peril. "Please, help me to the house," he begged as he reached out toward Luke.

Luke scoffed with laughter.

John could plainly hear the extent of Luke's loathing in his sardonic laughter. He could see the contempt in Luke's piercing green eyes as he looked down on him.

"Get to the house any damn way you can," Luke hissed as he turned to select the two horses he wanted for riding and the third for packing their belongings, which were meager at best. He saddled each horse with the finest saddles.

John still lay on the hard ground holding his leg and moaning from the almost unbearable pain. "How can I give you the money if you don't help me to the house?" he pleaded in agony.

"I'll tell Ruth you said to write a bank draft to me for supplies.

When Naomi and I leave, I'll tell her where to find her loving husband and just why you had a pitchfork stuck through your leg. If you try to send anyone to stop us, I'll kill him and come back for you," he stated emphatically.

John watched Luke and knew the young man of fourteen meant what he said. Yes, he was more of a man than a boy now. Well, good riddance. He could hire cheap labor but would likely need two men to do the work Luke had done. Ruth would need help in the house with Naomi gone. Damn it all, anyway! The two should be grateful he had taken them in. They needed to earn their keep. He knew Ruth would be hopping mad when she learned what had happened. Well, he'd just have to convince her it wasn't the way it seemed.

"Yes, indeed, she had an ungrateful brother and sister," John muttered to himself as he now lay in the silence of the barn wondering how long it would take Ruth or someone, anyone, to find him.

His life had been nothing but misery since he married Ruth. He had fallen in love with the pretty young woman with strawberry blond hair and twinkling blue eyes. Her figure was slim, with full breasts and rounded hips. She was most pleasing the first few months of their marriage. Then her ma died and dumped three young'uns on them. Her sister, Rachel, had been a pretty little thing too. He was itching to have her at least once, but she eloped with that Joseph Thomas before he could enjoy her pleasures. Naomi was coming of age and already snatched from his grasp too. Now he was left with Ruth to warm his bed. With each baby, she had gained weight and was no longer as appealing. Most of the time, he felt she tolerated his advances as any good wife was supposed to do. Maybe he could find a pretty young thing for a housemaid. He deserved some comforts in life for all he had put up with these past two years, he thought piteously.

~

"Ruth," Luke called as he bounded through the front door.

"Ssshhh, the babies are napping," he heard her say as she came to meet him.

"John wants you to write me a bank draft for five hundred dollars to buy supplies," Luke said.

"Goodness, why so much?"

Luke shrugged his broad shoulders. "Long list of stuff," he answered as Ruth wrote the draft and handed it to him.

Luke stood staring at the large amount of money and took satisfaction in knowing he and Naomi were about to be free. He felt a pang of guilt about leaving Ruth and the children at John's mercy. He raised his head and looked at his older sister.

"What I told you about the money isn't exactly true," he confessed.

"What do you mean?" Ruth asked, puzzled.

"I threatened to kill John and was about to run him through with the pitchfork when he begged me to let him live."

He saw Ruth's mouth gape open in shock.

"He hit me with that damn whip one too many times," Luke blurted out. "Besides the way he's treated me these past two years, I saw his lustful looks at Rachel before she married, and next he'll be after Naomi," he accused.

Ruth's face turned bright red with anger. She raised her shaking hands to cover it and began to sob.

"I'm going to take Naomi with me. We're going far enough that John will never find us. Don't worry, I'll take good care of Naomi," he said in a low, soothing voice. "You and the babies could come with us. Naomi could tend to them and we could find jobs," he suggested.

Ruth looked lovingly at her brother. "I'm so sorry, Luke. I had no idea John was mistreating you and lusting after my own sister," she said sadly.

"Come with us, we can make a go of it," he urged.

Ruth slowly shook her head. "I made vows for better or worse," she paused. "I better stay."

Luke hugged Ruth. "Don't let John mistreat you or the children," he cautioned.

"I won't," she answered. "Where is he?" she asked, letting out a deep sigh.

"In the barn holding his leg where I rammed him with the pitchfork," Luke smiled.

"Luke, it's getting dark. Where will we sleep tonight?" Naomi asked in a trembling voice. She looked about her but saw nowhere for them to hide from John.

Naomi felt nervous; butterflies started fluttering in her stomach. She knew Luke would take care of her, but yet, she was afraid of what might lie ahead. She was glad in a way to be away from John and Ruth's house. Ruth and the children were dear to her, but she didn't like or trust John. Lately, he had been trying to lure her to come sit on his lap or would put his arm around her and make it seem like an accident when he brushed his hand across her small budding breasts. It gave her the shivers whenever she found herself alone with him for even a few minutes. She had wanted to tell Ruth what he was doing, but she wasn't sure Ruth would believe her, and it would make her cry. Then she and John would argue and shout at one another. The children would get upset and cry, and everyone would be miserable. She had thought about telling Luke, but she was afraid of what he might do to John. Then things could become even worse. Yes, it was for the best they had left, she told herself as she gazed around, hoping to spot a safe place to bed down for the night.

"Stop worrying, Naomi. I know of a place up ahead where we can camp for the night. John certainly isn't going to follow us. I warned him if he sent anyone to try to stop us, I'd kill him and then come back for him," he said in a loathing tone.

Naomi felt the shock as his words washed over her. "Would you really kill him or anyone for trying to stop us?" she asked in dismay. She had never thought of Luke as being a violent person. Could it truly be his hatred for John ran so deep it would drive him to murder? Perhaps so, she reasoned. She knew full well the cruel treatment Luke had suffered these past two years. She had been more sheltered by her sister who refused to believe her husband did any brutal thing without just cause, but Naomi knew about John's unjust, vicious treatment of Luke.

"Please, Lord, let us get away without any bloodshed and protect us I pray. Amen," Naomi whispered.

Naomi had not attended church since their mother passed. She remembered the Bible scriptures their mother had read to them as children and had listened to her pray. Then she would teach them to say a prayer at bedtime. Naomi still prayed every night but often wondered if God really heard her prayers. Maybe other people had more urgent needs and God listened to their prayers first, she thought as they rode in silence.

John and Ruth lived fifteen miles from the nearest town, so they did not attend church. She and Ruth rarely ever went to town. All town business was taken care of by John or sometimes Luke or one of the hired men.

"Luke, do you think we can find jobs in a town? It would be nice to live in a town where there are lots of people and places to go," she said wistfully. A faint smile touched her attractive heart-shaped lips.

Naomi was like a butterfly emerging from its cocoon. She had always been a pretty child. Now she was emerging into an extraordinarily lovely young woman. Her long strawberry blonde hair lay in soft waves with the ends falling into soft curls. She had the same aqua-blue eyes as their mother, who had been a beautiful woman in her youth.

"Maybe, but not this town. We are going farther away, so we won't

be seein' the likes of John Martin," he answered. He knew he would
have to be especially watchful over Naomi as she aged. Men would
naturally be attracted to her unusual beauty. Luke feared some might
try to take advantage of her sweet nature to satisfy their own lustful
pleasure.

"How far will we go? Will we travel for days and days to get there?
Do you know the name of the place?"

Luke laughed at Naomi's seemingly endless questions.

"I don't know just yet, but we'll start asking about places with
plenty of work when we reach a bigger town tomorrow. Then we'll be
headed that direction," he told her with a smile. "There's the woods
just ahead," he pointed to a stand of trees near a creek. "That will do
for tonight. Don't worry, the horses will alert us if anyone comes
around, and I'm a light sleeper," he reassured her.

By late morning they were headed almost due south toward the
growing town of Abilene, Texas. Several men in the small towns had
told Luke that Abilene was building by leaps and bounds, and there
was plenty of work of all kinds for him and his sister.

"How many days did you say it is until we get to Abilene?" Naomi
asked again as she wiped the sweat from her eyes. The afternoon sun
beat down through her bonnet, and every stitch of her underclothes
was wet with sweat. She felt the layers of dirt covering her exposed
skin. The reddish film of dirt on her clothing was easy to see in the
sunlight.

"About three days at the most," Luke answered again. "We won't
reach the main road into Abilene until the last day's ride. Then we'll
see a few automobiles. In town there will be lots more. We'll have to
stay alert to keep these horses under control since they ain't been
around automobiles much."

"Just the one John bought a few months ago," Naomi answered, understanding Luke's warning.

"Do we have enough money to find us a room and get a bath before we go hunting for work?"

"Yes, I have some money, but we can't be spending it foolishly." He had not told her about the five hundred dollars, as he knew she would think they were rich and want to stay in nice hotels and so on. They had never had the money to stay in nice hotels and weren't going to flitter away the five hundred dollars on such frivolous things now.

"It will be cooling off in a couple of hours, and there is supposed to be a nice creek up ahead where we can camp. You can cool off in the water."

"Good, I'm about baked to a crisp," she said but not in a whining or complaining way like lots of girls seemed to do.

Late in the evening, they found the creek shaded by large cotton-wood and pecan trees that grew along the banks. It was noticeably cooler in their dense shade.

Luke found a suitable camping spot. Then he walked along the creek until he found a place Naomi and then he could bathe. The water wasn't clear as it carried the reddish color of the dirt, but it would be cool. They might come out a bit cleaner anyway, he thought as he retraced his steps.

Just after Naomi left for her bath Luke spotted two scruffy-looking men riding in. They gave Luke a friendly greeting as they dismounted and introduced themselves as Wayne and Buster Smithson.

The two men observed the three horses and Wayne inquired, "You travelin' with someone?"

"Yes, my sister."

"Where she be?" Buster asked as he looked around the camping area.

Luke felt a bit leery since he had just met the two men and didn't know what they might try. He didn't want to say she was bathing. "She just stepped into the brush for some privacy," he answered nonchalantly.

"Mind if we camp over yonder?" Wayne asked as he pointed to another clearing nearby.

"Not my land. I guess you can camp there if you want to," Luke answered, wishing they had gone somewhere else. He wouldn't get much sleep tonight with them nearby.

Naomi appeared from the nearby trees drying her hair on an old towel she had brought along.

"The water is really—," she stopped in mid-sentence when she saw the two strangers with Luke.

Wayne gave her a broad grin. "I'd bet you was gonna say really nice and cool." Luke noticed how his eyes roved over her but saw she was only a girl and quickly lost interest. Luke surmised he liked full-grown women that knew how to pleasure a man, and there was no need in causin' trouble over a measly kid.

Buster only nodded in her direction as though to acknowledge her presence but did not bother to speak.

"Where are you fellows from?" Luke inquired.

"We growed up on the high plains near Amarillo. Got damn, pardon girlie, tired of the cold winters where the North wind don't ever stop blowin'. Thought we'd check out Abilene. Hear tell there's plenty of town and ranch work goin' on there."

"That's where we're headed too," Naomi put in and then caught the look Luke was giving her. Then she realized she shouldn't have said where they were headed. Luke likely didn't want to have them as traveling companions for the next few days.

"That right, well we might as well travel along together," Wayne said with a cheerful smile.

"Come on, Wayne, let's get camp set up and go cool off in the creek before dark," Buster said as he started toward the other campsite.

When they were out of earshot, Naomi looked at Luke with regret showing on her face for telling them where they were going. "I'm sorry, Luke. I spoke before I thought about them wanting to travel with us. Please don't be mad at me."

"I ain't mad, but you need to be careful what you say."

Naomi thought for several minutes. "I know what we can do. In the morning I'll pretend to be sick and you can tell them to go on and maybe we'll catch up to them later," she said, hopeful that Luke would accept her suggestion.

Luke grinned at her. "You're pretty smart when you think before you speak," he told her with a slight grin.

The ploy Naomi had thought up worked. She moaned and bent over, holding her stomach and pretended to cry with pain.

When Luke told the two men to ride on, Buster looked at Naomi and commented with a note of sympathy for Luke. "Looks like you're stuck with a sickly sister. Likely her monthly curse comin' on. See you in Abilene." The brothers mounted up and were soon out of sight.

"How long should we wait?" Naomi asked as she watched Luke pour himself another cup of strong coffee.

"We better stay put till about noon. Waiting that long we won't likely catch up to them again. They might be all right, but we can't take a chance."

"Yes, I know. It's all my fault," Naomi answered with a tinge of regret in her voice.

"It's okay. I'd rather not travel with others no matter who they are."

Luke drank his coffee as he looked off in the distance contemplating their future. After a while, he turned his attention back to Naomi. "When we get to Abilene and start to look for jobs, I think we will have better luck if you say you're thirteen, and I am going to say I'm sixteen. People won't think of us as just kids if they think we are a bit older and might be more likely to hire us."

"That's not fair. You get to claim you're two years older, and I only get to claim one," Naomi said with a slight pout.

"I can pass for sixteen because of my height and build, but you aren't filled out enough to claim to be fourteen."

Naomi felt self-conscious knowing her brother had noticed she still looked more like a girl instead of a blossoming young woman. "I guess you're right," she conceded, ready to change the subject.

For three more days, they traveled on, enduring the relentless heat and constant wind that kicked up the red dirt that covered them. They rode for hours without a break. By the end of each day, they ate sparingly and soon collapsed exhausted on their blankets and slept.

Chapter Two

In the late afternoon of the third day they topped a rise and looked in awe at the sprawling city of Abilene.

Naomi gasped in panic at the site. She had never seen such a large expanse of structures where people lived, worked, and worshiped. They likely even had lots of schools, but she knew that would do her no good. She felt frightened as she looked at all of the houses and buildings stretched out before her. Naomi looked at Luke wide-eyed. "What if we get lost or get separated from one another? How will we ever find the other again in such a big place?" she asked with a tremor of alarm in her voice. "I don't think I'll like it here; it's too big. Please, Luke, let's go on and find a smaller town," she begged as her insides began to shake, and she couldn't stop the tremble in her hands as she clenched the horse's reins.

Luke was a bit shocked at his sister's reaction to the large town but could understand her fears. He felt slightly intimidated himself but didn't let it show. Naomi had hardly gone into the small town near the ranch, and never went anywhere without Ruth.

"It'll be okay, Naomi. We'll find a small rooming house and take a couple of days to look around together, so you won't feel so frightened," he smiled, trying to reassure her. Luke too was surprised at the size of the city but didn't feel the fear he knew Naomi felt. In fact, now that he had seen it from a distance, it had just the opposite effect on him. He saw opportunity to find a good job and new things to learn about for the future. Who knew, someday he may even own one of those sleek black automobiles he was beginning to see more and more as they rode into town. It was a place with a future free of the likes of John Martin and others like him. Oh, he wasn't a fool. He knew there would be some rough characters, but they wouldn't be mistreating him or his sister. Besides, in a town this size they were sure to have more lawmen to keep the peace, he reasoned.

"But what about when you go off to look for work? I won't know where you've gone. What if something happens to you? I won't know where to look for you," she stated as she became more agitated. Her blue eyes had grown larger as she gawked at her surroundings.

He realized how afraid Naomi was feeling, and he knew he would have to keep reassuring her until she became used to her new surroundings.

"Naomi, just calm down. I promise nothing bad is going to happen to me. I know how to take care of myself. Stop worrying so much," he answered in a stern voice. He couldn't let her become hysterical, or they might have to go elsewhere where there were fewer jobs and less pay.

"Come on, let's go find a place for tonight," he said as he nudged his horse forward and she followed.

They rode past little, shanty houses. The small yards seemed filled with children; chickens, a few pigs, and donkeys were running wild in the yards and street. A few scrawny dogs and cats roamed the area. Soon the houses became nicer and only a few children played in the larger, well-kept yards without barnyard animals. They entered the edge of the business district, and soon Luke spotted a small rooming house just off the main road. Pearl's Rooming House, the modest sign in the front yard of the two-story equally modest house read.

"We'll try this one," Luke said as he turned onto the side street.

They were met at the front door by Pearl, a middle-aged woman with her graying hair done up in a bun. Her plump face matched her round body. She greeted them with a pleasant smile. They could smell the aroma of food drifting toward the open door. Naomi's stomach gave a loud growl.

Pearl laughed when she heard the sound and ushered them inside. Before either could speak Pearl began her speech about the rooming house. "Rooms are eighty cents a day; bathing is an extra fifteen cents; I only serve breakfast and supper, which are forty cents each; so, most folks only pay a dollar and sixty cents a day, except when they take a bath."

The price sounded reasonable to Luke although he had little experience in the prices charged to stay in rooming houses or hotels. "We'll be needin' two rooms unless you have a room with two beds my sister and I could share."

Pearl looked them over for the first time. "I suppose she is a bit young to be your wife. Well, let's see. Yes, I do have the attic room that would be big enough for the two of you if you'll carry the beds upstairs yourself and pay for a week in advance," she looked at Luke as she spoke. "I don't normally rent it out. It ain't finished off with walls, just the open beams, but if it suits you, I'll hang a quilt to give you each some privacy and drop the price a bit."

"That sounds fine, Ma'am," Luke agreed as he reached in his pocket and counted out the week's rent. "Do you mind if we have some supper first and then we'll get settled? We'll each need a bath tonight."

Pearl smiled as she counted the money Luke had given her. "That will be just fine, Hon." Then she hesitated, "I don't recall you telling me your names," she said with a good-natured chuckle.

"I'm Luke O'Donnelly, and this is my sister, Naomi."

"How old are you?" she asked as she looked from one to the other.

"I'm sixteen and my sister is thirteen," Luke answered, knowing how Naomi hated to lie.

"Don't you two have any folks?" Pearl inquired as she led them to the dining room where several guests were already enjoying the evening meal.

"No, Ma'am. Our Pa and two young'uns passed a few years back, and our Maw and two more passed a few weeks ago, so it's just my sister and me." He glanced at Naomi for her reaction to his lie.

Naomi blinked with a startled expression but quickly regained her composure and did not give him away.

Naomi suddenly looked as though she might burst into tears. "Our Ma and two youngest sisters passed on my thirteenth birthday. I'll never like having birthdays again," she moaned with immense sadness reflected in her voice and continued to look as though tears were about to flow.

It was Luke's turn to be surprised at his sister's lie. My sister can be a little imp, he thought. What was she trying to do? Show him she could deceive people as good as he could or even better? Luke couldn't help but be shocked at Naomi's unexpected behavior.

Best people not know too much about them. He would have to warn Naomi to say as little as possible about their folks and stick to the story they had told even if it was a lie. Saying too much would likely get them tripped up in their own lies.

After breakfast, they walked for blocks exploring the area that made up the central business district. They passed all kinds of shops and occasionally Naomi would linger to peer at items displayed in the shops' front windows to lure in customers.

"If I could read and write better and knowed my numbers, I could get a job in one of these nice places. Look at all of those pretty ladies' dresses," she raised her head to peer at the sign over the door. "Gra-c-ie's Sh-op For La-di-es and Gir-ls," Naomi struggled to make out the words on the sign.

"Well, sister, I'm afraid you aren't likely to be workin' in one of these stores. Besides, you would only want to spend your money on pretty dresses that would be of little use to you."

Luke's statement stung a bit, but she knew he was right. She would forever be cleaning house for someone else and tending their young'uns. That was about all she really knew how to do well. But, how did she find such a job in a city where she didn't know anyone? Maybe Pearl would know of someone to hire her, she thought. They walked on through the streets that were becoming more crowded with folks on their way to work or shopping.

"Let's go over to the cattle pens near the railroad tracks. I heard one of the men at supper last night tell another they were hiring workers to load and unload the cattle from the trains."

The nearer they came to the cattle pens the less desirable the town became. There were plenty of bars, rundown houses, and boarding houses that looked far less desirable than Mrs. Pearl's. Several of the houses had women in scanty nightclothes lounging on the upper balconies. They all had dark eyebrows; their cheeks were painted pink and their lips bright red. As they passed several called out to Luke to ditch the kid and come up for a real good time. Then they would laugh as though they had made a funny joke. Somehow Naomi sensed these were not the kind of women Luke needed to be around.

Naomi kept her eyes straight ahead and whispered to Luke. "Let's go back to Mrs. Pearl's. I don't like it here."

Luke was wishing he hadn't brought his sister to this part of town too. It certainly wasn't a place for an innocent girl.

"Come on, we'll go back on another street. Maybe it will be nicer," he said as they turned the corner.

They had only gone a few paces when a drunk staggered out of a seedy-looking bar and bumped into Naomi, sending her sprawling into the street, landing with a hard thump in the dirt.

Luke instantly doubled up his fist as anger seized him. He was ready to land the fellow a few good blows when the man held up his hands in a sign of surrender.

"Hold it, young feller," the man slurred. "I didn't mean no harm to the girl. Just didn't see her in time when I opened the door."

Luke knew he was likely telling the truth.

The shabby, ill-smelling man staggered a few steps toward Naomi and reached out with his grimy hand. "Let me assist you up, young lady, and I do beg your pardon."

He was unusually polite for a drunk, Luke thought.

He reeked with the stench of alcohol and tobacco. His disheveled clothes were dirty and looked as though he may have been wearing them for quite some time.

"Keep your hands to yourself and step back," Luke snarled as he stepped between the man and Naomi. Keeping one eye on the man he gave Naomi his hand to assist her in standing.

She brushed the loose dirt from her dress and tugged at Luke's sleeve for them to go before there was more trouble.

They walked faster for several blocks and were soon back in the better part of town. Neither spoke. "Luke, please don't go back there lookin' for work," Naomi pleaded. "I'd be so worried about you with all of those, those, kind of people everywhere."

"Don't worry, sister, I can take care of myself. I made a mistake by taking you to that part of town. Now you know where to stay away from even if I get a job there. Don't be comin' to bring me food or for any reason. If you should need me, find some boy or man to come find me. Understand!"

"Yes, but surely there are better places to work."

"I'll look around but have to take the best-paying job I can find."

They walked on in silence, looking at a different set of shops on the street running parallel to the first street they had explored.

Naomi cleared her throat and gave Luke a quick look out of the corner of her eyes. "Luke, why were those women sittin' where people could see them dressed like that and callin' out to you?" she asked shyly.

Luke was a bit shocked by Naomi's question and certainly had never visited one of those places. However, he happened to know pretty much what went on there. He had overheard some of the ranch hands talking about such places they seemed to frequent on Saturday nights. But how in heck did he explain such a thing to Naomi?

"Well, well, Naomi. I ain't never been to one of those places, but from what I've heard the ranch hands say, it's a place where men go to play cards, drink a bit, and, and, look for a lady friend," he stammered. He could feel his cheeks grow warm from discussing such a topic with his sister and fervently hoped she didn't press the subject too far.

Naomi turned her head to fully look at Luke. "I ain't so sure those women were ladies. Real ladies don't go around lookin' like that and callin' out to strangers. I bet they are what Ruth and some of her friends called loose women. I ain't sure exactly what all that means, but I don't think they was very proper actin' like real ladies. Yep! I'll bet that's what they were, loose women," she finished, apparently satisfied with what she had figured out about the women.

Luke breathed a sigh of relief because he certainly wasn't going into any details about what he had heard the men say. Loose women might be a compliment compared to the things he had overheard.

After their walk around the part of town where they would likely find jobs, Luke saw no need to keep the horses, so he sold them within a few days. He did show Naomi where he hid the money in their room but emphasized it was only to be used in case of a real emergency.

Pearl gave Naomi several suggestions of places to go to look for work. The places she recommended were in the homes of the upper-class families of Abilene that usually employed several housemaids, and a few potential employers might need someone to care for young children.

On the third day, when Naomi was about to give up, Mrs. Margaret Newton, wife of one of the local bankers, hired her. Mrs. Newton was a tall woman. In fact, she was a good two inches taller than her average-height husband, Harold.

Mr. and Mrs. Newton seemed like an odd pair to Naomi. Mrs. Newton was a very poised, formal acting lady. She did not speak to any of the housemaids except Thelma, the head maid. Thelma then relayed her directions to the other maids. Mrs. Newton expected her instructions to be carried out immediately and to perfection. There was to be no unnecessary talking, and laughing was unheard of in the Newton household, except by Mr. Newton.

When Mr. Newton arrived home, he came in whistling and greeted each maid he encountered with a friendly smile and asked how her day had been. Of course, their answer was always, "Just fine, sir." To say otherwise would have meant an immediate dismissal by Mrs. Newton as soon as she learned they had given any other answer. Naomi wondered if Mr. Newton ever asked why some maid had suddenly gone. Likely not, she decided.

Naomi looked forward to six o'clock arriving so she could hurry back to Pearl's, where she could talk and laugh if she felt like it, and most evenings she was full of gossip to pass on that she had heard at the Newtons' house. Several afternoons a week Mrs. Newton seemed to have some type of entertainment or meeting, and the maids got an earful of the latest gossip.

Luke wasn't usually interested in the stories Naomi had to tell, but Pearl thrived on hearing every delicious morsel of the latest gossip. In a short time, Naomi felt at ease with Pearl as she shared the latest daily gossip with the older woman.

Luke finally landed a job at the cattle pens near the railroad. Naomi constantly worried about his safe return. He worked varied hours, so Naomi never knew when to expect him to return. She would often fret if he was too late in getting back to Pearl's.

Naomi felt a little better each time Luke reassured her he was fine and could take care of himself. Together they were making enough money to pay their room and board and put a little aside for that rainy day they heard people talk about.

Naomi found it hard to believe they had already been in Abilene for several months. In a way, it seemed much longer since they had left the farm. She missed Ruth and the children and wished she could hear from her and Rachel. Luke cautioned her about having anyone write a letter to Ruth or Rachel, as he still didn't trust what John might decide to do for revenge if he found out where they were.

Naomi didn't think much about it the first time she met Mr. Newton in the upstairs hallway and he gave her a brief hug. She thought he was just being kind, knowing how his wife treated the help. The second time, his hand slipped to her rounded hip where it lingered momentarily until they heard someone talking in one of the rooms. Naomi scurried away as quickly as possible and hoped it was just an accident that his hand had strayed where she felt it shouldn't be. His action reminded her of her brother-in-law, John Martin, trying to lure her to sit on his lap, and she didn't like those feelings.

Several weeks had passed with no further contact. Naomi had almost forgotten about Mr. Newton's little advances when one day she was bent over putting linens in the upstairs closet. Suddenly she felt an arm snake around her waist. Naomi gasped as she was pulled backward, pressing her backside hard against a man's front that obviously showed his desire. She instinctively knew it was Mr. Newton. She could feel his hot breath on her neck and recognized the unmistakable smell of stale tobacco on his breath. "Let me go," Naomi shirked. She tried to free herself by attempting to twist away from the arm that imprisoned her.

"Be still, you little fool!" she heard Mr. Newton's low, husky voice demand.

She was shocked at his forward behavior and certainly didn't intend to have him taking advantage of her in such a manner.

"If you don't let me go, I'll scream the house down, and I don't think you want your wife to find out about what you've been doing," Naomi threatened, meaning what she said. "If my brother finds out about what you've done, he'll come after you, and you won't like the way your face looks when he's finished with you!" Naomi hissed at him. She hoped her threat would scare him into letting go of her.

"Don't you threaten me, you little twit!" Harold Newton rasped. He gave her a fierce shove, banging the side of her face and shoulder hard against the doorframe.

The pain from the sudden blow swept through her entire body, making her feel queasy. She rubbed the side of her aching face and saw smears of blood on her fingers.

Harold Newton glared at her, showing no sympathy for what he had done. "Get out of here and don't come back until you've thought up a good story for what happened to your face," he murmured in a fierce tone.

As Naomi walked the eight blocks back to Pearl's boardinghouse, she wondered how she could explain the red mark along the side of her face that stung and throbbed. If Luke found out the truth, he would likely confront Mr. Newton and give him the beating of his life. Then she would lose her job, and they might have to flee again.

No, she would just say she had climbed on a chair to place some linens on the top shelf of the closet, and it slipped, causing her to fall and strike the door facing. Yes, that sounded likely. No one should question that story, she thought as she trudged along. She dreaded telling Pearl and especially Luke the lie. But it was for the best, she tried to convince herself.

When she opened the back door where she normally entered,

although they were paying guests, Pearl instantly saw the angry red welt along the side of her face.

"For goodness' sakes, child, what in the world happened to your pretty face?" Pearl exclaimed in near horror at her appearance.

Naomi repeated the story she had made up, and thankfully Pearl did not question what she said.

Pearl instantly dipped a clean white dishcloth in a pan of cool water and gave it to Naomi to hold to the side of her face.

Pearl started rummaging through the pantry searching for some ointment she kept on hand for all sorts of mishaps. After several minutes, she produced a bottle of thick yellow liquid and shook it vigorously.

"Hold that cool cloth on your face for about half an hour and then put some of this magic ointment on your face. By morning you'll be surprised at how much better it feels and looks," Pearl instructed.

"Thank you, Pearl. I think I'll go lie down until it's time for supper." No gossip session today, she thought.

"That's a good idea, Love. I'll call you when it's time to eat if Luke isn't here by then."

This was one time she rather wished he wouldn't return until after she had gone to bed for the night. Maybe by morning, he could hardly tell anything had happened to her face and wouldn't be too inquisitive.

Her wish was granted, although it still worried her to some extent when he hadn't returned by bedtime. She presumed he had to work late and would be along directly. She relaxed a bit as she drifted off to sleep knowing Luke wouldn't see her face until morning. There were no disturbing dreams to haunt her this night.

On some nights she had awful dreams that their brother-in-law was chasing after them with a dangerous gang of armed men. At other times she dreamed Luke had disappeared, and she was frantically searching for him up and down the streets of Abilene but could not find him. When she reached the street where the painted women lived, they were laughing and calling out, "Luke is mine, Luke is mine." She could see him standing on their balcony, but he would not come when she pleaded with him to come back to Pearl's with her. On those nights she would wake in a cold sweat and listen intently for the sound of his peaceful snoring on the other side of the quilt that separated their room.

Chapter Three

"Naomi," a hand shook her gently by the shoulder. "Naomi," the voice was louder and the shake more vigorous.

Naomi's eyes flew open to see, by the faint light of the old lamp, Pearl bending over her.

"Is it already morning?" Naomi asked in a startled voice.

"No, Love, it's the middle of the night. Two men just brought Luke home, and he's been beat to a fare-thee-well!" Pearl told her with a worried look as she puckered her lips and made a smacking sound.

"What happened?" Naomi asked in shock as she scrambled from her bed.

"The two men said a fight broke out at the loading pens, and the next thing they knew it had turned into an all-out brawl. Luke got knocked in the head with a board and fell into one of the cattle pens and was being stomped by scared cattle when these two managed to drag him to safety. They carried him to Doctor Fredrick's house, and he just come to long enough for them to bring him here."

~

It was quitting time, but the day's work wasn't finished. Luke knew they had to stay to finish the job no matter how tired they were. Two men working the next pen started quarreling. Each one blamed the other for not having the work finished.

Luke paid little attention to the two men cursing one another. It seemed every day words were exchanged between several of the men. Then he heard the sound of pummeling fists followed by the wrenching sound of a loose board being jerked from the side of the pen. Luke stepped up on the bottom rail for a better look at the fight. Instantly he felt the hard smack of a board smash into the left side of his head. Then he felt himself falling and falling, as though in slow motion, toward the cow pen full of cattle. Darkness overtook him.

Luke awoke to some man asking him his name and where he lived. The pounding in his head felt like someone was using it for a drum. He ached from the top of his head to the bottom of his feet. His skin stung as though someone had tried to skin him.

With great effort, Luke murmured his name and finally was able to tell the man he lived at Pearl's Boarding House with his sister.

"He's coherent enough to go home now, but tell his sister to keep a close watch on him. I'll be by sometime tomorrow afternoon to check on his progress," the doctor told the two men.

Then Luke heard Buster and Wayne say they would take him home if they could borrow the doctor's buggy.

He had been surprised to meet up with the two brothers again when he went to work at the stock pens near the railroad tracks. They had developed a close friendship during the past months. When they started home from work, he walked with them to their room in a seedier part of town. They had suggested he and his sister move there as the rent was cheaper, but Luke had refused to put Naomi in that part of town.

Naomi had put her hands over her mouth to hold back her scream of terror as she listened to Pearl.

"Put on your wrapper. They're bringing him up to his bed," Pearl told her as she turned toward the door.

Pearl motioned to the two men to bring Luke up the narrow stairs.

Maneuvering the tight passageway up the stairs proved to be no easy task. Buster and Wayne tried to move as carefully as possible, but it was impossible not to jostle Luke as they bumped against one wall or the other.

When the two men struggled past Pearl, who was holding the lamp high to light their path, Naomi instantly recognized the two men they had met on their journey to Abilene. Luke had told her about meeting up with them again and had said they seemed to be decent fellows.

Luke awoke briefly as the two men carried him up the stairs to his own bed. Every step they took sent excruciating pain through his body. It was a blessed relief when the darkness overtook him once again.

Naomi approached her brother's bed and looked in dismay at his bandaged head. Scrapes and bruises covered his body, and a row of stitches was neatly holding a long gash in his left forearm together. He only wore his pants that were filthy and ripped in numerous places. His left ankle was bound with a clean white bandage.

"It's a wonder he came out as good as he did," one of the men said as he watched Naomi and Pearl assess Luke's condition.

"Wh—what did the doctor say?" Naomi's voice trembled with fear.

"He has a concussion and you need to keep a close watch on him to be sure he's breathing good and will wake up when you call him or give him a gentle shake. The Doc thinks his ankle has a bad sprang. Doc said he needs to be kept clean so he don't get any infections in the wounds. He was in the cow pen, and well, you know that's pretty dirty," the man said with a slight chuckle.

The other man spoke up. "Doc said he'd be around sometime tomorrow afternoon to check on him."

Naomi turned her gaze to the two men. "We met you on our way here. I'm sorry, I can't recall your names."

"I'm Buster Smithson and this is my brother, Wayne," the one who had done most of the talking answered.

"Oh, yes. How can I ever thank you for taking care of Luke and bringing him home?" she asked with genuine gratitude.

"No need. I think he would have done the same for one of us," Buster answered.

"Well, you could invite us for a good home-cooked meal some-time," Wayne ventured.

Buster gave his brother a scathing glare.

"Ma'am," Wayne spoke up again. "Would you like us to take those ragged pants off and wash him off a bit before we head out?"

"Oh, yes, that would be most helpful. I'll get a clean pair of under-drawers for him if you don't mind. I'm sure those are dirty too," Naomi said with a slight blush.

Pearl looked at Naomi. "Go bring us a pan of water and a rag. I'll help clean him up," Pearl said as she set the lamp on a small table near the bed.

The two men tried to hide their smiles as they exchanged a brief glance.

Pearl caught their exchange out of the corner of her eye. "I'm forty-eight years old and seen it all so don't go looking funny about things. It's for sure it ain't proper for his sister to do such a task," she scolded.

"Yes, Ma'am, you're right about that. What happened to her face?" Wayne asked as they undressed Luke.

It took Pearl a few seconds to realize he was asking about Naomi. "Oh, she climbed on a chair to put away some linens on the top shelf at work. The chair slipped and when she fell, she hit the door facing. She works for Mr. and Mrs. Newton; he's President of the Bank of Abilene."

Pearl insisted the two men come the next evening for supper.

Naomi was glad, as she doubted they would have come if it had just been her inviting them to dinner.

Naomi lay listening to Luke's light snore and realized she had to keep her job at the Newton's now that Luke was hurt and couldn't work for a while. She would go early in the morning and tell Thelma she would have to be off a couple of days until Luke was better but would be back to work in two or three days. Hopefully, Mrs. Newton wouldn't fire her for missing a few days to tend to her brother.

Naomi also understood she would have to avoid any more encounters with Mr. Newton. She couldn't take a chance on giving him any opportunity to press her into doing something she knew to be wrong, no matter how badly she needed to work. She also knew the upper crust passed gossip about their hired help to one another. If she lost her job it would be hard to find another job, especially one that paid as well.

Chapter Four

B y Monday morning Luke was wide awake and out of sorts because he was mostly still confined to his bed. It was hard to manage the steep stairs, so Naomi had carried his meals up to him. Thankfully, by Sunday afternoon, he was able to maneuver the steep steps with the aid of a pair of crutches the doctor had left. After dinner, he sat for a while visiting with some of the men boarders. When he returned to their room, he assured Naomi he could manage well enough for her to return to work. He, too, realized it was important for her to work while he was forced to wait until he healed enough to handle the rough work at the cattle yard.

While Naomi was away Luke wondered if he should confide in her about where he had put the bulk of the five hundred dollars he had gotten from their brother-in-law. She still wasn't even aware he had money besides the little they had managed to save after arriving in Abilene. If something happened to him, she would likely give his coat to someone not knowing there was money sewn into the lining. Yes, he better tell her, he finally decided.

Luke remained downstairs for a short while after supper visiting with some of the men before climbing the stairs to the attic.

He sat on his bed and breathed a deep sigh realizing he was getting stronger each day but knew it would take many more days before he could go back to work.

"Naomi, there's something I need to tell you," he said as he listened to her moving about on the other side of the hanging quilt getting ready for bed.

"Yes, what is it?"

"You remember when we left John and Ruth's place, I stopped at the bank when we passed through town?"

"Yes, I remember," she answered.

"Well, I had gotten some money from John. In fact, I got five hundred dollars," he said, knowing full well he would have to confess what had taken place in the barn between him and John.

Naomi stepped to the end of his bed and stared at her brother with her mouth slightly agape. "How in the world did you manage to wrangle that much money out of him?" she asked in obvious dismay.

"He came at me with that damn horsewhip, and I had finally reached the end of my rope. I had already decided I wasn't going to let him or any man whip me again. I ain't no farm animal that needs lashing to do my job. I'd worked from morning to night and sometimes into the night for a roof over my head and little else. I picked up a pitchfork and charged him, fully intending to run it clean through his wicked heart. He jumped out of my way, but I managed to ram it into his leg and cripple him," Luke now spoke through clenched teeth as he remembered the anger John had provoked in him.

"Oh, Luke," Naomi whispered, sensing the pain her brother had suffered at John's hands. Strange, she thought, Luke had never said a word to Ruth or likely anyone else about John's cruel treatment. He had just endured it in silence, all the while seething with anger and hatred on the inside.

Luke took a few deep breaths to calm his nerves before he continued. He looked at his sister. "I knew he would be after you soon after

Rachel married. I'd seen his evil-hearted glances at her when he thought no one was watching. That's why I brung you with me. I wasn't about to let him get to you. If he had, I'd have killed him for sure," he finished with some relief.

"While he was rolling around in the dirt, like the low-down jackass he is, moaning and begging me to help him to the house, I told him I wanted three horses, the money, and provisions for several days. He readily agreed, to save his sorry skin," Luke paused. "I kept out ten dollars for our trip and the rest is sewed in the lining of my winter coat."

"Luke, why didn't you tell me before? Didn't you trust me?" Naomi asked, obviously hurt to think her brother didn't trust her.

"Oh, Naomi, I trust you. I was just afraid you'd think we was rich and want to stay in nice hotels and buy things you ain't ever had. I likely would have let you have your way if you'd put pressure on me. You're my little sister. I need to take good care of you," he finished, and Naomi could hear his love for her reflected in his voice and see it equally as plain on his handsome face.

"You have taken good care of me, Luke. You are a good brother and really all I have, that I can depend on until I'm old enough to marry. I don't want you to waste any money on me. I have all I need," she said with true understanding.

Luke looked at her and gave her a slightly crooked smile as his green eyes sparkled. "It wouldn't be a waste exactly. I have been making plans, and we need that plus any more money we can manage to save."

"What plans?" she asked as she sat on the end of his bed and continued brushing her long golden blond hair until it shimmered in the lamplight.

"I've learned a lot about ranching and especially about breaking and training horses. I'd like to get about a hundred or so acres and raise really fine cutting horses. All ranchers need good trained cutting horses. I think I could make us a good living doing that. To buy the land, build some sort of small house to start, a barn, pens, and get some good stock horses will take more than the money we have now. We'll need some money to live on, too, till I can really get the business going good," he said. A dreamy look lit his face as though he were seeing it as he talked.

Naomi felt she could see Luke's dream, too. A small house, all their own, where nobody would bother either of them.

"Luke, what would I do besides keep the house clean and cook? That wouldn't take much time," she asked. Naomi felt afraid that wouldn't be her fair share of the work.

"Well, I expect you'd need to raise a garden and can up some food for winter. We'll get some chickens and a milk cow. Don't worry, sister, once we get started there'll be plenty to keep you busy."

"Have you thought about where this is going to be?" she asked, eager to hear more details about their future home.

"Not just yet. I've been talking to the men that work the cattle pens about where they've been, the ranches they've worked on, and the land. From what I've learned so far, I'm thinking farther south, but first, we've got to work and save as much money as we can."

Now Naomi felt even more pressured to keep her job at the Newtons', and she wasn't about to tell Luke about what Mr. Newton had tried to do to her. She'd just be careful to stay out of his way, and maybe there wouldn't be any more trouble, she hoped as she rose to return to her own part of their room.

"How much longer will it take us to have enough money?" she asked as she lay in her bed thinking about their future.

"I ain't real sure about that just yet either," Luke answered. "The more folks I talk to the better idea I'll get about how much all that's gonna cost. Don't be frettin'. I'll tell you as soon as I know."

They both lay looking into the darkness trying to see a brighter future.

Luke broke the silence. "Say, Naomi, aren't you about to have another birthday soon?" Luke asked.

"You know I am. It's next week. I'll be thirteen, well, fourteen to other folks," she answered with a slight laugh.

Luke chuckled too. "You getting to be on old lady already. Maybe I could spare a little change to buy you some small trinket for your thirteenth birthday," he teased.

"No, keep the money for our future. That's lots more important than any trinket."

"Now don't you sound all grown up," Luke laughed and promptly fell asleep.

Naomi lay awake for a long time contemplating how she could be certain to keep her job at the Newtons'. After much thought, she settled on a plan she hoped would work.

As Naomi walked to the Newtons' the next morning, she went over and over her plan in her mind so she would be ready when the right opportunity presented itself.

At 5:00 p.m., Naomi, with feather duster in her hand, climbed the back stairs off the kitchen that led to the second floor. She walked down the long hallway to the far end of the opulent house. She entered the library that also served as Mr. Newton's office at home. The two interior walls were covered with bookshelves from the floor almost to the twelve-foot ceiling. Numerous books bound in rich leather with mostly gold lettering on the back spine filled most of the shelves. Intermittently placed among the books were intricately carved, decorative statues of horses and dogs. There were also some crystal vases placed on the shelves, which to Naomi's untrained eye looked a bit out of place. The dogs and horses were mostly cast in bronze or pewter.

In front of the north windows was a long library table with ornate trim around the top and S-shaped legs. It was the same deep, rich color as Mr. Newton's huge desk. An electric lamp with a rounded burgundy base displaying delicate white roses and a white rounded top globe sat in the middle of the long, narrow table. Flanking each side of the table were two plush armchairs covered in deep burgundy velvet material. Naomi supposed this must be where the Newtons sat to read, as there was usually one of the fine books lying on the table beside each chair.

Mr. Newton's large mahogany desk was placed with the chair back toward the east windows. He could easily swivel around to see up and down Pine Street, the main thoroughfare, from the north edge of town leading past their house south toward the central business district.

Naomi had observed the Newtons were creatures of habit. They followed the same routine on the days they dined at home and were not entertaining, which was a couple of times a week. On those evenings Naomi worked late but was paid for her extra time. That was incentive enough to have extra money to add to their savings.

Most days, Mr. Newton arrived home precisely at 5:20 p.m. He would go to his bedroom, take off his suit coat and tie, unbutton his top collar button, and walk down the hall to the library.

At 5:25 p.m., Mrs. Newton, not one of the maids, would bring two sparkling crystal glasses filled with a deep red wine sitting on a silver tray and enter the library, closing the door behind her. They were not to be disturbed unless it was a dire emergency, of which none had happened since Naomi had come to work for them.

The two would emerge promptly at 6:00 p.m. and enter the formal dining room. He would seat Mrs. Newton at the foot of the long table that could easily seat twenty people and then be seated at the head of the table. Thelma would appear with their evening meal and serve each from the sideboard. After the Newtons had finished their meal, in virtual silence, they would each amble to whatever room of the huge house they chose, rarely being the same room, and eventually make their way to their separate but adjoining bedrooms and retire for the evening.

Mr. Newton arose early and left promptly at 7:30 a.m. for the bank with Frank Brown driving him in the new Packard automobile. Frank would return to the Newton home to await any instructions from Mrs. Newton for the day until time to pick Mr. Newton up at the bank at closing time.

Margaret Newton usually arose around 9:00 a.m., depending on her day's agenda. Some days the servants did not see her until almost noon.

Naomi liked this room most of all in the lavish house. Although all of the rooms were beautifully furnished and decorated with lovely lamps, exquisite vases filled with fresh flowers of the season, huge mirrors with decorative wide gold frames, and beautiful landscape paintings also in sumptuous gold or wood frames, this room had a cozy feeling about it. Naomi wished she could read better so she could ask to borrow one of their many books. Surely, they wouldn't refuse such a request, or would they, she wondered.

At the appointed time she heard Mr. Newton's footsteps approaching the library. She had been running the feather duster over the shelves on the south wall where the door was open partway concealing her presence. The smell of Mr. Newton's tobacco filled the air, practically making her start coughing. He was almost to his desk when he became aware someone was in the room.

"So, you're back. Did you have a story ready for Mrs. Newton to explain the mark on your face?" he asked in an unpleasant tone as he scrutinized her appearance.

"I didn't need a story," she answered and turned her face so he could see there was scarcely a pink mark showing on her creamy, smooth skin.

"Good, I guess you weren't so bad off after all," he said as he sat down at his desk, swiveling his chair so he could look out the windows.

Naomi counted slowly to ten. Then she burst into loud giggles.

"Oh, Mr. Newton, now you stop that; it tickles!" she screeched and continued to giggle louder.

Harold turned and stared at Naomi as though she had gone daft. Before he could say anything, she let out another peel of uproarious chuckles and almost screamed with delight, "Now you stop that, you silly man, that tickles there too!"

Harold glared at her with a furious frown on his face. As he rose from his chair, he continued to stare at her, wondering what had brought on this peculiar behavior. An eerie feeling of uneasiness came over him, which led to a strong feeling she was up to something. Harold glared at Naomi as though he would like nothing more than to strangle her. Then a dawning expression crossed his face. Suddenly, he understood she was up to something he most assuredly was not going to like.

Before he could move toward her, she bolted from the room still giggling. She pulled up short just before slamming headlong into Margaret delicately balancing their wine glasses on the silver tray.

Naomi paused briefly and looked into Margaret's startled face. Naomi gave her a big impish smile. "Better watch the Mr. today; he's in a feisty mood," she said as she brushed past Margaret. She ran down the hall still shrieking with laughter. After she heard the library door slam, she slowed her steps and could hear shouting coming halfway down the long hall even with the door closed.

Naomi swiped at the beads of perspiration that covered her forehead with the back of her sleeve. She breathed a deep sigh of relief thankful that, so far, her plan was working as she had planned.

Naomi entered the kitchen door five minutes early and donned her white apron and maid's cap. As she came into the kitchen, she heard Thelma and Clarisse, one of the other two maids, whispering. When they heard Naomi's footsteps they turned, and Thelma motioned her to join them.

"Watch your step today," Thelma warned. "The Mrs. is already up and in a foul mood for sure."

Naomi acted surprised at that news, although she strongly suspected she may well be the reason, or part of the reason, for her rising so early and being in a snit. Mrs. Newton had never been up this early since she had started working here.

"What's happened?" she asked with obvious curiosity and wondering if it really did have something to do with her.

Thelma shook her head from side to side and frowned slightly. "I don't rightly know, but they had a big free for all before dinner last night."

Naomi looked puzzled. "What's a free for, what did you say?"

"A big row the likes of which I ain't never heard 'afore," Thelma stated with another shake of her head. Her normally pleasant face bore deep lines in her forehead as she frowned, perplexed.

"It happened just after you left. I was here in the kitchen finishin' their dinner when I heard the loud yellin', and next thing I knew they were comin' down the back stairs instead of the main stairs. They never use the back stairs! Well, anyway, they were yellin' and screamin' at one another like two alley cats in a fight to the finish. Mr. went out that back door and slammed it so hard I thought sure it was gonna fly off its hinges! She stood on the bottom step just watchin' him go. Then she turned to me and just cool as you please said, "Cancel dinner."

"Oh, my," Clarisse murmured as she raised her hands to both cheeks. It was plain to see her expression of dread because of what was going on.

Naomi looked from one to the other. "You didn't understand what they was yellin'?"

"I did make out her tell him to go find him a, well, you know what kind of woman, and leave her and her maids alone. Did he do anything to either one of you?" Thelma asked suspiciously.

Naomi felt her chest tighten as though she couldn't breathe. Should she really confide in Thelma and Clarisse about what Mr. Newton had tried last week and what she had done yesterday? She didn't want to put either of them in a position to get them into trouble or fired.

Clarisse looked down and then up with a slight blush touching her pretty, round face. "Several weeks ago, the Mr. caught me cleaning the upstairs washroom and tried to touch me," she tucked her head again in embarrassment.

The two women waited, but she seemed to not want to explain further what had happened.

"I need to know what goes on around here since I'm the head maid," Thelma said kindly and put her arm around Clarisse's shoulder to encourage and soothe her.

"First he tried to touch my breast," Clarisse hesitated again. "I pushed his hands away, and then he grabbed my behind and tried to pull me to him. I raised my knee and, well, you know where I kneed him," she finished with a slight smile. "That made him let go, and I dashed out of the room." She looked apprehensively at Thelma to see if she was in for a scolding for what she had done.

"Good for you! Don't neither one of you put up with his ugly ways!" Thelma stated emphatically.

Then Thelma turned her gaze to Naomi. "What about you, Miss?"

Naomi cleared her throat. "Last week he caught me in the upstairs linen closet and grabbed me from behind. He pressed his lower body against my backside and let out a moan. I tried to get free, and in the tussle, he pushed me hard and smacked the side of my face against the doorframe. It made an ugly red mark down the side of my face. When I got to the boarding house, Mrs. Pearl gave me a cool cloth and some sticky, yellow ointment to put on it, and by the next morning, it was almost gone. That was the night they brought Luke home hurt really bad. I was dreading to tell him what had happened for fear of what he might do to Mr. Newton. By the time he was conscious enough to look at my face it hardly showed, so I just said I accidentally scratched it on a low-hanging tree branch while walking home."

"Is that what you told Mrs. Pearl?"

"No, I told her I had climbed up on a chair to put linens in the closet. The chair slipped, making me fall hitting the door frame," Naomi answered.

Thelma shook her head and looked a bit dismayed. "Lands sakes, don't you know if you gonna lie, you tell the same lie to everybody?" she asked a bit exasperated. "Now what if Mrs. Pearl or Luke says something to the other about what happened to your face?" Thelma shook her head as though she was amazed at how naive the young could be.

"I didn't think about that, but you're right. I should think things through better before I say anything," Naomi confessed, feeling a bit foolish at her own inexperience.

"Now if Mrs. Newton asked either of you about what the Mr. has been up to, you answer her honest," Thelma advised with a serious expression.

"But she'll fire us, and I really need this job," Clarisse protested first.

"Me too," Naomi joined in.

"If you stick together, I don't think she will. She don't want no bad gossip goin' around about the Mr., so I think she'll not do it. Especially after what I heard her yell at him last evening."

"What about Maggie? Has he ever bothered her that you know about?" Clarisse asked.

Thelma gave a short snorting laugh. "No, child, she's too old and ugly for even him to be after. It's you pretty young ones he wants, so watch out."

Just as Thelma finished that statement, they heard Mrs. Newton ring the bell for service.

Thelma wiped her hands on her apron and straightened her maid's cap as she left the kitchen. She returned in a few minutes looking grim.

"She wants to see you," she nodded to Naomi, "in the library. Just remember, be honest. And don't be timid about it," she emphasized with a vigorous nod of her head.

Naomi trudged up the back stairway and down the long hall to the library. The door was closed so she knocked softly.

"Come in," came Margaret's familiar but expressionless voice.

Margaret was seated in one of the plush chairs beside the reading table.

"Come have a seat," she indicated the chair on the other side of the library table.

Naomi felt uncomfortable sitting on such an elegant and expensive chair. The maids never sat on any of the chairs, only in the kitchen where rickety wooden chairs surrounded the scarred table where they ate their meals.

Nonetheless, she did as Mrs. Newton had instructed. She did not lean back as Mrs. Newton was sitting but perched on the outer edge with her back straight.

Margaret stared at her for what seemed like an eternity but was actually only a few moments.

"I understand my husband has acted rather inappropriately with you as of late," she stated, still in her impassive manner.

Naomi could not bring herself to look at the woman so she looked down at her own hands, clasped tightly together, trying to will them to relax.

"Yes, Ma'am," Naomi answered in as strong of a voice as she could muster.

"I won't embarrass you or myself by asking for details of his inappropriate actions but do want to emphasize whatever happened is to never, never," she stressed, "be spoken of to anyone, and that includes the other maids."

Oh, if she only knew that was just what they had been talking about, she would have a holy tantrum fit, Naomi thought as she listened to what Margaret had just said.

"Do you clearly understand me?" Margaret asked in her arrogant tone.

Naomi turned slowly in her chair and looked directly into Mrs. Margaret Newton's solemn face.

"Yes, Ma'am, I do understand you perfectly well. I will tell you this though. If Mr. Newton ever, ever, tries anything else with me, I will put on my pretty new Sunday dress and present myself at the next Sunday morning service at the First Baptist Church. When the minister asks for folks to stand up and testify about their sins and ask for forgiveness from God and their fellow Christian brothers and sisters, do you know what I'm going to do?"

A look of sheer horrific terror crossed Margaret's normally stoic face. She sucked in her breath, as though in anticipation of never breathing normally again, as she prepared for what Naomi was about to say.

"I am going to stand right up and say how sorry I am that my body, that the good Lord blessed me with, is such a temptation to my boss that he can't seem to control his male passions when he's around me. Yes, Ma'am! That is exactly what I am going to do! Now if you don't want anyone to know about your husband's downfalls, you better warn him that if he bothers me again the whole world is going to know all about his sins!"

Margaret stared at Naomi. She seethed inside but could not find the proper words to rebuff the young woman. As Margaret studied Naomi, she saw a strength she had not noticed before and begrudgingly admired her grit.

Naomi rose and walked, with her shoulders back, toward the door.

As Margaret watched Naomi prepare to leave, she quickly realized she must regain control of the situation. "If you ever do such a despicable thing to embarrass us in public, you will NEVER work in Abilene again as long as you live!" Margaret screeched as Naomi reached for the doorknob.

Naomi slowly turned and looked at the deflated woman and knew with satisfaction she had undermined her self-righteous confidence.

"It's likely your husband never will either," she stated calmly and closed the door softly as she went out.

Chapter Five

T wo weeks after Luke was hurt, he was finally ready to return to work. He felt like a bird let out of a cage. It felt good to walk through the early morning quiet streets just before daybreak.

Poor Naomi had seemed a bit strained lately, and he felt certain it was because all of her pay was going to pay for their room, food, and his doctor bill. There was none left over for their savings, but he had assured her once he started working again things would change. At present they had five hundred and thirty-three dollars. Now their savings would grow, although it might not be fast enough to suit them.

Naomi spoke often about their dream of owning their own place and a small house all their own. He knew she didn't especially like working for the Newtons. They were uppity rich folks who made people like them feel far less than they really were.

He didn't like anyone making his sister feel beneath him or her, no matter who they were. He paid little attention to others' attitudes toward him, but he knew what other people thought bothered Naomi.

He whistled softly as he walked along. Suddenly he remembered tomorrow was his fifteenth birthday. Well, seventeenth to everyone but Naomi. He might mention it to Buster and Wayne. Maybe they could stop off for a hamburger at a cafe on their way home to celebrate.

At the end of the day, Luke did mention his birthday to his two friends.

"So, you'll be turnin' seventeen tomorrow," Wayne said in his usual jovial manner as he playfully slapped Luke on his back.

"Yeah, getting on up there I suppose," Luke answered with a grin.

"Oh yeah, up there towards manhood," Buster put in. "I think it's time you become a proper man," Buster said as he and Wayne exchanged a knowing glance.

Luke knew Buster was already twenty and Wayne was eighteen. He supposed they naturally thought of him as "the kid," kinda like a younger brother.

"What do you mean a proper man?" Luke asked a bit puzzled. Buster's statement left him with an uneasy feeling he couldn't quite figure out.

Wayne and Buster both started chuckling and then burst into laughter.

"Boy, don't you know nothin' about becomin' a man?" Wayne questioned as he playfully slapped Luke on his back again.

"Didn't they have any girls where you come from?" Buster asked, still grinning.

Luke felt a bit shocked to realize it must be obvious he didn't know much about girls or women.

"Sure, they had some girls, but I didn't have time to get to know any of 'em. All I did was work from mornin' till dark or later for my sorry boss!" Luke grumbled, letting his bitterness at the memory show. He didn't mention it had been his own brother-in-law. The less people knew about his and Naomi's background the better, he believed.

Wayne and Buster looked at one another with an expression of sympathy for Luke.

"Well, it's time to change things. By the time most fellows are seventeen they've had some fun, you know what I mean," Buster told Luke with a mischievous glint in his brown eyes.

Luke swallowed hard. It had just dawned on him what the two were talking about. He had to admit he had stolen a few glances at the painted women, lounging on the balconies in their scanty clothing, as he walked home from work, but it had never seriously entered his mind to try what they were offering.

Luke laughed. "No, no, I ain't spendin' my hard-earned money on them women we see on the way home! Besides, I know enough to know you can catch stuff you don't want from their kind."

Buster looked more serious. "You're right about that for sure. Well, I guess we'll have to do with a couple of beers and let you find your own gal."

"Sounds good to me," Wayne put in. "I'm ready for a beer any day after wrestlin' those ornery cows." Then he gave Luke another good-natured slap on the back. "I'd likely be too tired to wrestle one of them upstairs fillies myself," he said with another laugh.

Luke felt relieved at them not insisting he try one of the women or, worse, offering to pay for him a good time for his birthday. Of course, he was as curious about women as any young man but not those women. He expected in time he would find a nice girl to marry and learn about women the proper way. Their ma had taught them to respect others if you wanted to be respected. He figured that went for women too, especially when it came to being close like married folks.

The weather was turning a bit cooler as mid-October arrived, which was a pleasant change from the sweltering summer heat.

Luke had made several more friends at the cattle pens and continued to ask questions about where they had worked and the cost of land where they had come from. More and more he believed he would do well to move farther south, maybe to what they called the hill country. There were big ranches that he could supply with good quality cutting horses. He figured by next spring they would have enough money to move to a place called Bandera. One of the men said it was about thirty miles west of San Antonio, and the land was reasonable in price. He also said the grass was plentiful and most had a spring or river for a good water supply.

He would wait a while longer to mention this plan to Naomi. He knew she longed for their own place and would likely be after him for them to just go there and get jobs. That might be all right but the man that told him so much about the area said it was a very small town, so jobs might be harder to find. No, they would wait until spring he decided.

By then they could spare enough money for train tickets to San Antonio and then on to Bandera.

Chapter Six

All had gone well at the Newtons' after her talk with Mrs. Newton. Naomi avoided both of them, and it was obvious they avoided her, which suited her just fine.

Soon Naomi, Clarisse, and Mary became good friends. Naomi was excited to finally have the opportunity to attend church with her new friend, Clarisse, and her large boisterous family. She felt grateful and blessed when Thelma gave her two new dresses to wear in addition to her only nice dress. On most Saturday afternoons, they would meet at the soda fountain located in the Woolworth's Department Store and laugh and talk about their jobs and eye the cute guys that might also be hanging out at the soda fountain.

One Saturday, one of the young men she had exchanged several shy glances with approached their table. He had slightly wavy blond hair and striking blue eyes. He stood about five feet ten inches in height and looked rather muscular. She did notice his hands were not rough like Luke's, so perhaps he worked in a store, she surmised, as he smiled particularly at her.

"Good afternoon, ladies," he greeted them with a charming grin that revealed smooth white teeth.

"Hello," the three girls responded almost in unison.

"Please allow me to introduce myself. I am Arthur McGill. All of my friends call me Art, and I hope you will do the same."

The three young women giggled and, again in unison, said, "Hello, Art."

"May I join you for a few minutes?" Art asked as he placed his hand on the back of the empty chair at their table.

"Sure," Clarisse invited.

"May I inquire as to each of your names?" he asked pleasantly.

"I'm Clarisse Jones."

"I'm Mary Thomas."

"I'm Naomi O'Donnelly."

"My pleasure. Now, what do each of you lovely ladies do when you aren't sipping a cold drink here at the soda fountain?" Art asked with a charming smile. His eyes seemed to twinkle as he looked from one girl to the other.

"Clarisse and I work as maids for the Newtons, and Mary works as a maid at the Stoddard Johnson Hotel," Naomi answered.

Art quirked an eyebrow at Mary, "Wow! You work at that fancy place, huh?" Art let out a hardy laugh.

"Yes, indeed," Mary answered with obvious pride at having a job at such a prestigious establishment.

"The Newtons? I work for Mr. Newton at the First Bank of Abilene. Now, isn't that something," he laughed again.

"Oh yes, that's something," Clarisse stated with disgust. "I hope he's nicer to work for at the bank than he is at home," she continued.

Naomi nudged her with her foot in hopes she wouldn't say anything else until they knew this young man better. What if he went right back to the bank Monday morning and told Mr. Newton he had met two of his maids, and they hadn't spoken very highly of him? They would lose their jobs for sure.

Art looked at a loss for an answer to Clarisse's statement.

"Oh, I'm sure Mr. Newton is a fine fellow to work for at the bank. Likely by the end of the day when he gets home, he's just a bit testy because of the, the big responsibility of his job," Naomi said with a wan smile, trying to cover for Clarisse's unflattering remark.

Their conversation turned to lighter subjects and, before Art parted their company, he had suggested they meet him and a couple of his friends at the street dance downtown that evening. In fact, it was to be held at the intersection beside the Stoddard Johnson Hotel.

The girls agreed but decided to stick close together until they knew the fellows better.

Art smiled broadly when he spotted the girls seated on a bench waiting for him and his friends.

"Hi, lovely ladies," Art greeted them. "I'd like you to meet a couple of my good friends. This is Chuck Hobbs and Bob Bounds," he said.

"Nice to meet you," the fellows said in unison.

Soon they were laughing and exchanging partners almost every dance. Naomi had never danced but soon caught on to the steps and was surprised how easy it was to keep time with the music. Art was the best dancer and Naomi enjoyed dancing with him more than the other guys. Besides, he kept the conversation going and said some funny things that made her laugh.

The evening went well so the girls agreed to meet the fellows the next Saturday at Woolworth's soda fountain. The group enjoyed several long afternoon picnics in a nearby park before the weather turned too cold for outings. It was fun to just walk through the park chatting and laughing. Chuck brought his croquet set so the group would have something fun to do besides just walking around the park.

Mary and Clarisse still lived at home so sometimes the girls would meet the fellows at one of their homes to play parlor games. It didn't take long for the group to become couples. First, Mary and Chuck paired up and, then, Clarisse and Bob had shown a special interest in one another. That left Naomi and Art as the third pair. That was fine with Naomi. She enjoyed Art's company and he was a lot of fun. Art didn't press her to be his sweetheart but occasionally he would give her an affectionate goodnight kiss.

Chapter Seven

L uke trudged home later that same evening after a particularly grueling day at the cattle loading pens. Buster and Wayne had left about half an hour ahead of him so they could move to another rooming house nearer their work.

As Luke passed the brothel he happened to glance up and was surprised to see only one woman, alone, on the upper balcony.

"Hey, you," she called to him.

Luke wondered if he should pretend he didn't hear her and walk a bit faster before he was forced to acknowledge she was vying for his attention.

"Hey, you," she called a bit louder, so he couldn't pretend he hadn't heard her unless he were stone deaf.

Luke stopped and looked in her direction.

She had long dark hair, golden brown skin, and from this distance, her eyes appeared to also be dark in color. She was scantily clad in some red filmy thing that he supposed resembled a nightgown a woman like them might wear. It left little to the imagination. He had to admit she made an appealing picture as his pulse quickened and a surge of heat rushed through him.

She gave her head a nod in the direction of the open door indicating she wanted him to come upstairs.

Luke was in a quandary. What should he do or say? Then it came to him that she would certainly expect money for her services. He turned his pants pockets outward so she could see they were empty.

Luke managed to give her a pathetic smile and shrugged his broad shoulders as if to say, "I'm broke, sorry."

She leaned over the balcony railing, giving him an enticing view of voluptuous breasts that were a slightly lighter shade of brown.

"For you, darlin', so handsome with your green eyes and hair as black as the night, no charge. Aye, what you say to that?" she asked and gave him an encouraging smile.

Luke was shocked at her proposition. He had never thought of himself as being handsome. What man would turn down such an offer? If Wayne or Buster ever heard about this, he would never hear the end of them ribbing him about turning down a free offer.

As he stood staring up at the dark beauty, he could tell she wasn't much older than him. Yet, she had a look of knowing about life, knowing about the things rarely talked about except by men well out of the earshot of women. It was for sure she knew far more than he did about intimate things between men and women. Why would such a pretty girl get into this business? Luke asked himself.

The woman maintained her pose at the balcony railing, staring at him with a wicked little smirk playing about her pretty lips, waiting for his answer, waiting for him to cross the street and climb the side stairs to her room.

Luke wondered what her brown skin would feel like to touch. Would it be as silky soft as he was imagining as he gazed up at the inviting beauty?

"Luke, hey, Luke!" he heard Wayne calling from the corner on the same side of the street as the brothel. Thankfully, Wayne couldn't see the dark beauty beckoning to him.

Luke breathed a deep sigh of relief. Now he had an excuse for not crossing the street, not going to the woman.

"Yo!" he called back, turning his attention to where Wayne stood.

"Come help us get the rest of our stuff, and we'll treat you to a hamburger and beer," Wayne shouted.

"Coming," Luke answered and hastened his steps toward the corner to join his friend, away from the temptation of the pretty young woman.

When they reached Wayne and Buster's new room, Luke was relieved when he realized they would no longer be walking past the brothel. There would be no more tempting invitations from the young woman. It would also save him from being embarrassed at not taking her up on her offer.

Luke, Buster, and Wayne often visited some of the rowdier dance halls. Luke enjoyed dancing with a number of girls he met there. Some were a bit forward, but he was careful to not encourage them. Luke knew he wasn't ready for a serious relationship. Besides, he doubted they were the kind to be serious for very long.

Several times he had walked a few of the girls home. He was careful to keep a respectful distance and not let things go too far. He was fairly certain Wayne and Buster may have gone a bit further with some of the girls than he was willing to do, but that was their business. Sometimes one or both would disappear for the evening. Luke quickly caught on to not expect them to come back and would go on home when he tired of dancing. Buster or Wayne didn't try to persuade him one way or the other about the girls they met, and that suited him fine.

One cold December afternoon the three men stopped off at a cafe for hamburgers and hot cups of coffee on their way home.

Luke noticed Buster wasn't as talkative as usual. He had a pensive expression. Normally his brown eyes danced with mischief, but today they held a somber expression.

After a while, Wayne spoke up. "Buster, are you feelin' poorly? You haven't said a half-dozen words since we got here."

Buster heaved a deep sigh. "No, I ain't feelin' poorly. I just got a lot on my mind, that's all."

Wayne and Luke both laughed.

"A lot on your mind!" Wayne exclaimed.

"Yeah, a lot on my mind!" Buster retorted.

"What mind?" Luke teased as he and Wayne laughed even harder.

"Just shut up, you two nit-wits!" Buster growled.

Wayne and Luke exchanged a look of surprise. Buster was normally more jovial with little on his mind but his next Saturday night conquest.

"What's up, bro?" Wayne asked with a somber expression.

Buster heaved another deep sigh. "I've got a girl in trouble," he whispered as he looked from Wayne to Luke. "She says I better marry her, or she's gonna sic her pa and two brothers on me."

"Well, damn!" Wayne exclaimed in astonishment.

"Wooo! Are you sure it's yours?" Luke asked with concern for Buster's dilemma. He had certainly heard talk about such things. Some girls would blame any man that was handy, whether she knew for sure or not it was his kid.

Buster raked his fingers through his wavy brown hair with such force it almost looked as though he were about to grab hold and pull it out. "I guess it could be mine. I did, well you know, but I don't really know her very good. We only went out together a few times. She seemed nice enough but didn't back off when things got too heated up between us. She might have done the same thing with somebody else. I just don't know!" he muttered, expressing his doubts and frustration.

"Did you lead her on into thinkin' you were in love with her?" Wayne asked in a more serious tone.

"I told her she was pretty and sweet, but I said nothin' about bein' in love with her," Buster answered.

Wayne's face took on an anxious look. "What you gonna do? I guess me and Luke could help you out in a fight if you don't want to marry her." Wayne offered as he looked at Luke to see if he agreed.

Luke liked the two brothers but didn't really want to get tangled up in their personal business. Besides, he might get hurt again and have to miss more work. If that happened, it would delay his plan to move south. He also needed to be sure he could watch out for Naomi now that she was noticing the young fellows. He thought fast for a solution that would keep him out of their troubles.

"If you really have doubts, why don't the two of you just pack up and move on somewhere else? She wouldn't know which way you went. If you knowed her better and really believe it is your kid, that would be different," Luke suggested, hoping it didn't sound like he didn't want to help them fight the girl's pa and brothers.

"I think Luke's right," Wayne quickly agreed. "If you don't even know her that good, why marry her? She might turn out to be a real naggin' kind of woman. Besides, after she catches you, then, she might not want nothin' to do with you," Wayne expounded as though he had suddenly become an authority on women.

Buster sat quietly mulling over what his brother and Luke had advised. "Maybe you're right, but then, what if it is mine?"

Buster looked so downcast Luke really felt sorry for the man. He reminded himself that was another good reason to keep his own desires in close check. In time, when he was older and settled, there would be plenty of time to find a nice girl or woman for his wife.

The three got up and parted at the door.

Luke walked back to the boarding house wondering what the brothers would do. The next morning when he arrived at the cattle pens, Buster and Wayne were nowhere in sight.

That evening, as Luke lay on his bed waiting for the time to come to go walk Naomi home from the Newtons' late-night Christmas Party, he thought about the advice he had given Buster. Now he wondered if it had been justified. What if some fellow had done something with Naomi and then took off to avoid his responsibilities? Luke knew what he would want to do to a fellow like that, and it would likely be more than just a fight to make him marry her.

He needed to ask Pearl to talk to Naomi about what some young men would tell girls so they could have their way with them. After Buster's experience, Luke had become especially concerned, now that Naomi was noticing the fellows and they certainly seemed to be noticing her. Even he was aware she was quickly developing into a pretty young woman. She needed to be warned that fellows didn't always mean the things they said in the heat of passion. He was no authority on the subject but had heard enough talk at the cattle pens to know about some men's lack of scruples.

Chapter Eight

The annual Christmas Party Harold and Margaret Newton threw for the bank employees was indeed a huge, elegant affair. It was strange to see Art all dressed up and seated at the beautifully decorated long dining table with its glistening silver candlesticks holding tall red candles. They sat on an elegant red table runner that stretched the full length of the table, which was covered in a lovely white Irish linen tablecloth. The china plates, silverware, and stemmed goblets glistened beneath the extravagant crystal chandelier.

Art was seated next to a pretty girl with long brown curls and pretty hazel eyes. She wore a lovely red velvet dress with a white lace collar, and white lace cuffs enhanced the long, fitted sleeves. She and Art seemed to be well acquainted and often laughed at something the other had said. Naomi wondered if she was his date for the evening or if they just happened to be seated next to one another.

For the first time in her young life, Naomi felt a pang of jealousy. Art was her friend. She had never heard him mention a girlfriend. She tried to ignore them but had to be polite when she refilled their glasses. She also had to act as though she didn't know Art. She and Art had discussed the dinner party ahead of time and concluded that Mr.

Newton would not approve of his bank employee being friends with one of their housemaids.

About halfway through the long meal, Naomi had stationed herself beside the sideboard so she could observe the guests. The Newtons expected her to be ready to tend to any of their guests' needs. Naomi saw Mr. Newton rise and walk down the side of the table, between the seated guests and the sideboard. He spoke to each guest as he made his way down the long table. Just before Mr. Newton passed, he glanced at the opposite side of the table where Art was seated. At that exact moment, Art glanced at Naomi and gave her a flirtatious wink. She sucked in her breath at his unexpected action when she realized Mr. Newton was looking directly at Art. Instantly, Art's face grew red as he realized his employer had just observed his inappropriate action. Slowly, Mr. Newton turned his head and glared at Naomi as though it was her fault Art had winked at her. Her stomach tightened into a knot, as she dreaded what was likely to come because of Art's thoughtless action.

Much to Naomi's relief, when she arrived for work on Monday morning, Thelma informed her and Clarisse that Mrs. Newton had left on the Sunday morning train to Fort Worth as her mother was extremely ill.

"Now we can relax a bit while the Missus is away," Thelma told them with a playful smile. "When Mrs. Newton is away, Mr. will likely take his evening meal in the library and that will mean less work for me. I usually just take a tray up and leave it as he doesn't always eat right away."

They laughed and chatted as they went about their work. It was indeed pleasant to be able to relax, as they certainly couldn't behave in this manner when Mrs. Newton was at home.

"Oh my, wasn't the Christmas Party lovely?" Clarisse commented.

"Yes, indeed. The Newtons really know how to put on the dog, so to speak, to really impress everyone," Thelma answered with a little smirk.

"What do you mean by that?" Naomi asked, sensing Thelma was actually poking fun at her employers.

"I mean, in public they act so, so kind to one another, as though they really cared for the other, but, as we know, in private it's a different story."

"Yes," Naomi mused. "Why do you suppose they don't really care about one another? I guess they must have at one time to even get married," she said with a shrug of her shoulders.

"I don't really know. Just from bits and pieces of conversations I happen to overhear, I think the Mr. has always been one of those men with a roving eye. I know if my Frank acted like that, he would have had a rollin' pin smashed over his head to make him think twice about such carryin' on."

Naomi and Clarisse both shrieked with laughter at the thought of Thelma whopping Frank with her rolling pin.

"Maybe you should lend it to Mrs. Newton to use on the Mr." Clarisse suggested as they all broke into fits of laughter at the thought of such a scene.

On Wednesday, Thelma was obviously coming down with a cold. Naomi suggested she go home early to rest. "I can stay and make dinner for Mr. Newton and take it to the library. Go home and rest," Naomi encouraged Thelma.

Naomi felt fairly certain Mrs. Newton had warned the Mr. about not bothering the maids if he wanted to avoid any scandal. That thought should be enough to scare him into behaving himself, she reasoned.

"Oh, that would be so nice. I really feel awful and might make the two of you sick to boot," Thelma relented.

"Do you want me to stay with you?" Clarisse asked as the clock hands moved toward six o'clock.

"No, I can manage fine. I've already taken the wine tray to the library. I'll take his dinner tray in a few minutes and be on my way," Naomi assured her friend.

Although there was seldom any noise in the huge house except occasional muted conversations or the gonging of some of the old clocks, the house seemed unusually quiet. Naomi climbed the back stairs with Mr. Newton's dinner tray. She started down the long hall toward the library. As she approached his bedroom, she noticed the door was open. Just as she reached his door, she heard him call her name.

"Naomi, bring the tray in here tonight. I'm not feeling well and may nap a bit before I eat. Just put it on the table by the window," Harold said pleasantly.

Naomi crossed the room and set the tray where he had indicated. When she turned to leave, much to her horror, he stood against the now-closed door. He was clad only in a silk, maroon dressing gown with the front gaping open exposing his plump, naked body.

She gasped in revulsion at the thought of what he intended to do.

A sinister grin crossed Harold Newton's face.

"Now, my dear Naomi, I am going to teach you all about what pleases a man so when you flirt with the young fellows, you'll know just what to do to please them," he smirked.

He looked repulsive with his fat, flabby belly hanging out and his privates exposed. She found nothing alluring about the man standing between her and freedom. His round face with sagging jowls certainly wasn't appealing. His receding hairline made him look older than his forty-six years. He was a vile, wicked man! Naomi knew it would be a fight to the death before he would teach her anything about men or otherwise. It made her shiver to even think of his hands touching her, much less anything else.

Naomi braced herself for their impending confrontation. She stood straight and looked directly into his beady brown eyes.

"You best step aside, or I'll scream so loud it'll make your ears ring!"

Harold gave an evil, smirking laugh. "Just who do you think will hear you? There's nobody close enough to hear anything, so just scream all you want."

Naomi quickly removed the cover from the tray and picked up the steaming cup of hot tea. She ran toward him and flung the scalding liquid, hitting his chin and exposed blubbery body before he realized what she was intending.

He was the one to let out a yell of pain as he cursed and lunged toward her, managing to grab a fist full of her long hair and knocking off her maid's cap.

"You little bitch," he bellowed as he pulled her by her hair toward his huge bed.

In spite of the pain, she managed to twist her head and bite down hard on his arm just above his wrist.

When he let go of her hair to clasp his hand over his aching arm, he kicked her just below her knee, making her almost fall to the floor. As she regained her footing, she saw him grab at her again. Naomi catapulted herself onto the bed and stood up so she could move about while staying out of his grasp.

Harold made several unsuccessful lunges toward her as he lumbered around the huge bed.

Naomi suddenly realized he had worked his way to the far side of the bed from the closed door.

She jumped off the bed, grabbed her cap, and ran out the door. Panting for breath she continued down the hall toward the library. Her aching leg, where he had kicked her, was slowing her retreat. If only she could reach the library and bar the door, then she could use the telephone to summon help, she thought desperately as she ran.

When she reached the main stairway, she realized he was gaining on her. She quickly decided to make a run for the front door. Surely, he wouldn't try to follow her outside with his housecoat gaping open, she reflected. Naomi tried to ignore her aching leg as she ran down the wide stairway.

Suddenly, she heard a crashing thud accompanied by a loud, painful moan. Naomi glanced over her shoulder just in time to jump out of the way of Harold Newton's body rolling end over end down the stairs. Each roll was accompanied by a dull thump. He landed with a louder thud at the bottom of the stairs. Harold lay sprawled on the gray carpet with his housecoat gaping open. Blood was seeping from a gash in his head and trickled from his nostrils, making a dark stain on the carpet beside his head.

Naomi stood transfixed for several seconds letting the scene below her sink into her mind. Slowly she descended the remainder of the steps and stood at a safe distance as though she were afraid, watching to see if he may possibly be playing some mean trick on her. He might just be pretending to be unconscious or maybe even dead. She feared that, if she got too close, somehow, he would suddenly surge to life and grab at her again. He did not surge to life nor could she see any signs of his chest rising and falling with breath.

Naomi felt panic rising within her as she ran toward the side door off the kitchen, grabbed her coat from the rack beside the door, and kept running through the dark streets until she reached Pearl's boarding house. She was so frightened she had almost forgotten about her hurt leg. She stopped outside to catch her breath. As she started to run her hands over her hair to smooth it, she realized she still clutched her maid's cap and was wearing her apron. She quickly removed the apron and crammed them into her coat pocket. After a few minutes, she walked through the back door. She was thankful to find no one inside. She hurried up the stairs to the safety of her and Luke's room. Oh, how she hoped to find him there. She had to tell someone what had happened.

Thelma knew she was the only one left in the house with Mr. Newton. If he were truly dead, it was possible she could have a lot of explaining to do, and the law might not believe her. What if they thought she was trying to seduce him and somehow pushed him down the stairs? "Oh, dear Lord, what can I do? Please help me," she quietly prayed for divine guidance.

Naomi opened the door to their room. Relief washed over her when she saw the soft glow of the lamp. There were no electric lights in the attic.

"Luke," she called his name in a shaky voice.

"Yo!" came his reply from the other side of the curtain.

"Oh, Luke, there's real trouble," she managed to get out before she burst into tears.

Instantly Luke was beside her.

"What's happened? Are you hurt?" he asked, showing his concern.

"It's—it's Mr. Newton! I think he's dead, and they may blame me!" she blurted out as her tears flowed.

"Come sit down and tell me everything. Don't leave out one little thing," Luke told her as he led her to sit on the end of her bed.

Naomi told him every detail of what had happened.

Luke sat beside her, with one arm around her shaking shoulder, listening intently.

"Why wouldn't they believe you? Thelma, Clarisse, and even Mrs. Newton know what he was like."

"That's true, but who will believe the maids against the word of Mrs. Newton? She don't want no scandals so she's going to deny what we are saying. People will likely believe Mrs. Newton. They are rich people of high standing in the community. If I say I tried to resist him, will they really believe me? If I say he was chasing me and fell down the stairs, why would they believe that either?" she questioned as she looked at Luke for a solution to this looming problem.

Naomi muttered softly, "There was just the two of us there and only me left to tell the story."

"Luke!" she looked at her brother with huge frightened eyes and spoke his name in alarm. "My footprints are all over Mr. Newton's bed!"

Luke sat perfectly still, contemplating what to do to protect his sister. They could do what Buster and Wayne had done, pack their few belongings and catch the next train wherever it went. By the time Mr. Newton was found no one would know which direction they would have gone. But that would certainly make her look guilty and, if they were ever found, the fact that she ran would make it even harder to prove she hadn't done anything to the wretched man. So, why run when it wasn't Naomi's doing? He had to have time to think this through clearly.

"What is the earliest anyone will find his body?"

"I suppose tomorrow morning when Thelma goes to fix his breakfast, but she won't likely find him right away. She goes in about six-thirty but stays in the kitchen cooking until it is time for him to come down to eat. That's about 7:15 a.m. I suppose when he doesn't ring the bell for his breakfast to be served, she'll go check to see what the matter might be." Naomi's sobs had become less violent, but Luke could still feel her shaking.

"Okay, that gives me plenty of time to go check to be sure he is dead," Luke spoke softly, making his plan. If he spoke the words, maybe one of them would catch any mistake he might make.

"Luke, what if someone sees you going there?" Naomi asked, obviously worried about the chance Luke would be taking trying to protect her.

"I'll wear dark clothes and watch carefully to be sure no one is around. You said you left by the side door just off the kitchen, right?"

"Oh, yes, none of the hired help ever uses the front door."

"Do they lock the house at night?"

Naomi looked at her brother a bit puzzled. "No, why would they do that?"

"He is a banker, and they have lots of expensive things someone might decide to steal."

"Not in Abilene! I don't know anyone that ever locks their doors, do you?"

"No, but I don't know any rich people that might have anything worth stealing."

"Well, they never lock any of the doors," Naomi assured him.

"Don't turn off any of the lights, that would make it look more suspicious. Be careful if you go in the entry hall where he is because the lights are on, and someone passing by could see inside through the windows on each side of the front door. You can see him from the dining room, and it won't be as light," Naomi warned.

They went over the plan again and again to make certain Luke knew exactly how to go to the upstairs bedroom to remove any traces of Naomi's footprints on the bed.

They hugged briefly after he put on his dark coat and black dancing boots. It wouldn't do to leave any traces of the boots he wore to the stock pens. He put on his black western felt hat, slipped down the stairs, and out the backdoor of the boardinghouse.

It was about ten o'clock, so the streets were all but deserted as Luke cautiously walked toward the Newtons' house. Occasionally he spotted an automobile, horse and buggy, or a random pedestrian coming down the street and would quickly step behind a tree or into the shadows of nearby shrubbery. Luckily, he didn't encounter any barking dogs to raise anyone's suspicions.

When the Newton house came into full view, he stood in the shadows across the street looking it over for several minutes. There was one light on in an upstairs room, and the front entry hall was also lighted, just as Naomi had told him. He wished he could sneak up to the front door and peek in one of the windows, but he knew that was much too risky.

He looked up and down the street and saw no one about. Luke darted across the street and into the shadows of the trees and shrubbery that filled the expansive yard. He walked quietly toward the side door. He paused while still in the shadows and looked toward the upstairs windows of the carriage house where Thelma and Frank lived, but it too was dark.

Luke quickly entered the side door and stopped in the dark kitchen to let his eyes adjust to the shadow-filled house. A bit of light from the entry hall filtered through the formal dining room, down the hallway, and into the kitchen.

Slowly he made his way down the hall and entered the dining room where he could see into the lighted entryway.

Harold Newton lay sprawled on his back with his housecoat gaping open exposing his grotesque nude body. There was a dark stain on the carpet beside his head. Dried trickles of blood ran down one side of his forehead and from his nostrils. His complexion had that odd pallor look often seen after death. The color had drained from his face. His lips had taken on a bluish tint. His eyes had that blank stare emphasizing he saw nothing.

Luke stood looking at the scene before him. He noticed one very important thing. The sash of Newton's housecoat was dangling much longer on one side of his body and almost out of its belt loop on the other. It could easily be assumed that somehow he tripped on the dangling end of the sash and that caused him to fall down the stairs. But the question might be, why would he be going downstairs in this near state of undress? Then Luke remembered Naomi had mentioned the liquor was kept in an ornate liquor cabinet in the formal dining room.

Luke turned and saw the huge cabinet sitting against the far wall. He walked around the long table, opened the door, and selected a bottle of whiskey, of which there were several. The bottle appeared to be the kind of drink a rich man would choose, he thought as he closed the door.

Luke climbed the back stairs and walked silently down the hallway toward the shaft of light from the open door leading to Harold's bedroom. He looked inside and then entered. Oh yes, there were obvious footprints on the soft feather bed. He set the whiskey bottle on the bedside table. Meticulously, he brushed the dust from the bedspread and plumped the mattress so no footprints would be hidden beneath the bed covers. Then he plumped the pillows. He took off his boots, turned back the covers, and lay on the side of the bed next to the table where the whiskey sat. He got up and surveyed the print his body had left. It did appear as though Harold Newton had indeed taken a nap. Luke then opened the bottle of whiskey and sloshed just a bit on the pillow, floor, and table. He then took the remainder of the bottle of whiskey to the adjoining bathroom and flushed its contents down the toilet. He returned and sat the empty bottle back on the bedside table.

Now, the scene was set. Harold Newton had likely gone downstairs for another bottle of whiskey, and the poor fellow had tripped on the dangling sash of his housecoat and tumbled to his death.

Luke took one more cautious look around the room to make sure he hadn't overlooked any small detail. Satisfied, he retraced his steps to the side door.

Just as he slipped out into the darkness, the Newtons' cat, perched on the lid of the trashcan placed just outside the door, pounced, letting out a loud yawl as it hit Luke on his thigh, digging in with its claws. Luke almost let out a yell at the surprise attack as he felt the claws' piercing sting through his trousers. He managed to remain almost silent as he swore at the cat under his breath. With his heart racing from the near outburst that might have been heard by someone, he cautiously walked back to Pearl's boarding house. He could hear his own heart pounding from the scare that devilish cat had given him. Now he could tell Naomi about the scene he had set up to make it look like the accident it actually was, but it wouldn't involve her in any way.

Naomi could rest easy now knowing she would not be involved in the death of the prominent civic leader and businessman, Harold Newton, President of the Bank of Abilene, known to a few as a despicable, unfaithful husband, and no better than trash!

When Luke got home, he assured Naomi that no one would ever know she was there when Harold Newton fell down the stairs. He had a hard time calming his thoughts and lay awake for hours. When he eventually fell asleep his dreams were filled with strange events. Then he was standing across the street from the brothel watching the dark beauty beckoning to him. He heard his name being called but when he looked toward the corner where Wayne had stood, he saw another girl with long dark hair. He could tell she was fully clothed when she beckoned him to join her. He started toward her, but she quickly disappeared into the fog. The next morning, he briefly wondered about the two dark-headed women in his dream, both beauties in their own way.

The tragic death of one of Abilene's leading citizens blazed in bold headlines across the front page of the local newspaper.

According to the news report, Mr. Newton apparently accidentally fell down the long flight of stairs leading from the second floor to the main floor foyer of his home, resulting in a traumatic head injury believed to be the cause of his death. The report did not mention his near state of undress or the empty whiskey bottle found on his bedside table. It did, however, expound on his many accomplishments and leadership role in the development of Abilene. His widow, Mrs. Margaret Wayneright Newton, was listed as his only survivor.

The four maids and Frank continued to work for Mrs. Newton during this trying event. The telephone rang constantly, and someone was continually knocking on the front door. So much food was brought as an expression of sympathy and concern that Thelma didn't have to cook for over a week. "It's kinda like a holiday," she confided in the other maids, with that wicked little grin that slipped out on occasion.

The four maids and Frank had attended the funeral, and they all had noticed Margaret scarcely dabbed at the corner of her eyes with her lacy white handkerchief. Later they had discussed the fact that she was not grieving for the loss of her husband, but, as they all knew, it was likely a relief to her to be rid of the loathsome man.

They had been right in their assumption. Margaret was, indeed, relieved to be rid of Harold. This unforeseen accident had saved them from the scandal of a divorce. While attending her ailing mother,

Margaret had decided she could not bear to continue in their sham of a marriage.

She often wondered if she had ever really loved Harold. When they met, she was a young bank teller, and he was already one of the Vice Presidents of a bank in Fort Worth. He was twelve years older than she and appeared quite charming and sophisticated. Although not a handsome man, he did have a certain appeal.

She could see he had a promising future, and she definitely wanted to rise above her humble status and enjoy the finer things in life. They had married after a brief courtship. At first, they got on well enough, although she didn't particularly care for the intimacy that was expected between married couples. She had heard it was a woman's duty to please her husband, so she tried to please Harold until she discovered he was also finding pleasure in other places. From that day forward their marriage became one of mutual convenience for them both. She was an asset in promoting his career by entertaining business clients and co-workers at elegant dinner parties, and he provided her with all of the trappings of living the easy life and rubbing elbows, so to speak, with the upper crust.

Now he was gone and had left her a very well-off widow still in her prime. If she ever married again it would be for love, but perhaps she would just enjoy being a merry widow.

A week after the funeral Margaret called all of the staff together in the upstairs library.

"I must inform you that I will be moving to Fort Worth to assist in caring for my ailing mother. I have found a realtor to handle the sale of the house and most of its contents. We will spend the next few days packing the things I want shipped to Fort Worth. At the end of the week, you will receive two weeks' additional pay that will hopefully carry you over until you can find another place of employment. I will give each of you a letter of reference with your final pay," she informed them with her usual lack of emotion.

Mrs. Newton called the maids and Frank in one at a time to give them their final pay and letter of reference. Naomi was the last to be called.

Margaret sat at Mr. Newton's large desk. She studied Naomi for several seconds before she spoke.

"Naomi, I know it is tempting sometimes after you have left a place of employment to tell tales about your former employers and things that went on while you worked for them," she paused. "I hope you will not belittle Mr. Newton's name or mine now that we will both be out of your life. It will serve no good purpose to speak ill of the dead or the living," she finished firmly.

Naomi met her intense gaze. "I know what is proper and what is not. You needn't worry about what I might or might not say, but we both know the kind of man your husband really was."

With her head held high and back straight, Naomi turned and left the Newtons' house for the last time.

When she had walked a few blocks, she paused to look in the envelope Mrs. Newton had given to her. There was a letter, but she would have to get Pearl to read it to her to be sure what she had written. Then Naomi counted and recounted the money inside. There were not two weeks' additional pay, but enough pay for one month. Naomi smiled slightly as she shook her head. Her own mother's words came back to her: "Money is the root of all evil." Yes, Mrs. Newton was trying to pay her off to keep her mouth shut.

Naomi fretted over where she could possibly find another job that paid as well as the Newtons. She and the others had immediately started asking around about the more affluent families' needs for additional staff but only heard of one position. It involved the care of an elderly bedridden gentleman.

Naomi immediately went to apply for the position. The man's daughter-in-law asked her age. Naomi proudly told her she was fourteen. The woman deemed that, because Naomi was single, she was too young to give the kind of personal care her father-in-law required. Naomi left disappointed.

Several days later Mary came to tell her one of the maids had quit at the hotel. Naomi hastily dressed and accompanied Mary to the hotel since she was on her way to work. The manager interviewed Naomi thoroughly and finally, with a bit of reluctance, again because of her age, hired her on a one-month trial basis. Unlike Mary, she did not live at home with her parents so was likely to not be the kind to stay in one place very long, the manager feared. Naomi was elated and knew Mary would help her learn all she needed to know to keep her job.

Chapter Nine

The months passed quickly, and the weather was turning cold again. It was the second winter they would spend in Abilene, still planning and saving for the future.

Luke missed his two friends, Buster and Wayne, but soon made some new pals to hang out with, going to the dance halls or shooting pool, on Saturday nights. Most of the men he worked with were heavy drinkers and often visited the brothels, but Luke drank little and still avoided the brothels. He had met a couple of nicer girls he enjoyed dancing with and would walk one or the other home but only went as far as enjoying a goodnight kiss. He had to admit at times his mind wandered to other places, but he couldn't make a mistake like Buster might have done. He knew he wouldn't run away, even if he had some doubts, and he certainly didn't need a wife and young'uns to support. He needed to concentrate on saving the money he and Naomi would need to get their horse farm started.

As Christmas approached it was hard for Naomi to believe this was the second Christmas they would spend in Abilene.

Christmas Day Naomi had to work from six in the morning until six in the evening. Pearl planned a Christmas supper instead of the usual mid-afternoon observance. She knew Naomi and one other boarder had to work Christmas Day. After the scrumptious meal, everyone moved to the large living room with its brightly colored decorations and festive Christmas tree decorated in an array of handmade ornaments. They gathered around Pearl's old piano, which was slightly out of tune, and sang Christmas carols for a while as they enjoyed Pearl's special recipe of eggnog. After her second cup of eggnog, Naomi began to feel a bit lightheaded.

When Naomi and Luke went up to the attic, they each had a small gift for the other. They had agreed to only spend a small amount on Christmas gifts as it was far more important to keep tucking as much money away as possible for when they moved.

"Naomi, I think in about March we'll have enough money saved for two train tickets to San Antonio and on to Bandera," Luke told her with a broad smile and a twinkle in his green eyes.

"Oh, Luke, that's wonderful! Only a few more months and then we can buy our own place and start building our own house!" she answered, overjoyed. A sparkling smile lit her face.

"Yeah, that's my plan. The only part I ain't quite worked out is what we'll live in until we get the house built. It will likely still be chilly even that far south, and you know how bad some of the spring storms can be," he stated with a worried expression.

Naomi's brow wrinkled as though she were giving the situation serious thought. Then she brightened. "We can live in a tent. I've seen people living in tents right here on the outskirts of town, so why can't we? It shouldn't take that long to build a small house," she bubbled with excitement.

Luke smiled at his sister's carefree spirit. Naomi was tough in a lot of ways and never complained about their lot in life.

"It won't be easy living in a tent, especially during spring storms, but I'm game if you are," Luke answered with a cheerful laugh.

"Oh, Luke, just think, it's really within our grasp."

"Yeah," he answered a bit dreamily. "At least all of our hard work will be going to build our future and make money for ourselves, not for somebody else."

"Can I tell Mary and Clarisse?"

Luke thought for a moment. "Sure, but tell them it's still a secret so we won't lose our jobs."

As Luke drifted off to sleep, he vaguely thought about all that had happened during the past two years. He knew he was ready to move on.

On the morning of March 24, 1921, as Luke and Naomi waited to board the southbound train, they exchanged jovial smiles filled with pride. They had worked hard and quickly learned to be very frugal with their money. Luke now carried an additional $533.35 they had saved during the past two years, and they were moving closer to making their seemingly long-awaited dream happen. As Luke took his seat he mused they were at last ready to work even harder to start his horse training business and build their own house. This would be their own place where they were the bosses, well, their own bosses, he chuckled softly.

As the train rattled along, swaying slightly from side to side, they both eagerly looked through the dusty windows, taking in the changes of the landscape until sunset. The almost flat country turned to slightly rolling hills that turned to steeper hills as they wove their way along the flatter terrain. The vegetation became more abundant. The grass, just beginning to turn a lush green, was of a thicker quality, and more trees regularly dotted the landscape.

As night fell the porter lit the lamps that cast a soft glow throughout the train car. Their car was not overcrowded, so Naomi sat on the seat in front of Luke. No one was sitting close enough to hear what they were saying if they spoke softly.

Naomi finally turned to Luke. "Do you think we can start telling the truth about our real ages if asked? Sometimes it's hard to remember to lie," she said with a sweet but slightly impish smile.

"I think that'd be all right since we'll be working for ourselves. Just don't volunteer it or anything else about our past," he cautioned.

Now that Naomi had brought up the subject, it would be a relief to actually say he was sixteen and his sister was fourteen if anyone asked. He didn't particularly like telling a lie. Folks didn't need to know they had some family as neither would likely ever return to see any of them again, especially John Martin.

At last, the lull of the gentle rocking motion allowed them both to sleep.

Luke awoke about three-thirty in the morning and realized the train had once again made a stop. He stood to stretch his tall aching body from sleeping in a cramped position. Peering through the window he saw a full moon lit the surrounding area. They were apparently in some small town taking on water.

Luke walked to the platform at the end of the train car and breathed in the cool night air. The distant hills appeared quite steep, and the vegetation was thicker than he had ever seen. This must be some of the grand hill country the man from Bandera had described.

Luke found the chill of the night air refreshing. The man had said the summers here weren't as hot as in Abilene and there was generally a southeast breeze. He would have to remember that when they built their house so they could take advantage of that coolness.

Luke returned to his seat as the train started to move and continued to observe the moonlit surroundings for a short while before falling asleep.

Shortly after sunrise, they entered the outskirts of San Antonio. It was already a huge city, and Luke knew instantly they wouldn't stay here any longer than necessary. Abilene had been plenty big enough to suit him.

During their three-hour wait for their train west, they did walk a few blocks to a small cafe where they enjoyed a huge breakfast. Naomi was in awe of the old buildings. An old Catholic Church standing majestically on one corner instantly caught her attention.

"Luke, let's go inside and look at that church. It must be really beautiful," she suggested, pointing toward the old structure.

He could see the curiosity reflected in her aqua blue eyes as her gaze perused the stucco building with its high steeple and stained-glass windows.

"We ain't Catholic and don't have no business goin' in there ogling around," he answered firmly, as he started back toward the train station.

"I don't think anyone would care if we go in to see the church," Naomi protested as she hastened her pace to catch up with Luke. She certainly didn't want to lose sight of him in this huge place.

"We ain't goin' snoopin' around in any churches so come on," Luke answered a bit tersely, as he continued walking toward the train station.

Naomi glanced over her shoulder with a final longing glance at the lovely old church. Sometimes she didn't understand Luke's reasoning but knew she wasn't going to argue too much with him or disobey whatever he said they should or should not do.

Soon they were back on the train headed west toward their much-anticipated destination. The hills were steep. Small streams and pools of clear water were in far more abundance than either had ever seen. It was certainly different than anything they had ever seen in west Texas.

At times they wondered if the train would make it up the steep grade of the next hill as it crept along, but, at last, they would top another hill and pick up some speed on the downside.

"It is so pretty here!" Naomi exclaimed as she continued to watch the passing countryside. "Oh, Luke, I think you've made a good choice for a place for us to live," she said almost reverently.

"It sure looks different from anything I've ever seen. Now we just have to find the place we can afford and get started," he chuckled as he reached forward and ruffled Naomi's strawberry blond hair, which was already in disarray from traveling.

Mid-afternoon the conductor called out, "Bandera."

As they gathered their few belongings, Naomi gazed out the train window at the small town. It looked like it was built many years ago.

Just as they stepped off the train, they heard three rapid gunshots.

Naomi grabbed Luke's arm and flinched at the unexpected sound.

"Don't be afraid, Miss," the conductor said when he saw her reaction. "Bandera is still a wild place on the weekends. The cowboys from the ranches come into town Friday and Saturday nights to let loose and spend their pay. You folks go straight down this street to the Bandera Boarding House and stay put till morning. Do whatever business you have to in the morning and go back to the boarding house by mid-afternoon." Then he looked at Naomi. "Don't be going anywhere by yourself until the cowboys leave town Sunday," he advised as he helped the last passenger board the train.

Naomi looked at Luke with huge, frightened eyes. "I don't think I like it here after all. It may be pretty country, but I don't like the shootin'."

"Come on, let's get settled. Tomorrow morning we'll go find out about some land we can buy. Then we won't be in town when the men come in to let off steam," he assured her. Luke took Naomi by the elbow and guided her toward the Bandera Boarding House, which he could see at the end of the next block.

Naomi noticed most of the buildings and sidewalks were made of wood. The streets were still unpaved. Only a few of the buildings looked as though they had ever seen a coat of paint. There was a large stone structure farther down the street that she assumed might be the courthouse, and a stone church stood on the next corner across from the boarding house.

Naomi didn't mention attending church services as all of their clothes were wrinkled from traveling. They wouldn't be here long enough to get to know anyone anyway. Living in the country most of their lives, they had rarely attended church. That thought made her feel a bit sad as she just realized they would have few friends living out in the country. It would definitely be a lot different from living in Abilene, where they had friends and plenty of things to do. Maybe in time, they would get to know the neighboring ranchers and their families, she tried to console herself.

Just as they were about to enter the boarding house, which didn't look near as nice as Pearl's, two more shots rang out. Naomi flinched again and hurried through the door leading into a small lobby.

They followed the train conductor and boarding house manager's advice about staying off the streets until the next morning. All weekend, through the late afternoon and night, they heard occasional gunfire. The manager said that was what happened on most weekends. They only had the sheriff and one deputy to try to keep as much peace as possible, but just two men couldn't cover all of the saloons and brothels.

Saturday morning Luke and Naomi carefully selected two horses to buy that Luke could also use in his horse training business and made their way to a realtor's office, where they were shown a map of several possibly suitable tracts of land. They set off in high spirits to find their future home. The land was a bit more costly than Luke had expected but he figured they would find something suitable they could afford.

The first tract of land consisted of two steep hills and a small stream that looked as though it might go dry in the summer. The second was more desirable, with better water, but still too hilly to suit Luke. After another hour and a half of riding, they found the old Carter place that had sixty acres, fewer hills with a wide grassy valley where they could raise some feed crops, and a strong stream that even fed into a small lake.

Luke sat straight in the saddle slowly turning his horse so he could look closely in every direction, taking in every detail of the land.

Naomi followed his lead in surveying their surroundings.

At last, Luke threw his hat high in the air, letting out a loud, "Yahoo!" that startled the horses and Naomi. "This is it! This is it!" he shouted with obvious excitement as he jumped from his horse and danced a little jig.

Naomi laughed at her brother's outburst of enthusiasm. "Oh, Luke, it is perfect for us. Where will we put the house?" Naomi asked as she continued to look at the lay of the land. Before he could answer she pointed to where a hill sloped down toward the water then flattened out for some distance before its final descent of about eight to ten feet to the small lake. "How about there? It's high enough it won't likely flood and near the water."

Luke grinned from ear to ear. "I think you have found the perfect place for our future home. Our future home," he repeated, as though it were indeed hard for him to believe they were actually getting closer to making their dream come true. Neither would ever have to put up with working for another person again.

Yes, it seemed they had found their little corner of paradise.

By the end of the next week, they were resting comfortably in their tent at night, had built the necessary outhouse, and Luke had started digging postholes for the corral. Naomi had begun clearing a space for a garden. The supply wagons would arrive at any time bringing the building materials for the corral, barn, and house. It really was a dream coming true.

"Luke, do you think just the two of us can build a barn and house?" Naomi finally asked out of concern, as she eyed the simple outhouse they had finished that obviously leaned slightly to one side. At times that had been a challenge for the two novices.

Luke paused from his digging. "I've been thinking on that very thing myself. We are getting toward the end of our cash and still have to buy some horses to start our business. I don't know how we could afford to hire someone to help us build," he said as he wiped the sweat from his forehead with the back of his arm.

He had cut the sleeves out of his oldest shirt to wear while work-ing. His arms were becoming brown and Naomi could see his muscles bulging as he worked. It was true; Luke could easily pass for eighteen. He was tall and filled out more like a man than a boy-man of sixteen.

"We could ask the men that bring the building supplies if they know anybody that would work for room and board and stay on for some pay when we get some horses sold. I'm sure there would be plenty of work around here to keep someone busy after the building is finished, while you train the horses," Naomi suggested.

"I guess it's worth a try, but we have to be careful what kind of man we hire. I might have to leave on business and don't want to leave you here with just anybody."

"You know I carry that small pistol in my apron pocket and wouldn't hesitate to use it if I needed to," Naomi said with self-assurance.

"What if he snuck up on you unexpected and grabbed you? Then what would you do?"

"I'd kick, bite, scratch, or do whatever I had to if that happened."

"Well, I just don't know. Let me think on it a spell," he answered with a pensive look as he continued digging.

It was true, she had held off Harold Newton, but a younger more agile man might be a different story, Luke thought.

They did hire a man willing to work for room, a small tent, and plenty of good food to eat, and was willing to stick around for pay later. Jim Keller, age twenty-five. He revealed little about his past, but he did know how to build. He stood about six foot; his long hair was flaxen blond from spending hours out in the sun, as he wore no hat. He had piercing crystal blue eyes as pale as the mid-summer sky, that seemed to take in everything about him. He smoked one cigarette after another and drank nothing but hot coffee from morning until bedtime. He wasn't much of a talker but treated Luke and Naomi with the due respect one would treat their employers, although he was considerably older.

Naomi noticed he often sat by his tent in the late evening and read by lamplight for an hour or more before turning in for the night. She was curious about what he read but dared not go snooping around as the two men were never far away, even when working.

Within a short time, the corral was finished and the framework for the barn was well underway.

A few of the neighboring ranch hands had dropped by to make acquaintance with their new neighbors, and a couple had come on their day off to help with the building.

Luke had a strong inclination they had come as much to get a better look at his pretty sister and enjoy her superb cooking as to help with the building. That was fine since she was never out of his sight with any of them.

Toby March, one of the hands from the next ranch, invited them to a barn dance to be held the next Saturday night. Luke saw Naomi's eyes light up at the prospect of meeting some of their women neighbors. He knew she must feel lonely, stuck out in the country with no friends. He did have Jim and the occasional visitor to converse with, but she didn't have any female company.

Luke was a bit surprised when Jim said he would also go to the dance since he rarely talked, even to them.

Naomi got out her best dress and made sure it was in good repair as well as Luke's best clothes. She thought about offering to inspect Jim's clothes but didn't really feel she knew him well enough.

Jim was a strange man in many ways, standoffish. But Naomi couldn't fault his work. He worked from sunup to sundown and never complained. She just wished he were a bit friendlier. Although he was much older, she found him rather handsome. At times she found herself watching him as he worked alongside Luke. She couldn't help but notice Jim's blond hair glistening and the sheen of his bronze skin as he worked beneath the warm sun. He too was lean but muscular from hard work.

The three set off with Naomi and Luke in high spirits. The two were in awe when they topped the ridge looking down on the sprawling ranch belonging to Major Martin Markham. A massive rock two-story house sat just beyond a large gate with a triple MMM, apparently the ranch brand, at the top of a huge metal bow set in large rock pillars. There were several barns, corrals, one large bunkhouse, other outbuildings, and several smaller houses scattered across the headquarters. It was an impressive site.

Naomi felt a twinge of panic when she glanced down at her plain dress and then at the men's best everyday trousers and western shirts. She suddenly feared they would look very out of place, even at a barn dance, at such a magnificent ranch.

She gave Luke a nervous look. "Let's go home; we don't belong here," she spoke softly. Memories of the lavish parties she had served at for the Newtons flashed through her mind. She would feel like the maid at this party, compared to the way the other guests would likely be dressed.

"Toby said it's a barn dance. How fancy can it be?" Luke asked, seeing the doubt on his sister's face.

"I don't know, but I don't want to find out either!" she insisted as she turned her horse to return home.

At that very moment, they saw Toby waving his hat at them and motioning for them to come on down the hill.

"I think it's too late to retreat," Jim stated with a slight chuckle, as he nudged his horse and started forward.

"Let's give it a try, and if you really don't like being here, we'll leave. Just because they have money don't make them a darn bit better than us anyway," Luke said as he followed Jim's lead.

Toby acted as their personal host, introducing them to the ranch hands and their families and those attending from neighboring ranches. Everyone seemed friendly enough and, much to Naomi's relief, most of the women were dressed much like her. A few of the single young women had fancier dresses, but Naomi didn't feel too out of place after a while.

Luke finally asked, "Where is your boss? Don't he come to his own dances?"

Toby laughed. "Oh, yeah, always at least an hour late. He says he just can't seem to manage to get his women folks to get ready for anything on time."

"How many women folks does he have?" Luke asked with curiosity.

"Just his wife, Rose, and two daughters, Marianna and Sarah. They are right pretty but not as pretty as your sister. They'll likely be jealous when they see all of the cowboys lined up for a dance with Naomi," Toby said with a good-natured laugh as he nodded toward the number of men already waiting for a dance.

Luke looked around and, much to his own surprise, it did seem a line had formed for a dance with Naomi. He'd sure have to keep an eye on that situation, he thought.

Toby nodded his head toward the archway leading to the expansive lawn where the dance was actually taking place. Lanterns had been hung from trees and sat on numerous tables where folks sat together eating, laughing, and talking.

"Come on, let me introduce you," Toby suggested as they walked toward Major Martin Markham, Rose, Marianna, and Sarah, who had just arrived.

"Oh, yeah, they also have a son, Marcus. I don't know if he'll be here tonight or not. He's about worthless as they come but will inherit what Papa has built for him. He don't have the brains of a piss ant about running a ranch or much of anything else."

Luke quirked an eyebrow at Toby when he heard what he thought of the son.

"I'm warning you, don't let him near your sister. He's already ruined several girls' reputations and don't give a damn about anything he does. I'm telling you, he's worthless," Toby finished in a lower tone of voice as they neared the Markham family.

Major Markham didn't seem surprised to learn who Luke was when Toby introduced the two men.

"So, you bought the land just to the east of my ranch. I've been considering buying that piece of property myself, but it seems I've waited too long. Well, good luck. Hopefully, we can do business together once you get established," Markham said with a broad grin. There seemed to be something about his friendly manner that did not ring true in Luke's eyes.

After the other introductions, Luke got up his nerve and asked Sarah for a dance. She politely accepted his invitation but spoke little as they whirled around the wooden dance floor that had been erected for the occasion. When he walked her back to the family table, he was a bit shocked when he started to walk away but was halted by Marianna's charming voice.

"I'm disappointed that my sister is the only one to receive an invitation for a dance from our new neighbor," she said with an impish grin.

"I will be honored by a dance with you, Miss Marianna," Luke said politely as he returned to assist her to the dance floor.

There was a remarkable difference in the sisters. While Sarah had hardly spoken Marianna never stopped talking. Luke only needed to nod his head and occasionally say a word or two in agreement. When the dance ended, she clung to his arm and whispered, "Let's keep dancing. I see Calvin Rolls lurking near where we are seated, and he isn't there to ask Sarah for a dance," she said, with a coquettish grin.

Her attention was rather flattering to Luke. He judged her to be about his same age and Sarah slightly younger.

He saw Naomi had taken a break from the dancing and sat with two young women laughing and talking. He was glad she hadn't gone home and missed this evening of fun. Maybe she would get to know some of the girls and have some friends of her own.

Suddenly Marianna let out a low shriek of laughter. "Well, well, look who the cat drug home, my dear brother."

Luke turned to look in the direction of where her family was seated. A tall, good-looking young man stood beside his mother, smiling as though he owned the world. His eyes roamed the crowd and suddenly lit on Naomi.

Luke felt a chill run up his spine.

Marianna chuckled. "It seems he has already spotted your pretty sister. What a shame for the other girls. They won't likely get any of his attention tonight. He always likes something new, kind of like a new toy a child enjoys for a short time and then is through with it once the newness wears off," she said as though warning Luke about her brother's habits.

Luke understood what Marianna was telling him and knew he would definitely be keeping a close watch on his sister and Marcus.

Naomi saw the tall, handsome young man strolling in her direction just as one tune ended. The three young men that had been waiting for a dance suddenly dispersed in various directions seeking another partner for the next dance.

Naomi felt embarrassed as she felt all eyes were on her and the good-looking man who now stood before her.

"Miss Naomi O'Donnelly," he paused and gave her a slight bow. "May I have the pleasure of the next dance?" he asked politely but with a wicked little grin that told her he was accustomed to having his way.

No one had ever bowed to her. She hadn't even seen people do that at the Newtons' house when they gave elaborate parties. Was this fellow making fun of her in some way she didn't understand, she wondered?

"You seem to know my name, but I don't know your name," she said plainly before extending her hand as a gesture she had accepted his invitation.

"How neglectful of me. I am Marcus Markham. My family owns this ranch, the Triple M," he answered still smiling.

94

"I see," was all she said as she extended her small hand and placed it in his much larger one.

His skin felt smooth. He likely had never done a hard day's work. She suddenly felt self-conscious about how her hands must feel to him. Then she remembered just why her hands were so rough. They were working for a purpose. She couldn't help but wonder what he used his hands for, apparently not hard work.

He was an excellent dancer, and they whirled around the dance floor to one tune after another. Finally, she smiled sweetly and excused herself to get something cool to drink. As he started to follow her, she turned and politely thanked him for the dances. Then she told Marcus it was time to say good-bye to her friends before they departed for home.

Marcus looked at his expensive gold pocket watch. "Oh, surely you're not leaving this early," he protested. "It is only twenty past ten, and there is much more music and fun to enjoy," he almost insisted.

"It has been a lovely evening, and we do appreciate the opportunity to meet our new neighbors, but we have a long day of work tomorrow," she laughed slightly, "and the next day and the next day."

"Well, we must arrange another dance soon so you and I can become better acquainted," he said as he gave her a flirtatious wink.

"Thank you, that would be nice," she answered, but with some trepidation in her thoughts. Although Marcus had been a perfect gentleman except for hogging all of the dances, there was something about him that didn't appear forthright to Naomi. She felt certain he was accustomed to having whatever he wanted and that everyone, especially the hired men, gave into him without question. That quality she didn't like. He needed to earn their respect, not just be the pampered, only son.

As the three rode toward home, they discussed the various people they had met and were generally pleased with the evening. Finally, Luke spoke softly to Naomi.

"You need to be wary of Marcus. Even his own sister warned me that he is spoiled and has ruined several young women's reputations and doesn't give a darn about what he's done."

Naomi looked at her brother in the pale moonlight that was just emerging above the eastern horizon. "Yes, I gathered as much. I witnessed the part about being spoiled when the other fellows never asked me for another dance after Marcus arrived. I could tell he is likely spoiled and used to having his own way. Well, don't worry. I have no desire to do more than have an occasional dance with the man."

"Good, but just keep alert to his charms."

"That's good advice your brother is giving you, Miss Naomi," Jim put in.

Naomi and Luke were both surprised to hear Jim express his opinion, as he normally said nothing about what went on around him.

"Oh, look at the pretty orange glow the rising moon is causing. I don't think I have ever seen anything quite like that," Naomi remarked as she gazed at the brightness of the night sky.

"Yeah, it's certainly bright tonight," Luke agreed.

They rode a bit further, each admiring the brilliant shine of the rising moon.

"Damn!" Luke shouted. "That's not the moon causing that glow! It's a fire!"

The three nudged their horses into as fast of a run as they dared, hardly being able to see the uneven ground they were traveling. As they topped the next ridge the glow became a sparkling orange ball in the distance reaching far into the night sky.

"It's our place!" Luke shouted, as he felt his stomach tie into knots and a sick feeling raced through him.

"Slow down, Luke," Jim called as he saw Luke nudge his horse to an even faster pace. "We can't save it now. No need in breaking your neck getting there," Jim yelled at Luke to get his attention.

Luke immediately slowed his horse and the three halted. They sat in stunned silence watching the luminous fireball as flames flickered and danced in the darkness.

"What, what could have caused this?" Naomi finally asked in a small voice the two men scarcely heard.

"I don't know," Luke answered in shock, as he watched their dreams being reduced to ashes.

"If I was a betting man, I'd lay my cards on it having some help," Jim stated firmly. "I should have stayed here tonight. Maybe this wouldn't have happened," he said with a tinge of regret.

Luke looked at Jim, a bit puzzled. "Why would anyone want to burn us out? We don't even know these people and certainly haven't made any enemies."

Then Major Markham's words came back to him about how he had been thinking about buying this piece of property. But surely the man wouldn't have sent someone to burn them out. Or would he, or better yet how about Marcus? Oh, that was crazy thinking. He didn't have anything to really base such thoughts on but that one remark, Luke chided himself.

They rode toward the inferno still in shock as they watched the bright glow ahead of them. The story of God providing a pillar of fire for the children of Israel to follow by night ran through Jim's mind. But why would this happen to these two fine young people trying to build themselves a future, he pondered as they rode. Was there some message being sent by the fire they did not understand yet?

When they were close enough to feel the intense heat Naomi let out a high-pitched wail that pierced the night. The powerful sound instantly drew both men's attention. She sounded like some wounded animal in excruciating pain.

Luke and Jim saw the look of anguish reflected in her normally pretty eyes. Now they were filled with tears that flowed down her once lovely face that was twisted as though she were in deep pain. Her sorrow was evident in the continued moaning sound of suffering she emitted between deep sobs.

"Why, Luke, why?" she wept with a heart-wrenching sound.

Luke just shook his head in silence. How could he know the answer to Naomi's question when he could not yet fully fathom what was happening? Luke felt like joining Naomi in weeping but could not yet let go of his emotions. He felt sick to his stomach as his insides quivered with anger and disappointment. If he ever found out who had done such a despicable deed, he wasn't sure he could prevent himself from doing the person great harm.

The hatred he had for his brother-in-law flashed through his mind. He could almost feel the pitchfork in his hands once again and the overwhelming desire to use it.

Jim tethered their horses to a tree a ways from the fire so they wouldn't try to run.

After several hours of watching their dreams disappear into smoke and ashes, Naomi stretched out on the hard ground, resting her head on her saddle. She still gave little sobs even in her sleep.

The two men talked quietly after Naomi drifted off to sleep.

"I have enough money to pay you for what you've done since I won't need to be buying any horses," Luke told Jim.

"If you still need the money for you and Naomi to live on until you can find jobs, I can wait."

"No," Luke shook his head. "We'll have enough to tide us over. There isn't near enough to start over, and I hate owin' you when I can pay," Luke said quietly.

"What if you sold this land to the Major and bought a smaller place? Would you have enough money to start over?" Jim asked thoughtfully.

"Not really."

They sat in silence, still watching the flames eventually burn out until all that was left was just a smoldering heap of remains. That was much the same way Luke felt. Burned out, a worthless heap of ruins.

There was no choice but for him and Naomi to start again by finding jobs and saving their money. It would take much longer to save enough money to get started since they wouldn't have the five-hundred-dollar nest egg they had started with this time. Likely it would take four or five years to save the money they would need, but he saw no other solution. At least they owned the land, and he didn't intend to sell it to the Major or anyone else. Whoever did this likely wouldn't gain what they had hoped.

Luke considered leasing the land out to Major Markham or one of the other nearby ranchers. That would bring in some money. That thought made him feel a bit better about their future. The key was to find jobs where he could take care of Naomi. Maybe they should go back to Abilene where they knew a few people. She might get back on at the hotel, and he could work at the cattle pens again. He'd talk it over with Naomi in the morning.

Jim broke the silence. "I know a ranch down on the border where you and I can get jobs. The pay is better than most, but it's not a place you can take your sister," Jim spoke softly.

"Why not?"

"It's run by a bunch of ruffians and the few women there are not of very upstanding character."

"I take it you've worked there in the past."

"Yes, about ten years ago."

"Why did you leave?"

"It's a long story, but basically I couldn't take their rough way of life any longer. Not the work but the rest," Jim answered with a long sigh.

"Why would you want to go back there? You're a darn fine builder and could work most anywhere."

"I need to come to terms with my past. Besides, it would give you a chance to make some good money faster than most places. Then you and Naomi could come back and start again. I'll come help you build when that time comes."

"That part sounds fine, but what am I to do with Naomi meanwhile?"

Jim stretched out on the ground and gazed into the star-filled sky. "I figured we'd ride into Bandera tomorrow and ask the minister if he knows of a good family that needs some help."

Luke finally gave in to his weariness and lay on the hard ground, but turned with his back to the smoldering fire. He didn't want to see any more of it tonight.

"I'll have to think on it. What if something goes wrong? What would Naomi do with nobody around to look out for her?"

Jim said nothing more, knowing the final decision was up to Luke. He didn't want to try to influence him just in case something did go wrong. Then he would feel to blame. Luke would have to decide what was right for his sister.

Luke stared into the darkness for a long time before the weariness took him to a fitful sleep. He dreamed about his loathsome brother-in-law, John Martin, the despicable Harold Newton, and his friends Buster and Wayne. Buster was running away from two men with guns, and Wayne was yelling at him to run faster. Luke awoke when he flailed his arm and hit the side of his hand on a nearby rock.

He sat up and rubbed the sleep from his eyes, as he turned to see the smoldering ashes and the sun rising over the hill on the other side of the creek. Jim was gone but soon emerged from the nearby brush. Naomi was squatted beside the lake washing her face. Luke scanned the destruction of the previous night. Then he looked up at Jim.

"I'll talk to Naomi about finding a place for her to live and work. If she agrees, we'll head for the border."

At first, Naomi wanted nothing to do with Luke's plan and guessed right away it had been something Jim had suggested. After discussing it all the way into Bandera, finally, Naomi consented to give it a try, but only after Jim promised to give her an address where they could be reached if she needed Luke.

Arriving in Bandera, they reported the very suspicious fire to the sheriff, who indicated he would try to check around to see if anyone saw anything suspicious but added that witnesses were rarely found when things happened out in the country. The three left his office with little hope anything would be done to solve their mystery.

When they explained their situation to the minister of the Methodist Church, he surprised them by clapping his hands together and giving thanks to the Lord for answering his prayers. Then he went on to explain the reason for his outburst of apparent joy.

"My dear friend and brother minister, Isaac Templeton, of Castroville, is in desperate need of help. He and his cherished wife, Viola, had a child late in life, and the birth has greatly affected Viola's health. Little Matthew is four years old and in desperate need of someone with plenty of energy to care for him. Isaac and Viola need someone to take care of their unpretentious home and prepare meals. Pastor Templeton, like me, also teaches school to supplement his income. Although the small parishes do furnish us a house, the pay is modest at best. You would have your own room, and, I assure you, they will treat you well. I'll write a letter for you to take with you and will also send a telegram for them to be expecting you tomorrow," the minister beamed with delight.

The problem seemed settled in a matter of minutes.

As they rode toward Castroville, Naomi thought perhaps it was an answer to a prayer, but it wasn't her prayer. Her prayer had been for her and Luke to finally have a home of their own. Why was someone else's prayer answered instead of hers, she couldn't help but wonder. She also couldn't help but wonder if ministers' prayers had a better chance with God than just common folks' prayers.

Luke's thoughts ran along the same lines as Naomi's. Why was their dream of their own home snatched away so someone else could have what they needed? Were they really more deserving than he and Naomi? Perhaps so since it was a preacher that needed the help, he reasoned. He almost felt resentful toward the preacher he hadn't yet met; but, on the other hand, he hoped it would work out to be a safe place for Naomi since he would be miles away.

They stopped in front of an unassuming stone house surrounded by a stone fence about three feet in height. It sat next to a small church made of the same stone. The house and church were rather picturesque with the two sitting side by side and a small well-kept cemetery at the back of the church. The scene presented a mood of tranquility.

The door opened and a tall, neatly dressed man with light brown hair, a neatly trimmed mustache, and pale golden-brown eyes stepped outside.

He smiled as he walked to the edge of the porch. "You must be Miss Naomi O'Donnelly. I assume one of these gentlemen is your brother, Luke, and the other is your friend, Jim Keller," he greeted each one warmly. He had read each name from what appeared to be a telegram he held in one hand.

"Yes, sir," the three answered, almost in unison.

"I'm Luke and this is our friend, Jim Keller," he said, so the minister would know which one was Naomi's brother.

"Please, do come in. Matthew and I have managed to make a pitcher of lemonade and there may be a few sugar cookies left from the plateful Mrs. Barker brought yesterday," he said with an amiable smile.

The three dismounted and each shook hands with Reverend Isaac Templeton as they filed into the amply-sized living room with a wide doorway leading into a dining room and the kitchen beyond. The rooms were not large but comfortable, and the furnishings were serviceable as well as pleasant. Large windows covered with white lacy curtains let in plenty of light. Each window was flanked by dark, flower-patterned drapes to be pulled at night.

Suddenly, a small boy ran into the room and came to an abrupt stop, looking wide-eyed at the three guests seated on the sofa. The child strongly resembled his father in looks.

He looked up at his father and asked something shyly that none of the three understood, but the father seemed to have no difficulty understanding the child.

"Yes," the man answered with a warm smile. "This is Miss Naomi, who has come to take care of you and Mama while I am away. This gentleman is her brother, Luke, and this gentleman is their friend, Jim. Come help me get the lemonade and cookies," he told the child as he gestured toward the kitchen.

As soon as they departed, Luke looked at Naomi. He didn't have to say anything.

"Just stay in town a few days to be sure they are as nice as they seem," she whispered.

Isaac and Matthew returned with the refreshments and Matthew beamed as he passed the plate of cookies to each guest.

Once everyone was served, Isaac summoned Matthew to come sit beside him while the adults talked.

"As you have been told, my dear wife is in ill health, and we desperately need someone to look after Matthew and help care for my wife. The household duties are simple, and we eat plain foods. The laundry is taken care of by the widow, Mrs. Green. Do you feel you can manage all of those duties?" he asked Naomi with a hopeful expression.

"Yes, sir, I don't think that will be too hard for me to manage. I can do the laundry too," she offered.

"That is very thoughtful of you to offer. The little I pay Mrs. Green helps her since she has no other means of income except doing laundry," he said with compassion.

Naomi nodded her head in understanding.

"I would like to meet your wife, if possible, before my brother and Jim leave for the evening."

Luke cleared his throat. "We'll be stayin' a few days just to be sure this is going to work out for Naomi and you."

"Of course, that is a good idea. If you gentlemen will wait a few minutes, we will return shortly."

Isaac stood and led Naomi through the dining room and into a hallway that led to the three bedrooms. He tapped gently on a door and softly called his wife's name.

Naomi heard a weak voice invite them inside.

When Isaac opened the door and led Naomi into the semi-dark room, she was a bit shocked to see a pale woman resting against several pillows. She looked like a ghost. Naomi had heard ghost stories all of her younger years, and Viola was exactly what she imagined a ghost would look like. She had long, very blonde hair; her face looked to be almost void of color; and her eyes had dark circles around them, making them look sunken into their sockets. She wore a white night-gown and lay on a bed covered with white linens. It was all Naomi could do to hold back a gasp, but she did not feel afraid like she would have if the woman had indeed been a real ghost.

Viola gave Naomi a wan smile. "Please come sit beside me so I can see you better," she invited as she patted the bed.

Naomi took her seat on the bed and tried to give Viola a bright smile.

"I am sure Isaac has told you all about your duties. The most important one is taking care of Matthew. I need very little care as I spend most of my time right here. I don't expect the house to be spot-less," she finished with a small gasp for breath.

Somehow Naomi knew she was supposed to be here to help this family. She could not begin to explain the feelings she was experiencing. She knew in some strange way the fire had been for a reason. It appeared the reason was to send her to this family. Her earlier resentment of not having her own prayers answered disappeared. Someday perhaps she and Luke would return to their land and build their own home. Now she knew it would be a while, but she was willing to wait.

Chapter Ten

Three days later Luke and Jim rode toward the border, leaving Naomi behind. Luke felt satisfied she was in a safe place. Jim had written down the name of the ranch, Sycamore Creek Ranch, where they expected to be working. Jim said they would send a letter as soon as they were settled for sure, and then Isaac could answer for Naomi.

Luke had seen Jim reading late in the evenings but had not thought much about him being an educated man until he had listened to Jim and the minister converse. Apparently, Jim had a fair amount of education. Why would he be content to work for someone else as a cowboy or builder, he wondered? Why wouldn't he be some kind of businessman with the amount of education he apparently possessed? Perhaps, in time, Jim would tell him more about himself, but Luke wasn't one to pry. It would have to be when Jim was ready to talk about his past.

They rode almost due west for about a hundred and forty miles. The land changed from the lush green hills filled with trees and frequent, clear running streams to scrubby brush, smaller trees, scarce sources of water, and distant hills.

They camped at night when they found water and rarely saw another person. An occasional cowboy would happen by and spend a little time sharing a cup of hot, black coffee and telling them about the surrounding ranches.

Luke had noticed early on that Jim never drank alcohol of any kind. That suited him fine as he cared little for the stuff himself. Just an occasional beer was about all it took to soothe his taste.

In the late afternoon of the fifth day, they reached Sycamore Creek and followed it almost to the Rio Grande River.

Long before they reached the sprawling ranch house, they could see the headquarters in the distance. Farther west the mountains in Mexico, shrouded in purple, made a picturesque backdrop. It was a rather pretty site, or perhaps it looked good because Luke was ready for a hot meal, hot bath, and cot to sleep on instead of the hard ground.

The house was a wide, Spanish-style, one-story stucco structure with numerous archways along the front veranda that stretched the length of the house. The stucco walls looked as though they had once been painted white but now almost matched the dirt that surrounded the large house. The roof was made of red tile that now also had lost most of its color beneath the harsh sunlight. There were a few mesquite trees scattered across the yard, and several struggling rose-bushes added a spot of color near one end of the veranda. Luke thought it had once been a point of beauty and pride, but unfortunately, now its glory had faded.

As they neared the gate that led into the compound, several barking dogs met them. Almost instantly, two men appeared from inside. Each man held a Winchester in a relaxed position, but Luke knew that could change in a heartbeat.

Both men had long, scraggly, blond hair and scruffy beards. They were both about six feet in height. Their strong resemblance left no doubt they were brothers. Luke realized their look was familiar but couldn't figure out where he would have seen either young man before.

Luke and Jim continued their slow progress toward the house, dismounted, and hitched their horses to the hitching post a few feet from the porch.

One of the men walked to the edge of the porch, closely studying each of them.

All of a sudden, he seemed to recognize Jim and let out a whoop that startled Luke and the horses.

"If it weren't so damn hot, I'd think for sure hell had froze over! What the devil brings you back after all this time?" the man asked Jim in disbelief.

"We need a job that pays a decent wage," Jim answered, showing little reaction to the man's unusual greeting. "This is my friend, Luke O'Donnelly," Jim said in way of introduction.

Then he turned his gaze to the men on the porch. "This is Willie and that man is Floyd, two of my younger brothers," Jim said with little emotion.

Luke was shocked at this unexpected revelation. Why hadn't Jim told him they were going to his own home to work, and why would Jim's home be too dangerous for Naomi? Then he remembered Jim saying something about not liking the way they lived. Luke definitely had more questions than answers.

Willie turned slightly toward Floyd and barked. "Go get the old man!"

Before Floyd could move, the door flew open. A large man with a full head of gray hair and a long gray beard that hung halfway down to his waistline burst through the door. He walked with a pronounced limp and leaned on a sturdy wood cane. He had the same piercing blue eyes as Jim, but otherwise, there was little resemblance.

"Well, well! Shall we kill the fatted calf and have a celebration now that the prodigal son has returned?" his voice boomed in an almost jeering tone.

"Hello, Pa," Jim said in a noncommittal reaction to his father's greeting. "If you see fit to hire us to work, tell us where to sleep in the bunkhouse, and we'll eat with the other ranch hands."

The formidable man stood staring at Jim for several moments as he leaned heavily on his cane.

His mood seemed to soften. "This is your home. You always have a job here, and your friend too. I don't think much of the idea that you'd rather live in the bunkhouse than in your own room that is just as you left it ten years ago."

"I'd just as soon it stay as it was ten years ago," Jim paused, "or better yet, let someone else use it."

Jim untied their horses and, with a nod of his head to Luke, didn't say anything else. He led the way around the house toward where several corrals, two barns, several smaller houses, and a large bunkhouse sat.

Luke could feel the old man's gaze following them until they were out of sight. He walked slightly behind Jim with question after question buzzing in his head.

The foreman turned out to be Jim's next youngest brother, Gilbert, twenty-six years old. Gilbert and Jim favored each other.

Luke not only noticed a strong resemblance in their features but also in their manner. Gilbert spoke in a rather quiet but authoritative voice while Willie and Floyd appeared to be the blusterier type like their father. Gilbert seemed glad to see Jim but did not elaborate on his return.

Gilbert turned to Luke. "Well, Luke, welcome to the Sycamore Creek Ranch. I expect a full day's work for a full day's pay. Don't cause no trouble and we'll get along fine."

"Yes, sir."

He turned once more to Jim. "Some things have changed for the better since you left. Pa has got too old and infirm to raise hell like he did after Ma passed. There's far less wild carrying on like there once was before you left. If the cowboys want to raise hell, they go to town to do it. If they get put in jail, they stay, and when they get out, they get paid and sent on their way. It's a shame I can't do the same to some of our brothers."

Jim quirked one eyebrow, "I'd say that's quite an improvement from when I left. I suppose you and the others thought I took the coward's way out, but I just couldn't take it anymore, especially when the woman I loved married another man for fear of what would happen to her if she became my wife. I don't blame her. I couldn't be with her every minute to protect her from the drunks and skirt chasers. Pa being the ringleader didn't help. Well, anyway, I'm glad to see you're in charge and things are getting better."

"It's you that should be in charge, Jim. You're the oldest."

"No, just let me be one of the ranch hands and work my way back into things. I don't intend to take your job. Let me just help out however I can," Jim said and shook hands with his brother as though to seal what he had said.

Gilbert nodded his agreement.

Gilbert turned to Luke. He reached out and gave him a friendly slap on the shoulder. "Luke, you are about to become a river rider."

Luke didn't have a clue what a river rider did, and he wasn't sure he liked the sound of it since he wasn't much of a swimmer.

"What exactly does a river rider do?" he asked, a bit reluctantly.

"Jim will teach you everything you need to know about being a river rider," Gilbert said as he turned toward the bunkhouse. "Come on, I'll show you fellows where to bed down before you go to supper. Better turn in early. Jim knows we work from daybreak to dark thirty and sometimes longer," he said with a chuckle.

While they saddled their horses the next morning and rode northwest toward the first line shack, Jim explained to Luke they had three line shacks or river camps. The one to the north was twelve miles from that fence line. It was twenty-four miles to the center shack, and another shack was twelve miles from the southern fence line.

Riders would start from each shack and ride twelve miles toward one another or the fence lines checking for cattle or horses coming across the river from Mexico. At the twelve-mile mark, he would turn and retrace his route back to his assigned shack. If a rider saw livestock or signs of where cattle or horses had crossed the river, then he would ride inland toward the first fence line, which could be up to another three to six miles, in search of the Mexico stock.

"What do we do then? Run them back to Mexico?" Luke asked.

"No," Jim said with a mild chuckle, "It's not near that simple. First, you have to drive them to the nearest holding pen; inspect them for ticks that could cause tick fever and for signs of hoof and mouth disease. They can easily contaminate the land they cross, and, if they get mixed in with our cattle, we can stand to lose a number of much better cattle than usually crosses over. Most Mexican cattle are scrawny and not purebred. Some have brands that are easy to identify. If they are clean, we return the branded cattle to their owners. If there is no brand, first we get rid of their ticks. We keep the cattle and try to fatten them up for market. We break the horses for ranch use. The ranchers in Mexico don't have strict laws to follow on sending healthy cattle to market like we do. That's why we have to watch for any problems with their cattle."

"How do we get rid of the ticks or hoof and mouth disease?"

"If they carry ticks, we quarantine them and dip them several times until they are clean. If it is hoof and mouth disease, we drive them into a pit and shoot them. Then we burn them. Then they are buried. The land around the burn pit is also burned. We don't see as much hoof and mouth as tick fever. When we find cattle or horses infected with ticks, the pasture they were in can't be grazed for up to nine months to starve the ticks they likely spread."

Jim rode in silence for a few minutes. "Yeah, it's an unending cycle, day in and day out. Likely after a while, you'll get to dread the thought of finding signs of where livestock has crossed the river. It makes for a longer, harder day's work," he said as he let out a long sigh.

"I sure hope you intend to ride with me for a spell and teach me the signs to look for," Luke said, a bit worried.

"Me or one of the seasoned hands surely will until we feel you know what to watch for," Jim assured him.

"I'll show you how to look for tracks along the river and the normal crossings. After that I want you to work with Scout. He's an expert at tracking."

"Was he really a scout?" Luke asked out of curiosity.

"Yes, indeed. He is a black Seminole Indian Scout out of Fort Clark. They were one of the most elite fighting forces around during and after the Civil War for a number of years. He's quite a fellow, but once you get to know him, you'll enjoy his company and learn anything you want to know about tracking. He's one hell of a poker player, too, so watch out if you ever decide to sit in on a game with him," Jim laughed.

"That sounds like the voice of experience," Luke chuckled.

"It is indeed."

When they reached the line shack Luke saw the word shack described it quite well. It was a dilapidated-looking one-room hut with an outhouse that didn't look any better. Both buildings leaned a bit, and Luke wondered what it would be like to spend a windy or stormy night in the shack. There was screening on most of the windows. In their present state, most of the screens looked as though they might keep out some of the mosquitoes and flies. The door hung ajar to the frame, and Luke wondered if it would actually shut. Behind the shack stood a three-sided barn for the horses.

"Home sweet home for three weeks," Jim said with a grin when he saw the expression on Luke's face.

There were four men assigned to a three-week stint. Two men rode out each day in opposite directions, alternating each day, while the other two supposedly did chores, cooking, and were on standby if needed. To Luke, it didn't look as though they spent any time on fixing the place up.

"We have the extras in case there's a problem. If for any reason a rider doesn't come back within three hours of his expected return, the two extras go out in search. The other man has to keep riding the river."

Luke suddenly felt a lump in his throat. Was it fear? Perhaps! A lot could happen to a fellow out here, and it might be hours or even days before he was found.

"If you get hurt, the best thing to do is fire a shot about every half hour. The searchers should hear it and know where to find you. If for some reason you can't fire your gun but can yell, do that. It has happened a couple of times in the past a rider didn't show," Jim said in a serious tone.

"What happened to them?"

"One rider's horse bucked him off in a thunderstorm. He wasn't hurt but had a long soggy walk back to the shack," Jim chuckled. Then his mood turned serious. "One was eventually found shot in the back of his head, and another had been thrown off his horse when it was startled by a rattler. He had a broken leg and arm. He did manage to kill the snake and then signal for help." Jim turned and gave Luke a serious look. "The best thing is to keep alert and don't panic if something does go wrong."

Luke nodded his head but felt a sudden churning in his stomach.

Jim accompanied Luke during the first ten days of his river riding experience. Luke had been quite relieved when he realized he wasn't actually going to be riding in a boat or on a raft in the river but riding a sturdy horse along a well-worn trail beside the river.

During the second part of his first three-week assignment, he rode with Scout. Luke was amazed at the old Indian's knowledge of every track, plant, rise and fall in the terrain, indications of cloud formations, and the changing moods of the Rio Grande River.

Luke gained a better understanding of how the Indians survived in this harsh land. It was rough, covered with cactus, squat mesquites, sagebrush, and scrubby cedar. Rattlesnakes, copperheads, and cotton-mouth water moccasins were plentiful. Jim had warned him about the hot, almost unbearable summers and cold, north winds in winter.

Another surprising part of this job was the discovery of the number of gates the riders had to pass through each day in each direction. Luke learned the pastures were fenced toward the river where the bank sloped to the water so the cattle could drink. There were long stretches of high banks where the cattle couldn't get to the water. There was one two-mile stretch with six gates. The first twelve-mile ride he was assigned included fourteen gates to open and close each direction. He wondered if the other areas had as many gates, or could there possibly be more?

Over the next several months Luke rode the river for three weeks, then would go to headquarters for one week and then back to the river. When the men went to headquarters, they were rewarded with two days off and then one more day before returning to the river camp. There was a rotating pattern for partners to follow so you didn't spend the entire three weeks with the same two partners. Most of the time he found he liked the solitude of the river much better than the hubbub of all that went on at headquarters.

From Jim and Scout, Luke had learned to distinguish a variety of tracks and determine the direction they were headed. He was pleased that soon he could easily recognize cattle, horses, humans, wolves, and coyotes. He even found a few bear tracks.

Scout also amazed him by identifying huge varieties of plants and the medicinal purposes they served. Luke even drew pictures of the plants and had Jim write out the directions for making the potion. Luke couldn't read it yet, but he intended to learn. They had long days with little to do but play cards if he and Jim were at the cabin or when it rained, so he had decided that would be a good time for Jim to teach him how to read and write.

Scout had commented the river was like a loving woman. Most of the time she was kind and soothing to a man, but at times her ire rose, and she was like an angry bear. She could rise up against you and all you could do was stay out of her way.

A couple of months after Luke had come to the ranch with Jim, a rider came out to get Jim. His father had passed quietly in his sleep, and Gilbert needed Jim at headquarters. Luke knew Jim had not been close to his pa. Yet, he felt sorry the old man had passed so soon, too soon for them to make amends over the past.

The weeks faded into months and Luke gained more confidence in riding the river. He liked the days it was his turn to ride far more than the days he was stuck at the shack. He could go fishing or do a little hunting on those days, that helped pass the time, but had to stay fairly close to the shack in case of some emergency.

Luke was riding one morning when it started raining and continued a steady downpour all day and all night. By daybreak of the second day, the river was rolling and turned brown as it churned its way south. The rain continued and the river rose higher and higher, overflowing its banks. The normally hard ground became a bog, hard for the horses to maneuver.

"No cows crazy enough to come across until the river goes back inside its natural banks so we get to laze around and play cards," Scout said with a slight smile.

"Hope you don't play for high stakes 'cause I ain't got much money on me," Luke answered, remembering Jim's warning.

"That don't matter, I'll take your marker if you get into me too deep," Scout answered with a slight chuckle.

"I don't intend to get into debt to you or anybody else," Luke stated. "I have more important plans for my money than to throw it away for a few hours of pleasure," Luke said with a serious, yet faraway, look on his face.

Scout didn't directly pry as to what Luke's plans might entail but instead asked, "Does that go for spending time in the company of the town women the other men visit?"

His question took Luke by surprise. He took a few seconds to think before he answered. The lure of the young woman in Abilene suddenly appeared in his mind, and he had turned down her free offer. No, he wasn't likely to pay for the pleasures the town women offered, but he wasn't sure he wanted to make that known. He felt certain that would lead to quite a lot of teasing from the other men. Not that he couldn't take their teasing, but why open himself up to something if it could be avoided?

Then Luke looked at Scout. "I plan to save my pay so I can go back to the land I bought near Bandera and build a home for my younger sister and me. I'm all she's got to depend on."

"How old is your younger sister?"

"She's fifteen."

"Why does she need anyone to take care of her? She's old enough to marry and have a husband to take care of her. Where does she live now?" Scout appeared more curious about his sister than the answer to his question about Luke spending money on the painted women in town.

"She lives with the Methodist minister's family in Castroville. Naomi, my sister, takes care of the minister's sickly wife, and they have a little boy about four that she also cares for. It was the best we could do for now."

"How did you come by owning land near Bandera, being so young yourself?" Scout asked, as he scrutinized Luke a bit closer.

Luke hesitated for a few seconds, wondering if he should lie about his age and say he was close to eighteen or nineteen instead of telling the truth, that he was seventeen. Somehow, he had the uncanny feeling the older man would see through his lie.

"I'm seventeen," Luke stated as a matter of fact.

Scout made no further comment concerning his age.

"I bought the land with my and Naomi's own money from working

and saving every penny we could possibly manage." Luke felt no inclination to tell he had wheedled five hundred dollars out of his sorry
brother-in-law. That was no one's business but his and Naomi's. Nor
did he feel inclined to tell Scout or anyone else about being burned out
before they could get started. Of course, Jim knew but wasn't likely to
say anything either. Jim didn't pry into others' business or talk about
their affairs, and Luke respected him for that.

Scout sat quietly, as though he was mulling over what Luke had
told him. He finally spoke. "You are wise for your years. Don't let any
man or woman goad you into being any other way," Scout spoke softly
without looking at Luke.

As the months passed Luke worked with a variety of men. He found
most of them personable and willing to help a fellow rider if needed.

One evening a fellow by the name of Bud Carson rode in
complaining about having to track several cows far into one of the
pastures. He said there weren't many so, if one of the off-duty riders
wanted to help the next day, they could likely make a short day of
rounding them up and getting them to the holding pen to inspect
them.

Luke volunteered, as he much preferred being out riding to hanging
around the cabin doing what they termed "domestic chores."

Bud was an amusing fellow. He didn't exactly curse but had a
favorite saying whether he was surprised, amused, puzzled, or down-
right mad. Bud would come out with, "Damnation, damnation, I say."
He could put such a variety of emphasis on the words that it amused
Luke every time he heard Bud mumbling, saying, or shouting those
words.

They rode for a couple of hours before locating the intruders. There
appeared to only be six scrawny cows. Luke and Bud started herding
them toward the nearest holding pen, about a mile away. About half-

way there, one of the heifers appeared to not like being driven in a particular direction and made a break for it through the brush.

Bud took off after the wayward beast. Just as he was about to get close enough to rope her, she would out smart him and head in another direction.

Luke could hear Bud start with, "Damnation!"

The next time the heifer outwitted him by running under a few low hanging mesquite tree branches. Bud came out more forceful saying, "Damnation, damnation, I say."

Luke couldn't help but be amused. He started chuckling. Before long he burst into full laughter as he watched and listened to Bud's frustration grow.

The unruly heifer outwitted him once more, and Bud let loose.

"Damnation! Damnation, I say!" Bud bellowed as he chased after the feisty little critter, finally managing to snare it with his rope. As he led the heifer back to where Luke waited, he was threatening to cut out its gizzard and have it for supper.

Chapter Eleven

Naomi watched anxiously each day when Isaac returned home at the end of the day to see if he would be carrying mail in his hand. She hoped there would be another letter from Luke, although there was only about one a month. She knew he worked long hours and was away from headquarters for three weeks at a time. Jim would have to write the letter for him, but she longed to hear from her brother as much as possible. She often dreamed of the day when they could return to their own land and build their own house. Oh, what a joyful day that would be; although she liked the Templetons and they treated her well, she still longed for her own home.

Isaac smiled as he saw the look of hope on Naomi's face.

"This is your lucky day," he said as he handed the letter to her.

She would open the letter and then hand it back to Isaac to read to her.

He was teaching her to read and write, but she could not read Jim's scrawling cursive letters yet. After supper, when she had finished cleaning the kitchen, Isaac would give her lessons for about an hour. Then it was time to put Matthew to bed and help Viola prepare for the night. She would then return to the kitchen table and work on her lessons by the dim illumination of the single light bulb mounted high in the twelve-foot ceiling. Most evenings she would study until she heard the mantle clock strike ten o'clock.

Isaac put on his reading glasses and sat in his favorite chair near the fireplace.

Dear Naomi,

I hope this finds you doing well.

I am fine. I think in another month I can print and spell well enough to pen my own letter to you, and I feel sure you can do the same for me. Now, won't that be a fine day for the both of us.

It has rained for several days so things at headquarters are even slower than usual. It makes the days seem awfully long. It does give me more time to practice my lessons.

Give my best regards to the Templeton family.

Your loving brother,

Luke

Although he hadn't actually said much, she cherished every word.

She turned to Isaac, her big eyes filled with anticipation. "Do you think by next month I will be ready to pen my own letter to Luke?"

"Yes, I believe you surely will, Naomi," Isaac answered warmly.

Naomi had brought a breath of freshness to his otherwise rather dreary life. He often wondered if he could go on and on in such a solitary manner if it were not for Matthew. Viola's constant lack of interest in life or what went on around her left him feeling alone and empty. He tried to involve her in his daily activities by telling her about his pupils, church activities, and anything else he could possibly imagine might be of interest to her, but it all seemed for naught.

He had long ago schooled himself to suppress his manly desires knowing it was an impossibility with Viola, although he wasn't quite sure why. The doctor had never said they could not be intimate, but Viola appeared to feel it would drastically further impair her health, so he had moved to the adjoining room in an attempt to avoid any temptation. When Naomi arrived, he had moved to Matthew's room, which served the same purpose.

Naomi had shared her hopes and dreams of her and Luke being able to return to their own land and start again. Isaac sincerely hoped her wish would be fulfilled, although they would miss her terribly when she left. He had no idea how long it would take her and Luke to save enough money to start over, but he realized she spent very little of the small salary they paid her.

He felt certain Luke was doing the same from the sound of some of his letters. Isaac hoped, rather selfishly, Naomi would stay until Matthew turned six and could go to school. Only two more years, but that likely sounded like a lifetime to Naomi.

1922

One Sunday morning, in early spring, Naomi was shocked when she looked up and saw Marcus Markham sitting across the aisle from her. He smiled politely and turned back as though he were taking in every word Pastor Templeton was uttering in his sermon.

Naomi noticed a slight space between Marcus and the Beck family seated on the same pew. He must have come alone. But why would he come this far from home to attend church, she wondered as she tried to concentrate on Isaac's sermon.

Naomi had never seen Marcus in Castroville when she went shopping or to the drugstore to meet some of her friends. She mulled over inviting him to join the congregation for lunch and perhaps find out why he was visiting church today or any day for that matter. She remembered all too well his reputation with the young women. Well, maybe he has changed, she reflected. People often change when they get more mature and realize the error of their ways. He must be at least twenty or maybe older, she decided as she scrutinized his profile. She had to admit he was quite handsome.

As soon as services ended Naomi stepped across the aisle and extended her gloved hand to Marcus, who was smiling at her as though they were old friends. He took her hand and shook it gently with a slight squeeze.

"I must say I was surprised to see you visiting church here in Castroville this morning," Naomi admitted as she returned Marcus's smile.

"I would have been here much sooner if I had known you were here. It has taken me months to learn where you went. I don't see your brother anywhere. Doesn't he attend church?"

"Come join us for lunch, and I'll tell you all about what has happened since we saw you last," she invited.

Marcus bowed slightly. "Lead the way, Ma'am. I didn't know religion came with lunch, or I might have tried it sooner," he quipped as he followed Naomi to a large room next to the sanctuary. Folks were already gathering, and large platters of fried chicken, roast beef, and numerous side dishes were being placed on a long table covered with a white tablecloth.

"Sit here while I help get the food arranged, and then we can visit while we eat." Naomi indicated a chair at the end of one of the long tables lined with chairs.

He watched the lovely young woman as her skirt swished from side to side as she hurried to help the other women. Well, she likely isn't a woman yet, but it won't be long, he thought as he perused her figure that had already filled out more than when he had met her months ago. He'd have to find out her age. No need in getting in too deep if she wasn't old enough to enjoy the advances of a man like him. He wasn't much for just holding hands and giving a girl a quick kiss on the cheek when it was time for the evening to end.

Yet, he had to admit he had not been as attracted to many young women as he had been to Naomi. Although they had only danced for the better part of one evening, he had not been able to shake her lovely, fresh image from his mind. Something about her intrigued him. Possibly it was because she was the one that had gotten away.

They talked amicably during the meal, and Marcus seemed quite anxious to hear about where Luke had gone and when she expected him to return. He even suggested in a casual manner that she let Luke know if he ever changed his mind about selling their land that he and his father might still be interested in buying it.

Naomi assured him they would never sell their land.

Marcus gave her a charming smile. "Well, then, I will look forward to the time when you return to be my neighbor," he said and gave her a flirtatious wink.

"Come for an afternoon ride with me," he invited, when they had finished their meal.

"Did you come all this way by horse and buggy and think you have time for a ride?" she questioned, knowing it was a good half-day's trip back to his ranch.

Marcus laughed. "No, I came in my new roadster. Put on your coat and scarf, and I'll let the top down."

Naomi gasped in delight when they stepped out of the church and she saw the shiny black automobile parked in front of the church.

"Oh, Marcus, it's lovely. When did you get it?"

"As a matter of fact, it was my Christmas present this year," he said as he opened the door for her and then let down the top.

The vast differences in how the rich lived and the working poor lived struck Naomi once again. She couldn't imagine why on earth Marcus would drive all the way to Castroville to attend church and take her for a drive. She certainly wasn't of his class.

She did have to admit it was fun to whiz along the dirt road leading toward San Antonio. The scenery seemed to fly past at such a fast pace it was starting to make her feel queasy in her stomach. She wanted to ask him to slow down, but at the same time didn't want him to think she was a total country bumpkin.

Suddenly he slowed and quickly turned off the main road and bounced along a rough country road. She had never been this direction and wondered where they were headed. After what seemed like a long time the road suddenly came to an end at a pasture gate. Beyond the gate there were only a few cattle, peacefully grazing on the tall grass.

Naomi looked at Marcus with curiosity evident in her gaze.

"Why did you drive all of the way out here? It's going to be hard to get turned around," she commented as she looked at the tall brush on each side of the road.

"I was just looking for a place to be alone with you," Marcus answered with a wicked grin. He scooted toward her and put his arm across the back of the seat as he pulled her near him. "It looks like I found the perfect spot," he whispered as he leaned forward to capture her pretty, sweet lips with a searing kiss.

Unexpectedly Naomi felt as though she couldn't breathe. Feelings of panic gripped her as her thoughts returned to the obnoxious Mr. Newton when he tried to trap her in his bedroom. Now Marcus had her trapped miles from anywhere, and she did not like the feelings racing through her. She shoved at his hard chest trying desperately to put some space between them.

The harder she pushed, the more persistent Marcus became in his amorous advances. Somehow, she managed to remove the shoe from her right foot. She held it with a firm grasp. Exerting all of her strength, Naomi whacked Marcus on the side of his head with the two-inch wooden heel of one of her new pearl-gray pumps. She had ordered them from the Sears Roebuck Catalog. They had cost her $1.99, and she hoped she didn't ruin the pump. She couldn't afford another pair, but there was nothing else handy she could use to defend herself.

Marcus' eyes rolled back in his head and he slumped backward, hitting his head hard against the door handle on his side of the car.

Naomi looked at the inert figure sprawled across the front seat. Fear gripped her. For an instant, she wondered if, this time, she had indeed killed a man.

Marcus felt the stinging blow to the side of his head as darkness was overtaking him. He felt his body falling backward. Before the night engulfed him, he felt the final blow to the back of his head. Then blissfully the pain subsided, and he felt nothing.

"Marcus, Marcus, wake up, we need to go!" an angelic voice called to him from far away.

Then the angel was gently shaking him and calling again. "Marcus, Marcus, wake up, we need to go!"

Why must he be awake for his journey to Heaven, he wondered as the pain began to return to his head. His own grandmother had passed in her sleep and one of the older ranch hands too, so why couldn't he make his Heavenly ascent while he slept? Perhaps his head would feel better by the time he arrived. How long does it take to get there, he questioned, as truthfully, he was a bit surprised to think he was headed in that direction.

The shaking became a bit more vigorous and the voice a bit clearer. "Marcus, open your eyes! Marcus, open your eyes!" the sweet voice repeated with a tinge of concern.

He tried to obey the angel's command. A dim figure came into view, but it looked as though she was surrounded by fog, or perhaps it was heavenly mist. She seemed to be holding what must be a torch to light their way upward. But the torch wasn't lit. Slowly, the fog lifted, and the angel took on the form and features of Naomi. It wasn't a torch she grasped but a shoe.

Memory slowly returned as he blinked his eyes in an attempt to clear his vision. Then he knew why his head was pounding. She had clobbered him with that damn shoe.

"What's that thing made of, cement?" he asked as he attempted to right himself.

"No, wood!"

Marcus grimaced as he rubbed the lump on the side of his aching head and then moved his hand carefully to the back to gently massage the lump that protruded as a result of his collision with the door handle.

"For a few minutes I thought you had done me in, and an angel was calling me for my final journey!" he grumbled.

Naomi laughed. "Marcus, I can assure you, it wouldn't be any angel calling your soul to Heaven. Be grateful you have another chance to change your ways so, when your time comes, that is indeed the direction your soul will be headed."

"Huh," was his only reply. Then he eyed her still holding her shoe. "You can put that shoe back on your foot where it belongs," he moaned.

"I think I'll just wait until you have driven me safely back to the minister's house."

Marcus sat up straight and righted himself behind the steering wheel. He started the car and backed several yards to a slightly wider spot in the road. With much back and forward movements of the car, he managed to get the automobile headed in the right direction. He never said another word to Naomi and drove even faster on their return trip to Castroville.

When he pulled to a screeching stop in front of the Templetons' house, Naomi slipped her foot back into her shoe and quickly exited the car.

She took a few steps, not intending to have any further conversation with Marcus, then she heard him call her name.

"Naomi, I apologize for my behavior and must say you are the only young woman who has ever tried to knock some sense into my hard head."

Naomi was surprised at his words. She felt compelled to turn and look at him. She managed a sweet smile as she almost whispered, "Goodbye, Marcus." Then she turned and with self-assurance continued up the walk to the house.

Marcus watched her calm departure. He spoke quietly to himself, "Someday, Naomi, you and I will meet again." Then he drove away.

During the next year Marcus dropped by the rectory several times intending to ask Naomi out again, but she always managed to have an excuse for not going out with him. After their one encounter in his new roadster on a lonely country road, Naomi was not taking any chances of a repeat incident. Next time she might not be lucky enough to knock him out trying to defend herself.

Although Naomi had made several friends, both female and male, she missed Luke and looked forward to every letter. For now, though, she was content with her living arrangement. She especially enjoyed taking care of Matthew. He was a delightful child, and they were very fond of one another. At times she couldn't imagine leaving Matthew, although she longed to be with Luke too.

Chapter Twelve

After old Mr. Keller passed away, Jim spent a bit more time at headquarters helping Gilbert. It was obvious Willie or Floyd couldn't be depended on for any consistent help. They still had several friends hanging on that followed in their hell-raising footsteps. Little by little, Gilbert and Jim were weeding them out, in spite of Willie's and Floyd's protests about the way their friends were being treated.

Luke was glad to see that the atmosphere at the ranch was improving since old Mr. Keller passed. Gilbert was a married man and wanted a safe place for his wife and children. He tried to keep Floyd and Willie in line but put up with far more nonsense from them than the hired hands. They knew being kin was all that saved them and worked it to their advantage.

Once in a while, Jim managed to spend a few days at one of the river camps. He, like Luke, seemed more content riding the river than being stuck at headquarters.

Occasionally Luke had considered asking if Gilbert's wife might need some help so Naomi could come to the ranch, but he didn't trust what Willie or Floyd might try while he was at the river camp. He knew Gilbert and Jim couldn't keep those two constantly under their watch. It was likely better to leave well enough alone. Naomi was in a safe place with the minister and his family, he reassured himself.

1923

Toward the end of February, Viola took a cold that turned to bronchitis and then into pneumonia. Daily it was evident her body was growing weaker and weaker. Doctor Nimitz came regularly but could do little to stem the downward spiral of Viola's failing health.

Naomi was exhausted from her constant vigil over Viola. Her heart ached for Isaac. The poor man looked like a walking ghost. Lines of worry deepened around his bloodshot eyes, and his movements became those of a much older man. Little Matthew even sensed there was some change in the house and played more sedately with little demands for the usual attention he received, especially from Isaac and Naomi. Even before this illness Viola had spent less and less time with her only child, which surprised and saddened Naomi. She wondered if the boy would even remember his mother.

After three long weeks of her illness, late one night as she slept, Viola quietly passed from this life. Naomi rose to check for a pulse but found none. She leaned over the still woman and put her cheek next to Viola's slightly open mouth but felt no breath. She straightened, quietly walked to Isaac's door, and gently knocked. Isaac opened it almost immediately. He did not have to ask but knew from the tears in Naomi's eyes that the end had come for his wife of twenty-one years.

The church was packed as the minister from Bandera conducted the solemn service. Isaac, Matthew, and Naomi sat on the front pew.

Somehow the sad service seemed fitting for Viola, as her life had seemed somber and lifeless too. Perhaps when she had been younger, and in better health, she was different. Naomi had rarely heard Isaac speak of the earlier years of their marriage. She supposed his thoughts were too consumed with his responsibilities at the present to spend time thinking about a happier past. Naomi hoped the earlier years of their marriage had been happy ones.

Viola's passing would change Naomi's situation too. She had heard snatches of conversations as parishioners came and went from the house to pay their respects. The visitors did not hesitate to point out how inappropriate it would be for Naomi to remain in the widowed minister's house, especially at night. It didn't seem to matter that Isaac was twenty-six years older than she was. Surely, he wouldn't be interested in someone her age, but that didn't seem to matter.

Speculation about where she might stay had involved a number of suggestions, none of which sounded too inviting to Naomi.

After the funeral service and burial, they walked quietly back to the parsonage. Isaac carried Matthew, who was almost asleep, and laid him in his bed for his afternoon nap. He kissed his son on his rosy cheek and gently pulled the blanket over him, as a brisk north wind was bringing in clouds that looked to be threatening rain in a few hours.

Isaac returned to the front room where Naomi sat. Any other day they would have talked freely, but today casual conversation seemed awkward. He started a fire in the fireplace and then sat in his favorite chair staring at the flickering flames. Neither spoke. At last, Isaac lifted his head and turned toward Naomi.

"Naomi, you realize that you can no longer live here as before. I am sorry, but it would never do. It has been decided you will stay with the Widow Green."

Naomi instantly felt a queasiness in her stomach. Widow Green was not a very pleasant person to be around. She smelled of sweat and lye soap. There was a constant smear of snuff dribbles off of her chin, and she spat on the ground or in a nasty looking can. Naomi had been to her small, run-down shack of a house and knew for a fact it had only three small rooms—a parlor, a kitchen, and a bedroom. That meant she would have to share the bed with the smelly old woman. She wanted to protest this arrangement but felt this was not the right time to upset poor Isaac. She would make the best of it but would seek a better living arrangement as quickly as possible. She would plead with Luke to let her come to the ranch where he worked. After all, it sounded like a better place than Jim remembered from when he left years ago. Yes, she would write a letter to Luke today and get it in the post. Surely, he would let her come. At least she could see him every three weeks. Maybe Jim's brother's wife needed some help in the main house. Oh, please, Lord, help me, she prayed silently as a shiver ran down her spine just thinking of having to go to the Widow Green's for even one night.

Luke rode slowly toward camp checking for signs of cattle crossing the river. So far, he had found nothing out of the ordinary, which suited him fine. It seemed as though every time he had found tracks, the strays had already moved far into the pasture, and he spent several extra hours tracking the critters.

The mid-afternoon sun beat down on him. It was already unusually hot for April. They were likely in for a scorcher of a summer if this was any indication of what lay ahead. Rain had been scarce through the winter and spring, leaving the grass hardly green. He had overheard Jim and Gilbert discussing having to sell off part of the livestock if conditions didn't improve soon. That would mean some of the ranch hands would be laid off too. Only a select group was trained as river riders, and they needed all of them. He hated to think about any man losing his job. Luke knew, if he lost his job, it would take lots longer to save enough money to start his own business.

A sudden noise in the underbrush jerked him back from his wandering thoughts. He reined his horse to a stop and listened closely for the sound to come again. In seconds he caught a glimpse of movement in the brush and could hear the gnawing of teeth against bone. Luke sat stark still watching as a brown bear ambled out of the brush, ripping the meat from the bones of one of their sheep.

It was the first bear he had ever seen. He closely watched the bushy animal that would likely stand over five feet tall, and Luke guessed it would weigh three hundred pounds or more. Being so close to the vicious, unpredictable animal, his heart pounded. He feared any sudden movement might make him a prime target for the bear's next meal. Luckily, so far, the bear seemed intent on its current meal. Thankfully, he was downwind from the animal. He didn't really know how close he would have to be for the bear to catch his scent or that of his horse, but he wasn't taking any chances.

Slowly Luke pulled his rifle from its scabbard and took careful aim. In a way, he hated to shoot the imposing animal but knew there was really no choice. It was bad enough to lose some livestock to the creature, but what if the bear came across an unsuspecting human, like the Mexican children that played in the river or the women washing their clothes? He hesitated no longer. With just one blast aimed at the bear's head, it staggered for several steps, took on a walleyed look as it let out a vicious roar, and fell to the ground with a mighty thud. Luke let out a long breath as he stared at the bear lying no more than thirty feet in front of him. Luke nudged his horse forward and sat for several minutes staring at the downed bear. He felt a bit sad at having to kill such a splendid animal.

Luke could hardly wait to reach camp to tell the others about his encounter with the bear. The men had recently found the remains of a few sheep and goats but weren't sure what had been the culprit. Now they would know for sure.

As he rode into camp, he saw Curley Joe had arrived with the supply wagon. That was a relief since they had used the last of the coffee that morning.

Curley Joe greeted Luke with a friendly wave. Then he reached into his shirt pocket and waved a letter in Luke's direction. Luke nodded that he had seen the letter but continued on to the barn to tend to his horse before returning to the cabin.

Before Luke reached the shack, he had told the men about his close encounter with the bear. The riders that had been around for a while didn't seem too surprised. Apparently bears often wandered across the river in search of food, especially in dry weather.

"You're just damn lucky you seed that bear 'afore it seed you," Curley Joe said as he listened to Luke's story. "A few years back one of the river riders got mauled pretty good 'afore he could shoot that mean son of a gun," Curley Joe told Luke. Everyone seemed in agreement that Luke had been lucky, and that included Luke.

When he entered the shack, he saw the letter lying on the table. Luke read his name and address written neatly on the envelope. He smiled to himself knowing it was a letter from Naomi. He recognized her neat, cursive writing, like Jim and the minister used. A surge of pride for his sister's accomplishment swelled up inside Luke. They had both learned a lot over the past couple of years, and their future was looking brighter. Once they had enough money to return to their own land and build again, they could each read and write and do some math. They wouldn't need to depend on anyone else for help.

Luke removed the single page from the envelope.

Dear Brother Luke,

I hope this letter finds you well. I am in good health but had to change where I live.

Luke felt a moment of panic, wondering what had gone wrong with the arrangements he and Jim had made for Naomi.

Viola took sick in February and passed toward the end of March. That meant that I could no longer stay at their house since Isaac no longer has a wife. I have to stay with the Widow Green at night and even share her bed.

She stinks and spits snuff into dirty cans. I don't think I can stand it much longer. I have asked about another place to stay at night, but no one seems to have room for me.

Please, Luke, let me come to the ranch where you live. In your letters, it seems to be better than Jim thought. Maybe I could help in the main house for a place to stay and food. I don't know how I can help you save more money, but please ask Jim's brother if I can come there.

Your loving sister, Naomi

Luke slowly folded the letter and wondered if that would be a wise thing to do. Willie and Floyd lived in the bunkhouse but still had almost free rein in the main house. They were both still hell-raisers and couldn't be trusted around decent women. Gilbert had threatened to run them off more than once but never did it.

It had been close to two years since he had seen Naomi and missed her terribly. He had felt certain she was in a safe place and endured their being apart for her own good. He felt bad about what had happened with Mrs. Templeton's passing and that Naomi had to live with some smelly old woman. But, no, Naomi couldn't live where there would be a constant threat from men like Willie and Floyd. He knew the layout of the house, and her room would be at the far end from Gilbert and his wife. Anyone could sneak into her room, and they would likely never know. What, oh what, was he to do now?

Jim rode in about an hour later to fill in for the rider that had quit. As soon as he saw the downcast expression on Luke's face, he knew something was amiss.

Jim unbuckled his gun belt and laid it on the shelf above his bunk. "What's the long face for?" Jim asked without turning to look at Luke.

"Got a letter from Naomi."

"That usually puts a smile on your ugly face. What's happened?" he asked as he walked to the table where Luke sat, sipping a cup of fresh coffee.

Luke handed the letter to Jim without commenting.

Jim looked at the neat handwriting. He couldn't suppress a smile in spite of Luke's sour mood.

"Hey! This should make you proud. It looks like Naomi has written you a letter in cursive without the reverend's help."

"I am proud for that part. She's been doing that for quite a while but wait until you read what she says."

Jim took that as an invitation for him to remove the letter and read it for himself. First, he poured himself a cup of coffee and slipped off his boots. He pulled the single page from the envelope and read Naomi's sad news. When he finished, he replaced the letter and handed it back to Luke.

"That's too bad about the preacher's wife. Too bad, too, that now Naomi is having to live with the washwoman." Jim drank half of the cup of scalding, hot coffee.

It always amazed Luke how Jim could drink such hot coffee without even flinching. He felt sure it had to be burning Jim's mouth and throat.

"Well—well. What do you think about Naomi coming here? It's a hell of a lot better than it once was but not perfect," Jim said with caution. "But I don't know of any place that is, do you?"

"No," Luke answered as he slowly shook his head. "I certainly trust Gilbert and Marylee, but you know as well as I do that Willie and Floyd still come and go at the main house as they please. Naomi would have a room at the far end of the house from Gilbert and Marylee, so what's to stop one of them from bothering her or even one of the other men if they took a notion?" Luke asked, not trying to hide his exasperation with the situation.

"Well, I have some news that might help put your mind to ease."

"Oh, and what's that?"

"Our little sister, who isn't so little anymore - she's seventeen now, is coming home from school, so there would be someone near Naomi's age in that end of the house. They could watch out for each other. Believe me, Gilbert will kill anyone that messes with Georgiana," Jim emphasized the extent of protection his sister would receive. "Gilbert and I would expect all of the men, including our brothers, to treat Naomi with the same respect," Jim concluded.

Luke looked at Jim in dismay. "You've never mentioned a sister before!"

"Well, she was still so young when I left home not long after our ma passed. Not long after that, Georgiana was sent off to school in San Antonio. At first, she went to a Catholic boarding school for girls. When Georgiana turned twelve, she moved to the Millhouse Finishing School for Young Women. She'll be home in about ten days. I haven't seen her in all of these years, so I suppose I think of her more like some distant cousin than a sister," he said with a regretful look. "It's hard to imagine her a grown-up young woman."

"Now ain't that something!" Luke exclaimed, still in shock at this new revelation about Jim's family. Jim's news also gave him a sudden feeling of great relief. "Do you think Gilbert and Marylee would welcome my sister? She could be lots of help around the house, and, with Marylee about to have another young'un, I expect she could use some extra help with two little ones and a new baby too," Luke sounded hopeful.

"You're due to go in tomorrow. Go straight to Gilbert and Marylee and tell them about Naomi needing a place to stay and that she could be a lot of help around the house. It's up to them, but I think they might be happy to have her, and she would be company for Georgiana. After all, she isn't used to the isolation of ranch life, and having at least one girl as a friend might help her get settled too," Jim suggested as he finished his coffee and rose to refill his cup.

Luke followed Jim's suggestion and rode straight to the main house when he reached headquarters. He was glad to find Gilbert and Marylee in the big kitchen. When he told them about Naomi's situation, they exchanged an understanding look.

Gilbert smiled. "We'll be glad to have some extra help, and Jim was right; it will be good for Georgiana to have someone near her age here, too. Write to your sister to come whenever she's ready. We'll welcome her," Gilbert said as he smiled at his wife.

"Yes, we sure will," Marylee confirmed. "I think this one will be here pretty soon, and an extra pair of hands will be wonderful." Then she frowned slightly. "Gilbert and I have been wondering how much we could depend on Georgiana, since she has been at that fancy school and likely not had much to do in the way of housework or cooking and likely knows nothing about caring for two little boys. Your sister sounds like an answer to my prayers," she told Luke with a pleasant expression.

Luke felt like jumping with joy. He could hardly wait to write to Naomi and tell her to come immediately. Besides, he had missed his sister. For several years they had depended on one another. He was the oldest but remembered how she had taken care of him in Abilene after he got hurt. Yes, indeed, it would be good to have her near, and with Georgiana in the same wing of the house, his mind was far more at ease about her safety.

Chapter Thirteen

Two rather tall, slender young women stood beside several valises chatting as they waited for the 10:20 a.m. train west out of San Antonio. One girl had long, golden blonde hair that shimmered in the bright sunlight and piercing, cornflower blue eyes that enhanced her light complexion. Her oval face was lovely. Full cheeks complimented her features, and her supple mouth was touched with a pink blush. When she smiled, she displayed even, white teeth that added to her beauty. The other girl had ebony hair, the color of a moonless night, and black eyes that seemed to dance with excitement. Her skin was a light tan, depicting her Hispanic origin. Her high cheekbones indicated some Indian blood in her ancestry. She had a slightly pointed chin and lovely full lips. Both girls were striking in their looks, their new dresses, hats, and gloves of the latest fashion. Both seemed unaware of the admiring glances they were receiving from most of the men that happened by.

When the train whistle blew signaling it was about ready to depart, a porter rushed forward to gather the young women's bags and place them on the train. Once they were settled, he received a gracious smile and generous tip from each young lady.

The train rocked gently as it made its way slowly westward. It stopped at the small town of Castroville and took on three passengers. One was a pretty young woman who looked to be about the same age of the two girls who had boarded in San Antonio. She wore a plain green dress that had seen better days and only had one small valise, which she carried herself. She took a seat two rows behind the two smartly dressed young women, who paid little attention to anyone as they continued their constant chatter.

Naomi finally let out a long sigh of relief. She was really on her way to join Luke at the Sycamore Creek Ranch near Del Rio. It had been sad to say good-bye to Isaac and Matthew, but she was all too happy to be out of the Widow Green's smelly little house. Soon the train's mild rocking lulled her into a peaceful sleep. When she awoke it was late afternoon; a stab of panic gripped her. What if she had missed the stop in Del Rio and had gone too far? She looked around for the porter to ask but did not see him in the car. The two girls had ceased their constant chatter. One was looking out the window while the other had dozed off with her head resting on a pillow with a gleaming white pillowcase. Naomi wondered where she had found a pillow. She hadn't noticed any when she walked down the aisle of the train.

Finally, Naomi got up her nerve to ask the other young woman where they were.

"Excuse me, Miss, could you tell me if we have passed Del Rio yet?"

The girl with long blonde hair turned so she could look at Naomi. For an instant, Naomi thought the girl didn't intend to answer her question.

"No, we still have about two hours before we reach Del Rio. Is that where you're going?"

"Yes, my brother works on the Sycamore Creek Ranch near there. I'm going to join him and help in the main house," Naomi volunteered.

The young woman's mouth fell open in a slight gape. "Did you say the Sycamore Creek Ranch?"

"Yes."

"That's where I'm going. That is my home." Then she gave a sarcastic laugh. "I guess you'll be my new maid," she said and turned her attention back toward the passing scenery.

Naomi felt tears stinging her eyes at the girl's rebuff. What did she care if she did have to be that hateful girl's maid? At least she would be near Luke part of the time.

Gilbert stood on the depot platform ready to pick up the three young women. Since it was dusk, they checked into a nearby boarding house for the night. The trip to the ranch would take several hours.

The boarding house didn't look as nice as the one where she and Luke had stayed in Abilene. Well, the downstairs part had looked better than this place. The attic where she and Luke stayed wasn't very nice, but Miss Pearl had almost been like a second mother to them. This place needed a fresh coat of paint, and the inside didn't look much better. The wallpaper was faded and full of wrinkles, further showing its age. Otherwise, it was clean enough, but Naomi was more concerned with getting to the ranch to see Luke than the condition of the boarding house where she would only spend one night.

The three girls shared one room and Georgiana arrogantly instructed Naomi to hang up her traveling dress, get out a fresh dress for dinner, and to lay out her sleepwear.

Rosalinda Ruiz appeared a bit shocked at Georgiana's attitude toward the girl they had met on the train.

As soon as Georgiana and Rosalinda left to join Gilbert for dinner, Rosalinda whispered, "What's with you treating that poor girl like she's your slave?"

Georgiana laughed. "While you were napping, I found out she is going to be a maid at the ranch. I don't suppose she's my slave, as you put it, but she will be my maid," Georgiana said in a snooty tone.

Naomi had stayed in their room. She had an apple and cold biscuit left from her trip. She did not want to be humiliated further in front of her new employer by his spoiled sister.

"The Sisters would be very disappointed in your less than benevolent attitude to those not equal to your station in life. You would find yourself on your hands and knees, scrubbing the floors for such behavior," Rosalinda reminded her.

"I don't have to worry about the Sisters any more or any of the teachers at finishing school or what they think, so don't bother me with a lecture," Georgiana told her friend, not showing any remorse for her behavior.

Rosalinda shook her head, disappointed in her best friend's attitude.

Naomi pretended to be asleep when they returned. But first, she had done as Georgiana directed. She took the single cot, leaving the big fluffy bed for Georgiana and Rosalinda.

Naomi prayed that Gilbert's wife would be a kind woman. That would certainly make life at the ranch more tolerable.

The wagon bounced over the rough, rutted road that wound in a southeasterly direction out of Del Rio. Although the town was small, it was teaming with people. Naomi noticed a few stores, a school, and mostly wood-frame houses. They did pass a few large brick or rock houses as they neared the edge of town. Maybe a family that lived in one of those fine houses would need someone to work, and she wouldn't have to put up with Georgiana. If she came to town to work, she wouldn't get to see Luke much, so maybe putting up with Georgiana wouldn't be so bad once they got to the ranch, she reasoned as she looked at the countryside dotted with scrubby sagebrush and a few trees. In the distance to the west, she would catch an occasional glimpse of the river that Gilbert said was the Rio Grande, the border between the United States and Mexico. Far to the west in

Mexico, she could see a long mountain range. Gilbert pointed out the shape of the mountains and said they were called the Sleeping Lady Mountains.

This was a harsh land, not lush and green like their land near Bandera with clear running streams. Naomi wondered again how much longer it would be before she and Luke could return to their own land. She hadn't been able to save much money out of her small salary and had no idea how much Luke had saved. Hopefully, they could talk soon and make definite plans about their future.

"Mr. Gilbert," Naomi spoke to her new employer.

Gilbert chuckled. "We just go by first names at the ranch. Don't stand on formalities," he told her in a kind manner.

Naomi blushed slightly. "Is Luke waiting at headquarters?"

"No, he and Jim will be coming in tomorrow afternoon. Then we'll have a big celebration for our sister and for you, too."

Georgiana glanced over her shoulder at Naomi and made an ugly face. It was all too clear to Naomi that Georgiana didn't want to share the limelight with her or likely anyone.

Naomi couldn't help but wonder how a girl raised by the Catholic Sisters had become so self-centered and hateful. She had noticed that even Georgiana's friend, Rosalinda, seemed shocked at Georgiana's recent behavior.

Rosalinda saw what Georgiana had done and truly felt sorry for Naomi.

Rosalinda had suspected from time to time that Georgiana had put her own interest above others. On occasions Georgiana had made herself look superior to her classmates in the eyes of their teachers and the head mistress. However, most of the time she was fun and pleasant to be around. Rosalinda had always gotten along well with Georgiana in the past, but she didn't like the way Georgiana was treating Naomi. In fact, she wished Naomi were going home with her. Life at the hacienda would be lonely. There were a few other young women, but they were already married, and most had a baby or two. Rosalinda loved the babies, but she wouldn't have much in common with those young women anymore.

Gilbert pointed to a buggy and several mounted riders waiting at the juncture of the road they were traveling. "Rosalinda, it looks like the welcome committee is waiting for you," Gilbert said with a chuckle.

"Yes, Mama and Papa and likely some of my brothers," she answered with delight. Her dark eyes sparkled as she gazed toward those waiting to greet her.

After Gilbert stopped their wagon alongside the fancy buggy, he introduced Naomi to Señor and Señora Ruiz. They were an elegant-looking couple, and the four mounted riders were handsome men, who all favored their father. They were dressed in the traditional ornate Mexican attire, quite different than anything Naomi had ever seen before.

It was evident they were delighted to see their youngest daughter and promised to come visit soon. They also invited Georgiana and Naomi to come visit Rosalinda very soon.

Naomi knew she would not likely be invited to go when Georgiana went to see her friend unless she wanted her to act as her personal maid. Naomi didn't mind working but expected to be treated the way the Templetons had treated her. She certainly hoped this wouldn't turn out to be another situation like working for the Newtons. Gilbert certainly appeared to be a respectable man, and Naomi fervently hoped his wife would be a nice lady.

It wasn't much farther to the Sycamore Creek Ranch house. Gilbert summoned two of the ranch hands to help unload Georgiana's bags and carry them to her room and Naomi's one bag to her room. Naturally, Georgiana had a larger room, but the room Naomi was to occupy was larger and nicer than anywhere she had stayed. It was almost twice as large as her room at the Reverend's house in Castroville.

All of the furniture throughout the ranch house was large pieces made from dark wood. The dining table in the main dining room could easily seat twenty people. It reminded her of the long dining table in the Newtons' house in Abilene, but this was a far less formal dining room. In the kitchen, where the family took most meals, was a large round table with eight sturdy ladder-back chairs around it. Three long sofas and several chairs filled the main room. Each sofa held colorful pillows that you sank into when you sat on them. The bedrooms were furnished with large four-poster beds, dressers with eight to twelve drawers, washstands with a pitcher and bowl for washing, and a writing desk and chair.

Naomi stood in her own room admiring the pitcher and bowl that were covered in pink and red roses. She ran her fingers around the rim of the bowl and soon found a jagged edge along the back where it had been chipped. Oh, what a shame, she thought, that something so lovely wasn't as perfect as it appeared. At that instant, a picture of Georgiana's face flashed through her mind. Naomi gave her head a little shake to clear her thoughts. That isn't fair, she chastised herself. After all, she really didn't know the girl that well. Maybe in time, they would become friends.

Naomi counted five bedrooms in the wing she and Georgiana would share and supposed there were the same amount in the other wing that Gilbert, Marylee, and their children occupied. Naomi especially liked the long front porch with a variety of chairs and two porch swings. It would be a nice place to sit in the evening because of the shade and gentle breeze it provided.

As soon as supper was over and Naomi had finished helping Marylee clean the kitchen, she excused herself and went to her room. She fell across her bed exhausted from the long trip and quickly fell asleep. Hours later she awoke realizing it was dark and she was still in her traveling clothes. She found a candle and lit it to dress for bed. Just as she lay down, she heard a smothered giggle coming from the direction of Georgiana's room.

What would Georgiana be giggling about in the middle of the

night? she wondered as she listened intently for more sounds. Then she heard the unmistakable low rumble of a man's voice.

Briefly, she wondered if she should go check on the girl. Then she heard their hushed laughter and decided whatever was going on was none of her affair.

Naomi put her pillow over her head to drown out any further sounds and was soon asleep.

Most of the next day she helped Marylee in the kitchen. They were cooking a grand feast for the welcome home party that night in Georgiana's honor. Naomi was relieved to find Marylee a very pleasant, easygoing person and believed they would get along well.

Marylee and Gilbert insisted the party was also to welcome Naomi to the ranch. Naomi graciously thanked them for including her in the celebration. Mostly, she just wanted to see Luke.

When Gilbert came in at mid-morning for a cup of coffee and to check on his very pregnant wife, he gazed around the kitchen. "Where's Georgiana?"

"Still sleeping as far as I know," Marylee answered as she gave him a questioning look.

"Sleeping at this time of the day!" he repeated as though he could hardly believe what his wife had said. He rose from the table and walked briskly down the hall toward the girls' bedrooms.

Naomi and Marylee could hear him brusquely calling Georgiana's name before he reached her room.

"Get up!" they heard him almost shout. "We don't sleep the day away around here. There's work to be done!"

Naomi and Marylee exchanged a quick glance. They couldn't hear Georgiana's reply, only the clomping of Gilbert's boots as he returned to the kitchen with a scowl on his normally pleasant face.

Naomi was all too aware of the reason Georgiana remained in bed so late. She didn't want to cause trouble or become entangled in family matters by telling what she had heard in the middle of the night coming from Georgiana's room.

By late afternoon the yard was full of the ranch hands and the few men that had families. A long table was laid with huge platters and bowls filled with all kinds of delicious smells of food. All day the bunkhouse cook had been roasting a pig on a spit over a pit of hot coals. Naomi had fried enough chicken to fill two large platters, and another held thick slices of smoked ham. Bowls of potato salad, green beans, pinto beans, corn on the cob, and boiled squash lined the table. At the end were three cakes and several pies. The married ranch hands' wives helped provide some of the food for the celebration.

Several men were playing fiddles and guitars as the throng of guests loaded their plates and found a place to sit. Blankets had been spread on the ground for mothers with small children. Besides Gilbert and Marylee and the foreman, only three other ranch hands were married with families. The cowboys sat on the ground cross-legged as they wolfed down an abundance of food. Most of the men went back for seconds or even thirds.

Naomi kept scanning the crowd looking for Luke. She couldn't help but fret about Luke still not being at headquarters. She felt uneasy that something might have happened to him or Jim. Gilbert had said they would be coming to headquarters this afternoon, and she hated to bother Gilbert by asking more questions.

After a while, Gilbert noticed her anxious expression.

"Naomi, sometimes the men are late getting in from the river camps. It just depends on what's going on. If they have to go hunt down cattle, it might be tomorrow before Luke gets here. I'm sorry he may not make it for the big party, but that's just part of ranching. Work comes first," Gilbert said kindly. "Please try not to worry and enjoy yourself. Come on, let me introduce you to some of these handsome fellows that are just dying for a dance with a pretty girl," Gilbert told her with a big grin.

Naomi danced with quite a few of the better-looking cowboys and several of the ones who weren't as appealing. They were all courteous and polite, but they were in full view of their boss. She wondered how some might behave if she found herself alone with them. Memories of the affluent Mr. Newton in Abilene came back to haunt her. He had been a so-called pillar of the community in public, but in private, she had certainly seen a different side of him. As Naomi looked around at all of the men and only a few married women she realized why Luke had been worried about her coming to the ranch. She and Georgiana were the only single women within miles. Naomi knew she would have to be very careful about where she went alone and with whom she associated.

Chapter Fourteen

On his return ride to the river camp, shortly after latching gate six, Luke came across the unmistakable tracks of where fifteen or more head of cattle had come across the river. He rode to the top of the embankment and scanned the surrounding countryside. Far to the east he caught a glimpse of movement but couldn't actually tell from this distance if it was their cattle or the ones that had crossed the river. Wearily he turned his mount in their direction. No need to rush at this point. Judging from past experience, he wasn't going to make it back to the homestead tonight or maybe by the next night either. Knowing Naomi was waiting for him, and that she would be disappointed when he didn't ride in, made the delay even harder. Unfortunately, there was no choice in the matter.

Once he left the well-worn path along the river, riding became a slow go. Luke guided his horse, Bo, through the sagebrush, avoiding large and small patches of prickly pear cactus and low branches of the scrubby mesquites, and watched for any animal holes that might cause his horse to lose its footing. Luke had been assigned four horses to use for his rides. The riders traded them out as the horses quickly learned the routine and became bored and less dependable. Bo was the favorite of his string.

A deer suddenly bolted from the brush a few feet in front of him, momentarily startling the horse and Luke. Bo instantly made a quick, jerking sidestep that could have thrown a less experienced rider. After a few mishaps in his earlier days as a river rider, landing on the hard, rocky ground and in one prickly pear patch, Luke had learned to keep a firm grip and react quickly to prevent just such a calamity.

The sun was sinking toward the western horizon, casting a warm orange glow over the countryside as shadows lengthened, when Luke reached a point where he could plainly see the small herd of about twenty or so scrawny cows. One look at their size told him they had crossed the river. It would likely take three riders most of tomorrow to round them up, drive them to the nearest holding pen, and scratch each one for ticks. It took time to examine each cow from "A to izzard," as Scout would say. The men would spend hours feeling each animal, literally running their hands over the animal while using their fingernails to find the buried ticks. Luke had learned early on that cows, and especially horses, weren't the most cooperative critters on earth either.

"Ticks, why on earth were they put here?" Luke muttered with disgust. All they did, that Luke could determine, was cause trouble and extra hours of hard work for the riders. Well, that was the main reason for the job so no need in complaining; he mulled it over as he turned toward the river camp. It would be good dark by the time he got there. Luke hoped there would be enough supper left to fill his hollow belly.

Bo sensed where they were headed and tried to pick up the pace, but Luke patiently held him back as he guided the anxious animal over the uneven terrain toward home. This was no time to take a chance on the horse stepping in a gopher hole and losing its footing.

At daybreak, two riders followed Luke as he led the way back to where he had spotted the renegade cows. Toward the end of a long, hot, arduous day, they had rounded up twenty-three cows, searched the far-flung pasture for more strays, driven them to the nearest holding pen, scratched each critter, and, after finding the deadly ticks, given the cows their first dipping. It was late afternoon when they finished. Luke was too tired to think of riding any further than the river camp for that day. He felt let-down that his long-awaited reunion with his sister would have to wait another day.

"Naomi, Naomi," she heard some man's voice calling to her from far away. What man would be calling her late at night? It wasn't Luke's voice, Naomi thought, as she struggled to locate the distant voice.

"Naomi, wake up. Marylee is having the baby, and I need your help."

Naomi's eyes flew open as she suddenly recognized Gilbert's voice calling to her from the other side of her closed door.

"I'll be right there," she answered as she slipped out of bed and hurriedly put on her lightweight summer wrapper over her cotton nightgown. As she made her way by candlelight to the far end of the house, she dreaded what might be expected of her. She had never seen a baby born and had only heard sketchy gossip about what happened at birthing.

Just as she reached the doorway of the couple's room, brightly lit with several kerosene lamps, Marylee let out a loud moan and heaved her body in a backward motion in apparent agony. Her face was pale and wet with sweat; tears rolled from the corners of her eyes.

Naomi stood in the doorway transfixed as she took in the heart-wrenching scene.

Gilbert looked in her direction when he heard her give a short gasp.

"Sorry, Naomi. I need you to stay with her while I go get Maude Owens to come help. She delivers most of the babies around here," he explained as he rose to leave.

"You mean you're going to leave me alone with, with—" Naomi couldn't finish the sentence as alarming panic gripped her.

"I have to," Gilbert said, a bit impatiently. "It won't take long. I should be back with Maude in twenty minutes or so," he assured her as he quickly brushed past her without another word and was gone into the night.

Marylee let out an even louder groan that ended in a low scream. Her face became contorted into a grotesque expression, emphasizing the enormity of her pain.

Naomi had an overwhelming urge to run and keep on running. What on earth would she do if the baby started to come before Gilbert and Maude got back? She felt an almost uncontrollable alarm rising within her. It was hard to take in a sufficient amount of air to fill her lungs. Lightheadedness seized her and Naomi feared she might faint.

Maybe she should run to get Georgiana to come stay with them. She likely didn't know any more than Naomi, but at least she wouldn't be alone.

Naomi turned and ran headlong into a hard chest. She staggered backward, almost losing her balance.

"What's the matter?" she heard Jim's low voice ask as he grabbed her arm to steady her.

Naomi looked up into Jim's concerned face and crystal blue eyes that seemed much too close.

Jim released Naomi's arm as she stepped back to put some distance between them.

"Gilbert told me to stay with Marylee until he could go get Maude, but—but I don't know anything about delivering a baby. I was going to get Georgiana to stay with me until Gilbert and Maude get here," she confessed with a slight blush at discussing such a topic with Jim.

Jim laughed softly. "I doubt Georgiana would be of any help. I'll stay with you. I don't know why Gilbert didn't come get me to go after Maude. Not thinking straight, I suppose."

"Why are you up at this hour?" Before he could answer she rushed on, "Did Luke make it in from the river camp too?"

Jim shook his head. "No, likely tomorrow. I got back late and I couldn't sleep, so I walked outside to have a smoke. When I saw all of the lights over here, I decided I better see what was going on."

"I'm glad you did." Naomi gave a sigh of relief, knowing she was not alone. Then she asked a bit shyly, "Do you know how to deliver a baby if it decides to come before they get back?"

Jim quirked an eyebrow. "I've delivered plenty of calves and foals so guess we could manage in a pinch," he answered. Jim turned his attention to his sister-in-law as she let out another horrendous moan.

When she could catch her breath, Marylee lifted her head to see who was in the room.

"What are you doing here, Jim?" she asked in surprise at seeing her brother-in-law.

"I went outside for a smoke and saw all of the lights so decided I better check on things. I don't know why that knuckle-headed brother of mine didn't send me to bring Maude," he answered with an edgy laugh.

"OOOOH!" Marylee almost screamed.

Jim looked down at his scruffy boots and then at Marylee. "What can we do to help?" he asked with concern.

To Naomi, it sounded like he might be dreading hearing the answer almost as much as she did.

"Naomi, will you wipe my face with the damp cloth?" she asked, panting for breath.

Naomi moved to her bedside. She wrung out the cloth that lay in a basin of cool water and gently wiped Marylee's face, hoping against hope that Gilbert and Maude would arrive very, very soon. She glanced at Jim where he stood near the foot of the bed.

Marylee looked at Jim. "It would be a terrible thing if you and Naomi have to deliver this baby, but I don't think it's gonna wait much longer," she managed to bite out as another pain racked her body.

Jim cocked his head to one side; then, a slow grin touched his lips.

"I believe I hear them coming now so don't fret," he said kindly.

Gilbert burst into the room with Maude right behind him, giving him "what for" for waiting so long to come after her.

Jim touched Naomi on the elbow and motioned toward the door with a slight nod of his head. She gladly followed him out of the room, knowing Marylee was in much better hands now.

Jim had picked up the candle Naomi had left sitting on the table beside the door and relit it.

"I'll walk you to your room," he told her softly.

Naomi started to protest but, for some reason, did not say a word as they made their way silently through the dark house. When they reached her door, Jim opened it and handed Naomi the candleholder.

"Goodnight, Naomi," he whispered as he stepped slightly forward. Their bodies scarcely touched. Jim lowered his head and placed a tender kiss on her cheek.

With his nearness, the masculine smell of tobacco and soap floated lightly in the air. Naomi felt a thrill she had never experienced. She stood for several seconds stunned at his action. Then she timidly touched her cheek where she could still feel the faint brush of his lips. The feelings of that brief, gentle kiss and the slight touch of Jim's warm body against hers were so unlike anything she had ever experienced before. She certainly had not liked the unwanted attention forced on her by Mr. Newton or Marcus Markham, but these feelings were different, very different.

Jim turned and made his way through the dark house toward the back door. As he walked slowly toward the bunkhouse, he wondered what on earth had possessed him to kiss Naomi on the cheek. The startling part was once his lips brushed her soft skin, he instantly wanted to possess her sweet lips. A wave of shock at such an idea had surged through him. He was several years older than Naomi and far more experienced. Although many young women were married with children at her age, Luke had protected her. Jim sensed she knew as little about men as she did about delivering a baby.

As Jim stretched out on his cot, he reasoned that he must tread lightly in any pursuit of Naomi if his attraction to her persisted. She likely thought him much too old for her, and she was probably right. He didn't want to jeopardize his friendship with Luke by making unwanted advances toward his sister.

By mid-morning the next day Naomi had prepared breakfast, tended to Marylee and the newborn baby, and dressed the two boys. All the while Georgiana was still leisurely cleaning the kitchen. Naomi had gathered three basketfuls of clothes and was getting ready to wash. As she filled the last tub full of hot water, she saw Luke riding toward the house.

Naomi dropped the water bucket and ran to greet her brother.

"Luke, Luke," she shouted as the two met. He quickly dismounted, lifted Naomi as though she were still a child instead of a young woman, and swung her in a circle.

"Damn! It's good to see you, little sister," he grinned as he sat her on her feet and held her away from him. He looked her over from head to toe. "You've blossomed since I last saw you," he stated with a familiar teasing little grin.

Naomi felt a blush reach her cheeks. "Oh, Luke, you still like to taunt me, don't you?" she responded with a happy laugh.

"Of course. Even when you're sixty or seventy, I'll still be teasing you, if we're still around."

"Huh! I doubt either one of us last that long. Gosh! It's good to see you, dear brother!" Naomi beamed.

"You, too," Luke said as he gave her another brief hug.

Naomi scrutinized his growth of whiskers and hair that was longer than she had ever seen it before.

"Is this the new you?" she asked, grinning as she gestured toward his face and hair.

"We aren't exactly high on grooming while at the river camps," he answered with a sly grin. "How are things going for you here?"

"Oh, fine. Marylee had her baby last night," she said, with her eyes twinkling at the thought of the pink-faced newborn. "A pretty little girl this time."

"I always thought most babies looked alike, wrinkled and red," Luke answered.

"That's because you're a man," Naomi giggled.

"How are you and Jim's sister, I forgot her name, getting along?"

"Her name is Georgiana." Naomi gave a slight shrug of her shoulders. "She can be a bit trying at times. You know she went to one of those fancy boarding schools for girls in San Antonio. She doesn't know how to do much of anything around the house. I guess they just taught them how to act when they marry a rich man that can furnish maids to do all the work," Naomi observed, but not in a mean-spirited manner.

"Well, don't let her push you around. You're here to help Marylee, not be some stuck-up girl's maid."

"Don't worry, I can fend for myself, as you should know by now."

"Yes, I know, you've had lots of practice at that. Well, I'm glad you're here, but mind yourself around all of these men. Most are decent fellows and know you're my sister, but a few can't be trusted. Two of the worst are Willie and Floyd. They may be family, but they're both worthless so watch out. If either of them tries anything with you while I'm not around, you go straight to Gilbert. He knows how they are," Luke warned.

Naomi gave her brother an admiring grin. "I'll be careful. I don't want to cause any trouble, especially for you. Will you come have supper at the main house with the family and me tonight? I'm sure they won't mind since I'll be doing the cooking."

"Sure, I know that will be far ahead of the bunkhouse food." Luke answered as he playfully tweaked her nose.

Naomi set about preparing one of Luke's favorite meals - chicken fried steak with cream gravy, mashed potatoes, green beans, buttermilk biscuits, and apple cobbler for dessert. She hummed as she worked in the warm kitchen. Today she didn't mind the heat. This was a special meal to celebrate their being reunited.

It was Georgiana's job to set the big table in the dining room for the evening meal. Naomi told her that her brother would be joining them for supper.

"Willie went to town so he can have his chair. I sure hope he bathes before joining us for a meal. I detest being around these smelly men with their hairy faces. If I didn't know better, I'd think we lived among a bunch of bears. You would think there wasn't enough water for a bath more than once a month, the way they act. Some of the men I danced with the other night almost made me gag," Georgiana complained while holding her nose as though she were keeping out their obnoxious odors.

Naomi laughed. "I agree, most aren't the cleanest people I've ever met. I'm glad Luke isn't like that." She felt sure he would at least bathe before coming for supper, but she wasn't sure he'd shave off all of those whiskers.

"I hope not since he'll be sitting next to me," Georgiana concluded as she continued to place the eating utensils just so on the table.

Naomi had overheard Georgiana telling Gilbert she intended to order a set of china, silverware, and crystal goblets for the dining table. He had laughed and told her she better order a double set as they likely wouldn't last long around this bunch.

Naomi thought that finery would look a bit out of place in the ranch house dining room. This was an entirely different atmosphere to the Newtons' elaborate home where that sort of thing was appealing. She kept her opinion on the matter to herself knowing Georgiana was going to suit herself no matter what anyone else thought.

Just as Naomi finished setting the platters and bowls heaped high with the delicious-looking and smelling food on the table, the family started to take their places. Luke and Jim were the last to enter. Jim took his chair and motioned Luke to the empty chair beside Georgiana.

Naomi instantly saw the look on Georgiana's face. She didn't like the look of sheer delight that lit Georgiana's eyes as she gazed in awe at Luke. He had indeed bathed, shaved, and even attempted to trim his own hair. Luke had turned into a handsome man, but Naomi knew he wasn't the man for Miss Georgiana Keller. He would never be rich enough to suit her.

Naomi took a deep breath to steady her nerves before she spoke.

"Georgiana, I'd like you to meet my brother, Luke. Luke, this is Georgiana, the only girl in the Keller family," she said, trying to sound pleased to make the introduction.

Luke nodded politely as he took his seat.

The entire family chatted freely during the meal. Luke had apparently taken many meals with the family before her arrival, as they seemed accustomed to his presence at the family table.

Georgiana couldn't seem to keep her eyes off Luke. By the end of the meal, Naomi was beginning to worry. Luke seemed quite pleased with her attention. Now it was her turn to remind him about Georgiana being so spoiled and trained to be the wife of a rich man. In her opinion, Luke would be wise to watch his step around her.

Every evening Luke came to the main house for dinner, and every time Georgiana arranged for him to be seated next to her. Willie and Floyd soon got the idea that Luke's company was preferred over either of them, even if they were her kin. Naomi saw Jim eyeing Georgiana and Luke. She hoped Jim might say something to Luke as a friend. Maybe she could prompt Jim in that direction.

Naomi had not been alone with Jim since the night he kissed her on the cheek. She didn't want to appear to be chasing after him, so she had stayed busy and made no effort to seek out his company. Finally, on Friday evening, she did seek out his company as he sat on the big front porch after dinner. She wasn't aiming for another kiss but wanted to see what he thought about Luke and Georgiana being so friendly.

Naomi had seen Luke and Georgiana walking slowly together toward a nearby pond where there were big shade trees. It too was a pleasant place to sit in the late evening. It was also a bit secluded from the main house.

Naomi opened the front door and saw Jim sitting on one of the front porch swings engrossed in reading.

"Evening, Jim."

Jim lifted his head and saw Naomi approaching. He scooted to one side of the swing to make room for her to join him.

"Come sit a spell. It's much cooler out here," he invited.

"Thank you. Yes, it certainly is cooler than inside the house and especially the kitchen," she commented as she joined him on the swing.

"What are you reading?"

Jim turned the book so she could see the front cover but read aloud, "Of Human Bondage, by Somerset Maugham."

Naomi peered at the book cover but only commented, "That's a strange name, Somerset."

Jim smiled, knowing the books he read wouldn't likely capture Naomi's interest with her meager education. Jim thought it was a real shame she never had a chance to become better educated. She was obviously smart. He was drawn to Naomi's youth and beauty. Over the past few days, he had wondered if he could ever truly be happy with a wife so far less educated than him. He had always envisioned spending his life with someone who shared his interests, who enjoyed reading the same books, and who could engage in in-depth discussions about their content. He shouldn't have kissed Naomi on the cheek. The only purpose that served was to ignite his desire for a woman, a wife. It was time he married and started his own family, but yet—. Naomi still seemed very young to him and too young for him, he admitted.

They sat in companionable silence for several minutes.

"Jim, what do you think about your sister and Luke being so...so chummy?" Naomi ventured.

Jim stretched his long legs and gave the swing a slight push. "I haven't given it much thought."

Naomi turned and looked at Jim. "Well, don't you think they are spending a bit too much time together? I don't think they're suited for one another. Luke is just a plain workingman. Georgiana needs—, well, I think she would want a man with far more than Luke can ever offer." She paused and took a deep breath. "I don't want to see my brother hurt."

Jim quirked an eyebrow, "What about my sister getting hurt?"

Naomi cleared her throat to give herself a moment to think of how to answer Jim without saying anything unkind about Georgiana. "I'm thinking about both of them. After all, Georgiana was educated to be a lady, a rich man's wife." Naomi gave a small nervous laugh.

Jim laughed out loud. "You're right about that, Naomi. From what I can tell, she certainly hasn't been much help around here."

"Well, I don't think Luke will ever be a rich man, so why start something that may hurt them both?" Naomi persisted.

"The thing is, I respect Luke and don't think he will let things go too far. He doesn't need me, or you, telling him what to do."

"I don't know. He hasn't had any steady girlfriends that I know of. He's likely flattered by Georgiana's attention and may lose his head and heart."

"Naomi, I learned long ago, it is best to let other people tend to their own business. Who am I to tell Luke who he should or shouldn't spend time with? Besides, Luke is a grown man," Jim stated.

Naomi wondered if Jim still thought Luke was older than he actually was, or was he referring to another matter about him being a man? She didn't know what Luke had been doing during the time they were apart but didn't feel comfortable asking Jim to elaborate on what he had said.

Naomi realized she wasn't going to persuade Jim to intervene. It seemed it was up to her to try to put an end to Luke and Georgiana's relationship before it got too far along.

Jim felt tempted to slip his arm across the back of the swing and then—what? No, he needed to be careful about any advances he made toward Naomi until he was certain of his own feelings about their differences. He needed to resolve in his own mind about her lacking education. Would that stand between their true happiness as husband and wife? Jim also felt concern about their age difference. Yes, he needed to be cautious, he thought. As a way of letting Naomi know their discussion had ended, Jim opened his book and continued to read.

Naomi was a bit let down when Jim opened his book and started reading, as though she weren't there.

Maybe she had misjudged his interest in her. His kiss must have just been a sudden impulse and nothing more. She felt a pang of disappointment, although she wasn't sure she could ever want a serious relationship with Jim. After all, he was a lot older than she and would be an old man while she would still be relatively young. Besides, he read books she certainly couldn't understand or wouldn't likely be of interest to her either. He needed to find somebody like a schoolmarm or a woman that worked in a bank or something like that for a wife. Yes, Jim needed an educated woman nearer his age.

A few days later the immediate problem with Luke and Georgiana was solved without Naomi's interference.

One of the river riders rode in from one of the river camps to tell Gilbert two of the men were down sick. It seemed they had eaten spoiled beans and were taking turns in the outhouse or bushes and throwing up.

Gilbert called for Luke and Jim to head out to take their places.

Before he rode out, Luke went to find Georgiana to explain what had happened. He found her sitting in the large living room perusing the Sears-Roebuck Catalog. On the table beside her lay a pen and paper with a long list of items she was planning to order. When he entered, she looked up and greeted him with a delightful smile.

"Luke, I was just about to come find you. Come sit," she invited as she patted the cushion beside her. "I want to order you some new shirts and pants but didn't know your size."

Luke chuckled, "Now why would you want to do that?"

"Because, silly, I was thinking maybe we could persuade Gilbert to take Marylee and the kids and us to town some weekend when you're at headquarters. You and I could go out."

"Go out! Out where?" Luke asked, surprised.

"Oh, we could go to the Opera House or to a dance or go to one of the nicer cafes for a meal, alone! Doesn't that sound like fun?" she asked, flashing him a charming smile.

"Yes, but don't plan on that happening any time soon. I have to go back out to the river camp."

"Why? It's not time for another week."

"Two of the men are sick, so Jim and I have to go early to take their places. Besides, I'm not sure Gilbert will favor taking you and me to town for a weekend on the town, even if he and Marylee are along."

"Why wouldn't he?" Georgiana asked, a bit miffed.

"Georgiana, I am just a hired hand. The only reason I have the privilege of coming to the main house is because of my friendship with Jim and my sister being the cook. I doubt your brother is in favor of us becoming too close."

Georgiana stuck out her lower lip in a pretty little pout. "I don't give a fiddle-d-sticks what my brother likes or don't like. I am my own boss!" she fumed.

Luke rose as he looked at the attractive young woman, "Don't buy me any clothes, Georgiana. I can't afford to be spending money on fancy clothes or going out either."

"Why not? What are you planning to do with your money?"

"Naomi and I own some land near Bandera, and we plan to return there someday. We were about to build a place for me to train cutting horses and a small house, but we got burned out. We are both saving our money to rebuild."

Georgiana looked up at Luke and snipped. "No more than the two of you will make working here, you'll be old and gray by the time you have that much money, so you might as well forget it and enjoy life."

Luke knew she didn't understand how important that land and dream was to him, and she likely never would. She had everything she could possibly want. Yet, he had feelings for the flighty young woman, but those were feelings he would have to be cautious to control.

When Luke stopped in the kitchen to say goodbye to Naomi, she felt sad he was going but relieved he would be out of Georgiana's clutches for a while. Maybe by the time he returned she would have turned her attention to someone else, Naomi hoped. Georgiana didn't strike her as the kind of girl to wait around long for a guy's attention.

Chapter Fifteen

L uke rode toward the southern boundary of the ranch. In this leg, there were fewer places along the river for cattle to cross over from Mexico, so there were only eight gates to pass through. The last gate was near the southern fence line.

A scorching hot wind blew out of the southeast as the afternoon sun hung overhead. Luke paused to dampen his kerchief in the river and ran it over his head, face, and neck. He folded it in a triangle and put it over his head, tying it in the back. Then he put his straw, wide-brimmed hat over it. Its dampness brought some measure of coolness for a while.

The river had a sharp bend about a hundred yards before the boundary line. Just as Luke started around the curve, he heard men shouting and the rumble and bawling of fast-moving cattle. That was strange, he thought. There weren't supposed to be riders in this pasture to bring the cattle to water for two more days. Besides, he knew they wouldn't be coming as fast as these cattle were moving toward the river.

He moved his horse cautiously ahead and stopped in a small clump of trees for a better look.

"Rustlers! Damn it all," he mumbled.

Luke recognized their leader, Blondie. He was a notorious, ghostly white man with a jagged scar down one side of his face. He was the leader of a group of Mexican *banditos* that were feared along the border, from Del Rio south to Laredo. They were herding about thirty or so head of cattle across the river. Luke knew better than to tangle with four armed men. It galled him to have to sit by and watch the thieves stealing Sycamore Creek cattle in broad daylight.

His horse didn't seem to care for it either and whinnied in protest. Luke started to dismount to stand beside his horse, hoping there was enough brush to block them from the rustlers' view.

A rider on the other side of the small stand of mesquites must have caught a glimpse of his movement. The bandit turned to stare in Luke's direction as he rode past the clump of brush.

Luke instantly knew he had been spotted. He wheeled his mount and put his spurs to the animal's flanks. A shot rang out! Luke instantly felt the fiery sting of the bullet as it ripped into his upper right arm, rendering that gun hand useless. His horse plunged on through the scrub brush at a break-neck pace. Luke winced in pain as he struggled to stay mounted. Luke's shirtsleeve was soon soaked from the flow of warm, sticky blood. The piercing pain seemed to pound each time the horse's hooves hit the hard ground. He wasn't sure but hoped the bullet hadn't shattered the bone. Luke knew beyond any doubt that if he lost his horse, with the rustlers so near, he would be a dead man.

At last, he realized the rustlers were not pursuing him. Luke reined his horse to a walk and headed for the next watering hole along the river. The pain in his arm was almost unbearable. His sleeve was soaked with his bright crimson blood. He needed to wash away some of the blood and use his neckerchief as a bandage. Now he was far enough from the rustlers that he no longer felt in immediate danger.

Luke dismounted and waded just far enough to dip his neckerchief in cool water. He dared not venture too far, just in case he needed to take cover. Luke was one of those fortunate people that could use either hand equally well. If necessary, firing a gun wouldn't be a problem.

Luke gritted his teeth and cursed as he began to wash the blood from his sleeve and arm. He held the chilly kerchief to the wound to lessen the blood flow. The coolness of the water eased the pain slightly, but it soon returned with a vengeance. He cursed the pain and his helplessness to defend Sycamore Creek property. Finally, he wrung out his neckerchief and tied it around his arm as best he could one-handed. He felt a bit weak and slightly dizzy. Luke knew he needed to get back to the riders' shack as quickly as possible before he lost too much more blood and passed out. If that happened, it would be hours before he would be found. That might be too late, he reasoned. A dread of that happening plagued him as he pushed his strength to remount.

He rode toward the cabin, passing through gate after gate. Unlatching and latching each gate one-handed proved to be more of a chore than he would have ever expected. He felt weaker and weaker the farther he rode. The afternoon sun beat down on him, sapping his strength. The trees and brush became a blur, and he couldn't focus on the path ahead. Luckily his horse knew the way back to the shack and plodded along in what Luke knew was the right direction.

Luke struggled to unlatch the final gate. At last, the latch slipped and he managed to drag the gate far enough for the horse to pass through. He knew he was too weak to attempt to re-latch the gate but rode on in a daze. He leaned forward, letting his arms dangle on each side of the horse's neck. For a while this seemed to give him balance, but then Luke felt his body slipping from the saddle. He met the hard ground with a thud. Blackness overtook him.

His horse, Big Red, nuzzled his fallen rider, but the man did not respond. The horse nibbled some nearby grass and meandered on toward the riders' shack.

~

Jim sat in the shade of the porch that extended across the front of the cabin, as he rolled several cigarettes. He always liked to keep a few ready-rolled for when he had the urge to smoke. Jim was trying to wean himself off smoking so many cigarettes and drinking too much coffee but did enjoy a smoke, especially after a meal.

Jim looked up when he heard the whinny of a horse. He stood, staring at Big Red, when he saw it was Luke's horse minus its rider. A foreboding dread came over Jim as the horse stopped beside the porch. Then he saw the unmistakable smudges of dried blood on the horse's right side. That told him Luke had lost a considerable amount of blood as he had likely slumped forward from weakness.

"Bud, Norm, get ready to ride!" he called to two of the riders who were inside the cabin. "Luke's horse just showed up without him, and it has dried blood on its right wither running down toward its leg."

The two men bounded out of the shack to take a closer look at the horse.

"Damnation, damnation, I say!" Bud exclaimed, as the three men stared at the blood smeared on the horse.

The three men headed for the barn to saddle up. Jim took a few minutes to move the saddle to a fresh horse he would lead, in case Luke could ride. Jim had a sinking feeling. If Luke had been able to ride, he would have made it all the way back to camp.

The three riders headed south along the river trail in hopes of finding Luke near the river. If they didn't find him, they would have to start riding the expansive pastures, and that could take hours, if not days, before they might find a wounded man.

As they rode, they each listened for a shot or even a shout from the downed rider. They heard nothing except the normal sounds coming from the river and pasture.

On they rode for nearly two miles, toward the first gate leading to the next pasture with a watering hole. The sun was quickly sinking toward the western horizon, marked by the mountains in Mexico. The late afternoon sky was awash with streaks of orange, yellow, deep blue, and purple. It was a breathtaking sight, but the three riders paid little attention to its rugged beauty. Their eyes were constantly scanning the brush near the river path for some sign of their fellow rider.

"There!" Bud called out. He pointed toward a boot protruding from the thick brush not far from the open gate.

The three men dismounted and soon stood looking down at Luke's inert body. Although his face was pale it did not carry the color of death. His right sleeve and the bandana he had used for a bandage were soaked in blood that had now dried to a dark, reddish brown.

Jim squatted beside his friend and gently shook his leg. "Luke, Luke, can you hear me?" he asked, despite the tightness in his voice that reflected his unease. His feeling of anxiety was evident in the lines of worry that creased his normally smooth forehead, as his eyes searched Luke's face for some response.

Luke gave a low moan but did not open his eyes. He could hear a voice from far away calling his name, but, try as he might, he could not open his eyes. But, at the same time, some instinct of self-preservation told him if he woke or moved the pain might come back with a stronger vengeance.

"Looks bad. He's lost lots of blood," Jim said.

"Damnation!" Bud vowed, wishing he could see Luke break into a big grin hearing him use his favorite expression.

"Norm, you better ride to headquarters and tell Gilbert what's happened. Tell him to bring the wagon and Naomi. She can tend to Luke on the way to Del Rio. He needs a doctor," Jim stated with a nervous look.

"Do you think he'll make it that long? Jostlin' around in the back of a wagon ain't gonna help him none," Norm declared, as he started to mount up.

"I don't know what else to do. He's in a bad way; he's lost a lot of blood, and the bullet is still lodged in his arm. He needs a doctor to get it out."

"Damnation! Get going, Norm!" Bud snarled at Norm. "No need in wastin' more time jawin' about it. Damnation, I say!"

"I'm goin', I'm goin'!" Norm shot back as he rode off at a gallop.

"In a while, I'll build a fire near the river so they can find us when Gilbert comes with the wagon. We can stay up here in the brush, so we won't be an easy target, in case them low-down varmints that shot Luke are still around," Bud offered.

"What makes you think there was more than one man?"

"Unless he ambushed Luke, one man wouldn't have a chance of shootin' him. Luke's been practicing a lot and is damn fast with a gun!" Bud said, as he rose and walked toward the river to gather kindling for a fire.

Darkness fell. A slight breeze picked up, as the creatures of the night started their various serenades. Their long wait seemed endless. Both men constantly scanned the darkness for any indication of the *banditos'* return, but they saw nothing.

Jim pulled a clean handkerchief from his pocket and wet it in the cool water. He gently washed the dirt from Luke's face. The touch of the wet cloth made Luke stir slightly, but, still, he did not open his eyes. Jim considered removing the bandage and attempting to clean and redress the wound. Thinking it over, Jim was afraid he would cause it to open up again, and Luke would lose more blood.

A half-moon lit the night sky and millions of stars shone brilliantly above the three men near the river.

Several hours passed before Jim and Bud heard the rattle of the ranch wagon and the pounding of horses' hooves. The wagon rolled to a stop beside where Jim and Bud sat cross-legged beside Luke.

Naomi jumped from the back of the wagon before it came to a complete stop. She ran a few paces to where her brother lay on the hard ground. She held her lantern over Luke and gasped at the lack of color in his pale face.

Wide-eyed, she looked at Jim.

Jim nodded his head in answer to her unspoken question. "He's alive but in bad need of a doctor. The trip to town won't do him much good, but we don't have any choice. He's lost a lot of blood," Jim told her as he looked at her stricken face. He knew she was extremely close to Luke, him being her only living relative. Jim could hardly stand the thought of Luke not making it, for Naomi's sake as well as the dread of losing a good friend.

The wagon rattled over the uneven road leading toward Del Rio. Jim sat beside Gilbert as he drove, trying to miss the worst ruts. The familiar road was fairly visible in the pale moonlight. Gilbert had traveled this road countless times.

The two men quietly discussed what had happened to Luke.

"Maybe we need to double up on the riders for a while. If rustlers get by with stealing once, they'll likely try it again. I don't want to take a chance on losing any men," Gilbert said.

"You're likely right, but won't that run you short-handed at headquarters?" Jim asked.

"Yeah, but we'll just have to manage. It'll run me short if anyone else gets hurt or killed, so it's better to use some caution."

"That sounds like as good an idea as any."

"Are you going to report this to the sheriff?" Jim asked.

"I suppose so, although I don't think there's much he can do about it."

"At least the sheriff will know what happened."

Naomi sat quietly beside Luke listening to the two men talk. She hadn't realized the potential danger the river riders were in, but now she understood a man alone up against outlaws didn't have much of a chance. Luke was lucky to still be alive and have a fighting chance. The thought that he still might not survive made her shiver. Instinctively, she reached out and gently touched his cheek and then touched his hand for reassurance he was indeed still alive.

The wagon rattled on through the night toward Del Rio. At last,

Luke began to stir when the wagon hit a rut in the road and bounced its occupants more than usual. Luke would moan in pain and start to thrash about. Naomi instantly tried to soothe him so he wouldn't further injure his wounded arm.

Eventually, Luke opened his eyes and stared at Naomi as though he was trying to figure out where they were and why he was in so much pain.

"Naomi, where are we?" he spoke hardly above a whisper.

"We're on our way to Del Rio."

"Why, what happened?"

"You were shot in your right arm," Naomi answered, with obvious concern.

Jim heard them talking and turned on the wagon seat to better hear what Luke was saying.

"Luke, do you remember what happened?" Jim asked.

Luke appeared to be searching for an answer but at first, found it hard to remember. After several moments he finally answered.

"I was near the southern boundary and saw some rustlers. I think there were four of them. They were driving about thirty or so head of cattle across the river to Mexico. It was Blondie and his gang. One of them spotted me and fired. I remember riding away fast, trying to make it back to the river camp, but don't think I did," he answered, as his voice grew weaker from the exertion.

"No, you fell off of your horse just after you made it through the last gate. Lucky for you, Big Red came on to the cabin. I saw the dried blood running down his right shoulder toward his leg. Bud, Norm, and I found you beside the river."

Luke nodded his head and closed his eyes.

"He's too weak to talk anymore," Naomi said. She watched his every move and listened to his labored breathing. What would she do if she lost Luke? That seemed a selfish thought, but she could not prevent feeling apprehensive about the future, especially without her brother. She would never return to Ruth's house and endure what John might dole out. *"Dear Lord, please let Luke make it; he just has to,"* Naomi fervently pleaded. *"You know how much I love and need my brother,"* Naomi whispered, as they continued on through the darkness.

In the wee hours of the morning, they finally entered the quiet little town. Gilbert brought the team to a stop in front of Doctor Rivers' dark house.

Jim jumped from the wagon and knocked loudly on the front door. Soon a light was visible through the front window.

Doctor Rivers opened the front door and held a lamp high to peer into the darkness, trying to determine who had awakened him at such an hour.

"Doc, it's Jim Keller from the Sycamore Creek Ranch."

"Hello, Jim, what brings you to my door at this late hour?" the slender man with salt and pepper grey hair inquired. His neatly trimmed white beard shimmered in the lamplight.

"One of our river riders got shot in his arm by some bandits. The bullet is too deep for one of us to take out, and he's lost lots of blood."

The doctor opened the door wide. "Bring him in and let me see about that wound," he said, as he followed Jim to the wagon.

Jim, Gilbert, and Naomi carried Luke as carefully as they could, as they followed the dim light of the doctor's lantern. They laid Luke on a large table in what appeared to be a room set aside for the doctor to see patients.

Doctor Rivers turned on the electric light and one lamp. He sat the lamp on the table next to Luke's head so he could see the jagged wound the bullet had caused as it ripped into his upper arm.

"Um! That looks like a bad one. I hope it didn't hit the bone," he mumbled more to himself than those standing nearby.

Mrs. Rivers appeared in the doorway in her long nightdress and wrapper.

"Good morning," she greeted the early-morning visitors.

"Margie, will you heat some water so we can clean this fellow up after I remove this bullet?"

Margie Rivers nodded her head and disappeared down a long central hallway.

"What is his name?" Doctor Rivers inquired.

"Luke O'Donnelly," Jim supplied.

The doctor bustled around the room gathering supplies needed to remove the imbedded bullet. When everything was in place, Doctor Rivers looked at Gilbert and Jim. "You two better hold him down. He's too weak to give him anything for the pain." Then he looked at Naomi. "Are you his wife?"

"No, I'm his sister, Naomi O'Donnelly."

"I see, well, you better step into the next room. This isn't going to be a very pretty sight, I'm afraid," the doctor said with uneasiness when he looked at Naomi's pale face.

"No, I'd rather stay," she stated without hesitation.

"Well, if you start to feel faint you better get out of here. I won't have time to stop to tend to you," Doctor Rivers told her emphatically.

"Don't worry. I won't faint, and I won't leave my brother," Naomi returned with just as much fervor.

The surgery had torn at Naomi's heart when she saw the pain Luke endured. By the time Doctor Rivers had finished, Naomi realized she had tensed her muscles to the point of aching, as though she had done an unusually hard day's work.

Gilbert told Naomi to stay with the doctor and his wife to help with Luke. He knew her mind wouldn't be on her work at the ranch. As he and Jim departed, he jokingly told her he would get his cattle prod after Georgiana if necessary. That was the only time the two brothers had seen Naomi smile since Luke had been injured.

Luke convalesced for four days. The second night the dream came again. It was so real. Luke was back in Abilene, standing across the street looking at the dark-haired beauty as she tried to lure him to the brothel. She was so tempting. Then he heard the girl at the corner call his name. As he hurried toward her, she faded into the shadows. When

Luke awoke, he couldn't help but wonder why the strange dream kept haunting him.

By the end of the third day, he was chomping at the bit to get back to the ranch. Doctor Rivers patiently reiterated all of the reasons he needed to be stronger before returning to river riding. Naomi reinforced what the doctor told Luke and was grateful Gilbert did not reappear until the fourth day. The moment she saw him, she knew there was no longer a chance of holding Luke back from returning to the ranch.

Naomi and Luke said goodbye to Doctor Rivers and his wife. They followed Gilbert outside and stopped in shock when they saw a fine-looking farm truck waiting to carry them back to the ranch instead of the usual farm wagon and team of horses.

Chapter Sixteen

"Weee!" Luke let out a long whistle. "What in the world is this all about?" he asked with a big grin.

"Decided it was time to get in on the new way of ranching. Besides, in case you get shot again, it takes too long to get you to the doctor in the farm wagon," Gilbert returned with a teasing grin.

The truck bumped over the dirt road. Even so, it felt as though they were speeding toward the ranch. There was plenty of room in the cab for the three of them, and the back held the normal load of supplies with ample room left for twice as much if needed.

"We've been sending extra riders to go with the river riders in case there was more trouble, but now we need those men on other parts of the ranch. There hasn't been any more trouble, so today the riders started going alone again," Gilbert told Luke.

"I'm glad there hasn't been more trouble. I'm not afraid to ride alone. Don't worry about me," Luke assured him.

Gilbert let out a long breath. "I wish I could afford to send two riders all the time but just can't at this point. I know it is one of the more dangerous jobs on the ranch. It's not just because of the rustlers.

If a rider goes down for any reason, it can take a long time to find him, and that's dangerous too." Gilbert's worry was evident in the tenor of his speech as well as the expression on his face.

Gilbert had been mulling over another big change that would take the extra money it would have cost to hire additional river riders.

"Oh, yes, I've changed up the riding schedule a bit. Now you go out for two weeks and come back to headquarters for two weeks. I think that will keep the riders from getting so worn out and bored, and they'll be more alert," Gilbert reasoned.

The two weeks on and two weeks off didn't suit Luke. The truth of the matter was he wouldn't mind staying out an entire month, but he certainly didn't want to be at headquarters longer than two weeks. He liked riding the river. Although it was a desolate ride, for some reason he found it more exhilarating than being at the ranch headquarters. That was except for the charming company of Miss Georgiana Keller.

In spite of what Naomi said, Luke found Georgiana's attention flattering since she could have her pick of any of the men. It didn't hurt to enjoy the company of such an educated, beautiful woman. He knew she was spoiled and doubted their relationship would last long.

As Gilbert, Luke, and Naomi made their way back to the ranch, Gilbert reflected on his own responsibilities. Now, when he caught a glimpse of his reflection in the mirror, he thought he looked like a man who appeared considerably older than a man in his mid-twenties. The lines in his forehead and around his eyes and mouth were more pronounced. But what could he do? Jim had made it clear he wasn't ready to take on the responsibility of running the ranch, and his other brothers showed no interest in ranching.

Their father had died in his sleep about a month after Jim had returned. Charles and John had chosen the town life over the ranch and neither was ever likely to return. Charles had married the oldest daughter of one of the local bankers and gone straight to being one of the vice presidents. John worked for the Southern Pacific Railroad and showed no interest in returning to the ranch. Then there was Willie and Floyd. Gilbert instantly frowned as he thought about his two youngest brothers. What had gone wrong with those two? Unfortunately, he knew the answer all too well. They had been at a gullible age when their mother had passed. Their father had taken to drinking and carousing with women of questionable character. Willie and Floyd had fallen into the trap any irresponsible youth would likely follow. Unfortunately, neither could be counted on to even do a full day's work much less take any real responsibility in running the ranch.

Gilbert's thoughts turned to Jim. Jim was the oldest and should be the one in charge, but he had left and stayed away for ten years. He had lost the love of a young woman because of the uncivilized, shameful conditions at the ranch. He couldn't blame Jim for leaving. But now he was back. Still, he was reluctant to even become the foreman but had agreed to manage the bookkeeping. That would be a great load off of Gilbert's shoulders and give him far more time for managing the ranch.

Jim would be the perfect manager. He was well-educated and had even attended college on his own for two years. Gilbert had always known Jim was the smartest one of his siblings and was a whiz in mathematics. Since returning Jim had seemed content to ride the river, but lately, it seemed he was beginning to take more interest in the ranch in general.

They drove into the yard shortly before supper. The unfamiliar honking of the horn quickly brought a throng of curious onlookers. Marylee stood holding the baby, grinning at her husband as he lifted their two boys into the seat. The boys' eyes sparkled as they touched everything they could reach.

It was hard to tell if there was more excitement over the farm truck or Luke's return.

Once the excitement was over, Gilbert and Naomi gathered the supplies that went to the main house.

Georgiana had not come out to see the new truck or to greet Luke. She stood at the huge wood-fired cook stove stirring a big pot of soup.

"It's so hot I could just up and die," she complained before she realized Gilbert and Naomi had entered through the back door.

When she heard Gilbert laugh, she whirled to face them. Her face was beet red from the heat and took on a look of outrage when she heard Gilbert's laugh at her complaint.

"You should have to stand over this hot stove and cook a meal for this ungrateful family, and that includes you," she screeched, and her eyes flashed as she pointed the long-handled spoon toward her brother.

"I'm grateful and am sure everyone else appreciates your efforts," Gilbert tried to soothe his sister.

"No, you're not! All you and the others do is complain and say how happy you'll be when Naomi gets back. Well, she's back! She's welcome to this unbearably hot job!" Georgiana shouted. Then she lifted her skirt and marched out of the kitchen with her nose pointed upward.

Gilbert looked at Naomi and quirked an eyebrow. "It looks like you were indeed missed." Then, he lowered his voice. "It's true, we all missed your good cooking. Georgiana tried, but she doesn't know how to season anything. Everything she cooks don't have much taste," he said with a low chuckle.

Naomi smiled and walked to the cook stove. She stirred the boiling soup, took a small taste, and grimaced. She reached to the shelf above the stove and began to add some seasoning to the concoction.

Just as Naomi turned to put two pans of cornbread in the oven, she caught a glimpse of Georgiana as she quickly crossed the kitchen and slipped out the back door. She had changed her dress and put her hair up. Naomi fretted. She felt certain Georgiana was on her way to find Luke to welcome him home.

Georgiana was truly glad Naomi had returned, not because she missed her companionship but to take over the endless chores. Georgiana felt most of the household duties were beneath her. After all, she was educated. She was meant to be a lady with maids to do such mundane household tasks.

Georgiana ambled toward one of the corrals trying to look inconspicuous while observing the men working the horses. An impish smile caressed her full lips. She was certain Naomi had seen her leave the house and likely thought she was going to find Luke. Let her think whatever she pleases, Georgiana thought as she continued her walk.

Her eyes brightened when she caught sight of him on the far side of the corral. Their eyes met and a secret signal passed between the two. Georgiana hastened her pace slightly as she rounded the corner of the first barn. Now she was out of sight of the ranch hands and knew her sweetheart would soon join her.

Chapter Seventeen

The day Luke returned, he did not join the family for dinner. Naomi noticed Georgiana had not set the table to make a place beside her for Luke, as she had done previously. She was glad but was curious as to the sudden change. Did she and Luke have a quarrel? Had she found someone else while they were away? Naomi couldn't help but wonder about Georgiana's strange behavior.

Toward the end of the meal, Luke appeared in the doorway. "Sorry I missed supper, but the guys insisted I eat at the bunkhouse. They had stories to tell," he chuckled.

"I'd bet half of them were lies or strongly embellished," Jim laughed.

"You're in time for peach cobbler," Naomi said. She rose to serve Luke, but he motioned for her to remain seated.

He served his own cobbler and took the empty chair next to Naomi, across the table from Georgiana.

Georgiana put on her pouty look. "I came to look for you, thinking you might be outside. I didn't see you anywhere, and I certainly don't go near the bunkhouse." She sounded peevishly agitated.

Luke continued to eat. "I saw you walking toward the corral but couldn't break away in the middle of a conversation. Then I saw some fellow I didn't recognize following you toward the barn. Who is he?" he asked, giving Georgiana his full attention.

Her gaze instantly darted toward Gilbert and back to Luke. "I—I don't know his name. He just happened to be going the same way as me."

Gilbert glared at Georgiana. "If it's the new horse breaker, his name is Clint Swift, and you better steer clear of him!" he warned.

"Well, if he is someone to steer clear of, why is he working here?" she asked defiantly.

"He's a fine horse trainer, but, from what I've heard, not a man of very high moral character, so you keep your distance. You know better than to associate with the hired men anyway."

"I associate with Luke. Are you forbidding me to see Luke too?"

Gilbert looked exasperated. "No, Luke is the one exception. I don't want to hear anything else about it," Gilbert finished, as his knife and fork clattered against his plate.

It was rare to see Gilbert out of humor. He was normally a jovial man, but it seemed if anyone could irritate him, it was his sister.

Now Naomi knew why Georgiana hadn't set a place for Luke. She was pouting because he hadn't come running after her when he saw her. Oh, how she wished Georgiana would leave Luke alone.

Four days later Luke returned to the river camp.

Luke was content to be riding the river again. To be honest, he didn't actually miss Georgiana's company as much as he had first thought he might. Things had seemed different after his return from town. Several times he had seen her walking toward the barn. In the past, she had walked toward the pond in front of the house. He wondered why she had suddenly changed her habit. About the third time he saw her he observed Clint Swift soon headed in the same direction. Luke couldn't leave what he was doing to go see what the two were up to, but he had his suspicions, especially since Gilbert had forbidden her to see the man. It seemed Georgiana did whatever she pleased, especially if it was something she wasn't supposed to be doing.

The first few days were routine rides. He encountered some of the wranglers bringing cattle to the river for water. For the most part, the rides were quiet. Once in a while, he would see some of the Mexican women washing clothes along the far side of the river as their small children splashed in the shallow water.

Luke rode slowly toward the river camp checking for signs that stray cattle or horses may have crossed the river. On this ride, he had found nothing out of the ordinary, which suited him fine. It would save time in hunting any stray livestock or horses, in the event they had moved away from the river toward the herds of cattle.

The relentless mid-afternoon sun beat down on him. Rain had been scarce earlier in the spring. This entire summer appeared to be one of those long scorchers with only a few random showers bringing brief relief from the heat. The grass was mostly brown with only a few patches of green beside the river.

He had overheard Gilbert and Jim discussing the possibility of selling part of the livestock if conditions didn't improve. That would mean some of the hands would be laid off. It would likely be the wranglers that would be let go. He felt fairly secure at this point that conditions would have to become really drastic before Gilbert laid off any of the river riders. He hated the thought of any man losing his job, but he and Naomi were depending on every paycheck to save enough money in hopes of rebuilding their own place.

A lot of the wranglers seemed to drift from ranch to ranch looking for better working conditions or a little better pay. If Gilbert had to lay off some of his hands, it was likely the other ranchers would have to do the same. It would be a bad deal all the way around for those men.

An unexpected splash in the river abruptly caught his attention. He reined his horse to a stop near a clump of trees. He could hardly believe what he was seeing. To his amazement, a woman was apparently bathing in broad daylight. From his secluded vantage point, he could plainly see her naked shoulders and back gleaming in the sunlight.

It wasn't uncommon to see the Mexican women washing their clothes on the far bank of the river, but he had never seen anyone naked, except the children.

Luke knew he was across the river from the Ruiz Ranch. She was likely one of the women from that family. But what would possess her to bathe when it was highly likely one of their own ranch hands or one of the Sycamore Creek men could ride by?

Although she had her back to him, he could see her long dark hair glistening in the sunlight as it dipped beneath the surface of the almost clear water. Unexpectedly she stood, revealing her shining brown body to just below her trim waist. Luke swallowed hard as he observed the gentle curve of her hips.

Almost unaware of his own movements, he nudged his horse forward, intending to make his presence known. Before he could do so she turned toward him, apparently still unaware of his presence. He almost gasped aloud when he plainly saw her firm, full breasts with droplets of water cascading down her sleek tan body. She ran her hands over her face to brush away the water as she pulled her long dark hair back over her shoulders.

Luke felt his chest tighten and a rush of desire as he stared at the striking young woman who had emerged from the river like some mermaid he had read about in one of Jim's books. She was the most stunning creature Luke had ever seen.

Instantly she opened her eyes and they were staring at one another across the narrow distance of the stream. Her huge brown eyes collided with his green eyes that had grown darker with longing. She did not shriek or try to cover herself, as Luke would have expected most women to do. Instead, she gave him a haughty look, slowly turned, and waded toward the far bank, exposing her entire backside to him.

Luke felt another wave of heat rush through him and fully understood the overwhelming desire a man could feel for a woman he didn't even know. This was a strange feeling he had never experienced. It was a very different feeling than what he had experienced when the pretty young woman had tried to entice him into the brothel in Abilene.

With a jolt, his dream about a dark-haired beauty came into focus. Maybe this woman was her. She had called to him from the corner, beckoning him away from the temptation of the brothel, but as he neared the corner she had disappeared. He hadn't thought about the dream for a long time. Could it have been a forewarning?

Luke had enjoyed the company of several young ladies at dances and shared a few flirty goodnight kisses. None of those experiences had prepared him for this overpowering feeling.

He sat mesmerized as he watched her emerge from the river, slip her feet into her sandals, and pull a loose peasant dress over her head. She never looked back as she strolled toward a path that led through the brush to a hacienda that stood on a slight hill a hundred yards beyond the river.

Luke still did not move as he watched the top of her head gently bobbing above the top of the brush.

After several minutes, he wiped his brow with the back of his hand and let out a low whistle. He nudged his horse forward and continued on toward the river camp. He was tempted to find a spot further up the river and take a swim to calm his burning desire.

As he rode onward, he told himself she likely belonged to one of the Ruiz brothers. But it was possible she didn't belong to any of the Ruiz men. Maybe she was a visitor and didn't know about the possible danger of bathing in the river where anyone might happen along.

After some thought, he decided he wouldn't tell any of the men what he had seen. He didn't want any of them looking for the mysterious young woman, hoping to catch a glimpse of her bathing. He felt certain some of them might try to take advantage of such a situation.

Each day was much like the previous one, with little to break the routine of the ride. He spotted a few strays at the edge of the river but quickly herded them back to Mexico before they could do any harm. Luke felt disappointed when he didn't see the lovely young woman at the river with the other women. Perhaps she really had been just a visitor and hadn't realized the possible consequences of bathing during the day.

It wasn't uncommon to come across vaqueros crossing the river in search of ranch work. Luke had learned enough Spanish to tell them if Gilbert was hiring or some other nearby ranch was. They were hard workers and rarely caused any trouble.

A week later, Luke and Jim rode to headquarters just before suppertime.

"See you at the house," Jim said, as he led their horses toward the barn.

"I may eat with the men at the bunkhouse tonight. Don't feel like cleaning up yet," Luke replied.

"Naomi and Georgiana will be mighty disappointed."

"Yeah, I guess I better make the effort," Luke answered. He was dead tired. They had chased down a small herd of horses the day before and spent most of this day tending to them.

As Luke entered the large dining room, he was surprised to find the table had been extended and there were several additional places set.

"What's the occasion?" he asked as he gave Naomi a gentle hug.

"Georgiana's friend, Rosalinda Ruiz, and her parents are dining with us tonight."

Luke looked at his faded pants and shirt. "Maybe I better go back to the bunkhouse for supper. I'm not dressed for company."

"You look just fine. Besides, Georgiana has already told Rosalinda that Jim's friend, my handsome brother, will be joining us tonight," she replied with a slight scowl.

"Why are you making a face? Don't you think I'm handsome?" Luke teased.

"Yes, I do, but Georgiana acts like she owns you or something."

"Well, she doesn't, so don't get all huffy."

"Oh, Luke." Whatever Naomi was about to say was cut short as Georgiana and Rosalinda entered the dining room.

"Luke," Georgiana gushed as she almost ran to embrace him. She looked at his faded clothes and sighed. "I should have sent word we were having company so you would have dressed nicer to show off your good looks to my friend from school."

Luke felt embarrassed by his ordinary clothes. "I could go change," he offered, knowing his best clothes didn't look much better.

"It's too late," she sighed.

Georgiana turned to the other young woman and motioned her forward.

"Rosalinda, this is Luke O'Donnelly. Luke, this is my dear, dear friend, Rosalinda Ruiz," Georgiana beamed.

Luke stared at the lovely young lady dressed in a pale blue, pleasing to the eye, summer frock, the very same young woman he had encountered bathing in the river. Although she was dressed beautifully, he preferred the sight of water cascading down her brown sensual body. That memory made Luke smolder with desire. He hoped no one noticed his reaction to the young woman.

Rosalinda stared back at him with huge brown eyes that seemed to be begging him to not reveal they had met before. Well, they hadn't exactly met, but it was all too evident she did not want him to indicate in any way they had ever seen one another before this very minute.

Luke cleared his throat and extended his hand. "It is indeed a pleasure to make your acquaintance." The touch of her soft skin against his rough hand made his pulse race.

"It is a pleasure to meet Georgiana's friend and Naomi's brother," she replied, graciously, in a low alluring voice.

The captivating sound of her voice grabbed Luke's attention. He had never been this awestruck by any woman. Not even Georgiana provoked the feelings he was experiencing just looking at Rosalinda. Every gesture, the soft lilt of her voice, and her expressive eyes were all-encompassing. It was as though she had cast a charismatic spell over him, and he was powerless to resist her charms.

Once again Luke was seated across the table from Georgiana, as Rosalinda was seated where he had once been expected to sit. Naomi was seated to his right. She was expected to refill glasses, fetch more warm bread during the meal, and serve the dessert.

It often rankled Luke when Georgiana made no effort to assist with any of the chores. Well, she was the sister of the owners, and Naomi was only an employee like him. He realized they were given special privileges because of their friendship with Jim and his recent involvement with Georgiana.

As of late, he had found Georgiana's charms of less interest. When they first met, he had looked forward to his return to headquarters, anticipating her welcoming attention. While he was hurt and away from the ranch, something had changed in their relationship, but he wasn't quite sure what had changed.

As Luke sat across the table during this meal, he found the lovely Miss Rosalinda far more fascinating than Georgiana. In fact, he could hardly draw his attention away from her unless directly addressed by someone else at the table. Most often that someone was Georgiana. A couple of times he noticed a slight frown on her face when she was vying for his attention.

After the meal, the men adjourned to the front veranda to smoke and discuss the pros and cons of ranching. The drought and scorching summer heat were two widely discussed topics. Gilbert, Jim, and Señor Ruiz eventually ambled toward one of the barns for Ruiz to see a new foal. Luke remained in the lengthening shade of the porch to enjoy the faint coolness of a slight southeasterly breeze.

The door slowly opened, and Rosalinda quietly walked toward Luke where he sat on one of the porch swings.

"Thank you for not saying anything about—about, seeing me in the river," she murmured softly, as she sat next to Luke.

"I wouldn't want to embarrass you in any way, but you do need to be careful about bathing in the river," Luke answered. "Some men wouldn't hesitate to ride right into the river and join you, whether you wanted him to or not," he cautioned.

"Yes, I know. It was a foolish thing for me to do," she said, keeping her eyes averted from Luke as though she were too embarrassed to look at him.

"I had been working in the garden. The heat was so intense I felt I had to cool off. I had looked about before I went into the water. I didn't see anyone and only meant to stay a few minutes to cool off. I thought it was safe, but I guess I was wrong," she said softly.

"Well, you were safe from me but, as I said, that might not always be the case, so take care."

"I will. Thank you for not letting anyone know what happened," she said as she rose to leave.

"Oh, there you are," came Georgiana's voice from the doorway. "I should have known I'd find you trying to flirt with my fellow," she said with what might have been intended jest, but it didn't quite ring true.

Rosalinda blushed slightly, unsure about the true meaning behind Georgiana's remark. She certainly didn't want to cause any trouble between the couple. It was plain to see why anyone would be attracted to Luke. He was quite handsome and personable as well.

Luke saw little of Georgiana during his time at headquarters. She seemed to be occupied with one thing or another. Then she had also spent several days in town with her brother and his wife. Luke really didn't mind as he found his thoughts were centered more on her lovely friend, Rosalinda.

How could he get to know Rosalinda better, he wondered? He knew the hacienda across the river from near the middle river camp was where her family lived. He had heard the Mexican customs in such matters were quite different from on this side of the border.

He considered several possibilities to advance his cause. Should he just ride over and announce he had come to call on Rosalinda? Did he ask her father, first, for permission to see his daughter? Since he wasn't knowledgeable about the customs of courting in Mexico, maybe he should ask Jim before he made a fool of himself, he decided. Since Jim had grown up along the border, surely, he would know the proper way for him to go about courting Rosalinda.

Luke anxiously awaited their next assignment and was grateful when he learned it was going to be at the middle river camp. As soon as he and Jim were on their way, he quickly broached the subject of going to see Rosalinda.

Jim smiled when Luke confessed his interest in Georgiana's friend.

"Georgiana's not going to take kindly to you throwing her over for her best friend," Jim half teased.

"Things have changed with Georgiana and me. I don't know what took place while I was hurt. Since then, things haven't been the same. I really think she may be seeing someone else but haven't actually caught her with anyone."

Jim looked worried. "You might be right. I have noticed she doesn't seem as smitten with you as she did earlier. I'm afraid I know who she's been seeing but can't prove it either."

"Would you be thinking it's Clint Swift?" Luke asked.

Jim looked at him a bit surprised. "Yeah, how did you know? What makes you suspect it's Clint?"

"When I first got back, I noticed her walking toward the barn instead of toward the pond. Then I saw Clint headed in the same general direction. I saw that happen a couple of times. When I mentioned it, she acted like she had just chosen a different place to walk. Remember a while back at supper when Gilbert told her she better not be seeing Clint? But you know how Georgiana is. That was probably all it took for her to do it just to show Gilbert she could do whatever she wants."

"You might be right. If that is the case, Gilbert is really going to be mad if he finds out. You're likely better off without my sister. She is spoiled and headstrong. Back to you seeing Rosalinda, well, the Mexicans definitely have their customs for courting. First of all, you need to find out if she is already promised to some man for marriage."

"Promised!" Luke was stunned by that thought.

"Yes, in the old aristocratic families, who are usually quite wealthy and may also have political ties, it is quite customary to have arranged marriages among their children, almost from the time they are born. These arranged marriages can seal their family's wealth and power. I'm fairly certain Señor and Señora Ruiz share such a marriage. It is also not uncommon for the men to take lovers, but a woman must be extremely discreet if she chooses to see another man."

Luke's jaw dropped, but he knew Jim was serious. "So, it doesn't matter if they love or hate one another, they have to marry anyway?"

"That's right, it does seem most of the marriages are compatible. Of course, there is no divorce since nearly all are Catholic."

Luke frowned. "That seems like a mighty old-fashioned way to still be doing things. This is the 1900's."

Jim laughed. "It is here, but things change much slower just across that narrow river. Well, literally it may be narrow, but the gap is very wide in most other ways."

The two men rode on in silence for several minutes.

"My advice, for what it's worth, is to forget about both women. If you're thinking about settling down, then go to town and find yourself a nice churchgoing girl, and learn to love her," Jim suggested.

"I'm not exactly ready to walk down the aisle but just want to go courting and see where it leads. What would happen if I just rode over and asked to see Rosalinda?"

Jim sighed and tipped the brim of his hat back with one finger. He gazed at Luke for a long moment. "I can't rightly say but let me know before you go. In case you don't show up, I'll know where to go looking for you. Sometimes visitors from this side of the border are not always welcome," Jim said. Although Jim smiled, Luke could sense seriousness in what he said.

Chapter Eighteen

As Luke rode south the next morning, he scanned the far bank of the river for any sign of Rosalinda or the other women, but there was none. By mid-morning, the heavy bands of clouds started rolling in from the south. Within an hour, the first rain started and grew heavier each hour. By late afternoon, on his return trip, the ground was soaked. Throughout the day the clouds had grown heavier. It didn't look as though the rain was passing over quickly. It came in waves of heavy to light, and then the cycle would start all over again. Luke knew by morning the river would likely be on a big rise.

By the next morning, Luke knew the river would be rolling. Although it wasn't likely any livestock would be trying to cross, Luke was curious to see how much the water might have risen. After breakfast, he decided to ride out for a look.

As he reached the first watering hole, he could plainly see the river had widened considerably and was running swiftly. Luke could already tell there would be a sizable amount of fence to replace. He knew with the continuing rain the floodwaters would rise much higher.

Luke glanced across the river and saw several cows already trapped in the rising water, too far from the bank to swim against the swift current to reach safety. Too bad, he thought. They will be washed downstream and drowned.

A rider appeared at the top of the far embankment and rode at full speed down the slippery slope. The cowboy never tried to rein in his mount but plunged into the edge of the rushing water.

Luke took in a deep breath, knowing the rider was also headed for doom if he ventured any further. Luke gestured and shouted for the cowboy to go back, but it appeared the rider was going to ignore his warning. If the horse lost its footing, which was likely, the vaquero would meet an unfavorable fate. Even a strong swimmer couldn't survive. The heavy weight of soaked clothes, boots, and gun belt, plus the cumbersome rain slicker meant his chance of survival was slim to none. This must be a young, inexperienced ranch hand to not know better than to take such a chance trying to save a few cows, Luke surmised, as he watched the looming disaster.

Luke thought fast and hoped if he shot the cows the rider would surely turn back. Without further thought, Luke pulled his rifle from its scabbard, took careful aim, and shot the cow nearest the charro in the head. The loud rapport of the rifle echoed above the roar of the river. The rider did not move, and did not retreat as Luke had expected. Luke took aim and shot the second and third cow.

The vaquero did not move, did not react.

Again, Luke yelled and motioned for the rider to back away.

The rider hesitated only seconds before turning his mount and scrambling to the safety of the embankment. Upon reaching a secure position the cowboy turned toward Luke and jabbed the air with a raised fist and shouted words that were muffled by the roar of the churning water. Luke felt sure he was being cursed for what he had done, but he wasn't sorry. Maybe in time, the young fool would realize he had likely just saved his life.

~

Several days passed before the floodwaters receded and the damage could be assessed. There was a significant amount of fence to be replaced. The river riders and some of the ranch hands worked several days setting posts and stringing barbed wire.

When Gilbert rode out to inspect their progress, Luke told him about the incident during the flood and that he had shot three of Ruiz's cows in an attempt to save some young ignorant ranch hand. Luke generously offered to ride over to tell Señor Ruiz what had happened. Gilbert agreed that would be a good idea, in case the cowhand had told a different story about the dead cows.

Luke bathed, shaved, and put on his cleanest clothes for his journey to the Ruizes' hacienda. He wasn't as concerned about confessing to killing three cows as he was about asking to court Señor Ruiz's only daughter. He couldn't help but wonder if he would even be considered worthy of such an honor, even if she weren't promised to someone else. What if her father asked what he had to offer his daughter if their relationship became too serious? All Luke owned was a small number of acres and not enough cash to do anything but keep saving for the future. The wealthy Mexican might not consider him much of a prospect for his daughter.

Luke was graciously welcomed into the Ruizes' home and ushered into Señor Ruiz's expansive office. The walls were lined with dark wood shelves filled with leather-bound books, a large globe sat on an intricately carved stand near a large window, and the furnishings were made of ornate dark wood with plush upholstery. It was impressive and spoke of great wealth likely handed down for generations.

Suddenly Luke felt far less sure of himself than he had on his ride to the ranch.

Señor Ruiz poured them each a whiskey.

"To what do I owe the honor of your visit?" Señor Ruiz inquired with a pleasant smile.

"I come to tell you about shooting three of your cows during the flood. One of your riders rode into the flooded river, apparently intending to try to save them. I know from experience that was a foolish mission, so I shot the cows to save the rider's life. It was likely one of your younger ranch hands with little experience during floods. People don't always realize the power of rushing water," Luke stated in a matter-of-fact manner. He certainly didn't want to appear boastful since he wasn't sure how Ruiz would react to him killing three of his cows.

"Aye, yes, I was told one of the Sycamore Creek riders had killed three of our cows. However, the rider did not reveal that she had entered the river in an attempt to save the cows," he said with a tight smile.

"She!" Luke blurted out.

Señor Ruiz took a long swallow of whiskey. "Yes, my daughter, Rosalinda, was the rider." He hesitated slightly. "I am grateful to you for intervening and saving her life."

"I had no idea it was her."

"Apparently you were more concerned with the safety of another human no matter who it might be, and that is an honorable thing. As I said before, I am most appreciative you took action to save a life and especially the life of my only daughter," he said with warm affection. "She did not grow up here on the ranch and is unaware of many dangers. She means well and wants to help, but now I see she must be watched more closely for her own good," he said with a deep sigh.

The two men spent some time talking of ranching matters. Finally, Luke realized he might be on the verge of overstaying his welcome and plunged ahead in asking if he could come to call on Rosalinda.

Señor Ruiz refilled his own glass but did not offer another drink to Luke.

"Mr. O'Donnelly, I have no objection to you in particular, but my daughter is already promised to another man. Visits from you, or any man, would not be appropriate. Our customs are quite different from yours. I hope you will respect our customs and not make any attempt to see my daughter. She is young and impressionable. Any uninvited attention may only serve to confuse her as to what is expected of her in the not-too-distant future.

Luke felt as though he had been punched in the gut, although Jim had warned him of such a possibility.

"I see," was all he could manage before saying good evening to Señor Ruiz.

Luke rode slowly toward the river feeling more dejected than he could ever remember. He was normally a happy sort, but tonight he felt miserable, downcast, and even a bit angry. He saw the greed that provoked these arranged marriages as inhumane.

Luke remembered that Jim had indicated that Señor and Señora Ruiz had an arranged marriage. Surely, they weren't as happy as if they had freely chosen one another. How could they subject their daughter to the same loveless future? Luke wondered about Rosalinda's future and many other things as he rode slowly into the darkness.

He passed through a small stand of trees before reaching the river crossing. As he emerged, the pale moonlight illuminated the shadowy figure of a rider in the middle of the river. The shadow remained still, and Luke hesitated, not knowing who lay in wait for him to cross. If the person intended him harm, surely, they would hide in the shadows he reasoned. Just as he nudged his mount's sides, the rider called softly.

"It's me, Rosalinda."

"What are you doing out here at night by yourself? Your father may think I planned this meeting if he finds out," Luke said as he rode to meet her.

"I'm not afraid of Papa. Besides, he won't find out," she answered, apparently very sure of herself.

"What if he goes to your room to see if you are tucked in for the night?"

"I fixed my bed with pillows to look like that is exactly where I am," she said with a giggle. "I even put one of my dolls with long dark hair in my bed with her hair fanned out over my pillow. Papa will think I am asleep and won't disturb me," she said with an impish chuckle.

Luke was a bit surprised by her deceitfulness. "Why did you do all of that?"

"Well, I was listening outside Papa's office when you asked permission to come court me, and he told you I was already promised to another man. He's old! I don't want to marry some old man! I've only met him twice and don't really know him. How could they expect me to become his wife and be happy?" she moaned.

Luke was astonished to hear her family had promised her to some old man. An arranged marriage between two people of similar age would be bad enough, but a great age difference seemed especially cruel. Why, oh, why would her family do such a coldhearted thing? He couldn't help but question their motives. It must be for political reasons, as they appeared to be well-off. Or perhaps they weren't as rich as they appeared. Luke wasn't sure what to think. He knew he didn't like what was going to happen to Rosalinda, and he felt totally helpless to prevent what was about to take place.

"I don't know what I could do to help you, so why are you here waiting for me?" Luke asked, cautiously.

Rosalinda didn't answer immediately. When she spoke, her voice was soft, and he could hear her sadness.

"I know there is nothing you or anyone can do. I just want to spend some time with someone I really like before I am doomed to this—this awful marriage."

"If your papa catches us together, there will be hell to pay."

Rosalinda sighed deeply. "You are probably right. I am sorry I bothered you." She nudged her horse forward a few steps, so they sat side-by-side facing one another. She leaned toward Luke and whispered, "Will you kiss me just this once?"

Luke felt his pulse race and leaned in for the waiting kiss. "Rosalinda, this may only make things worse," he murmured as their lips met. The kiss was gentle, but, oh-so appealing. Her lips were as soft as the morning dew on a rose petal, making him want to drink in their sweetness. Luke pulled away, afraid of what might happen if he prolonged their intimacy.

They both sighed as their lips parted. Rosalinda reached up and gently caressed his smooth cheek. "Just think, that one kiss from the man I believe I could truly love may have to last me a lifetime."

Before Luke could think what to say, she nudged her horse and rode away into the darkness. He could hear the gentle splashing of her horse's hooves in the shallow water, and then the sound faded into the distance.

Luke did not move for quite some time. He listened to the gurgling water as it rippled over the shallow rocks. The river gently flowed, undisturbed by their dilemma, southward toward the Gulf of Mexico. The river separated him and the woman he felt sure he loved. Jim's warning came back to him. The river is narrow, but the gap between the two cultures is wide.

Luke rode into camp feeling trapped in a hopeless situation. As he unsaddled his horse, he told himself to take Jim's advice. Forget about Rosalinda. Forget about Georgiana. He would be better off without either of them to distract him from his goal of saving enough money to go back to Bandera and start over on his own land. Yes, he needed to stay focused on his future, not only for himself, but for Naomi.

Chapter Nineteen

The scorching heat lingered through the long summer into late September. A few late afternoon heat showers passed over but were of little benefit.

Gilbert worried constantly about the toll the drought was taking on the ranch. He was forced to sell a considerable amount of livestock and could no longer avoid having to lay off six workers. Another worry concerned not only the number of cattle and horses crossing the low river but the natural predators now attacking the sheep and goats. While searching for food they spread the dreaded ticks over more pastureland. Several pastures were already infested and lying empty for months, waiting for the tick infection to wane. He dreaded the thought that lightning from a storm might strike the dry brush and start a fire or that rustlers would toss a lighted cigarette, setting a fire to cover their trail.

Gilbert was thankful Jim was shouldering more of the responsibilities of running the ranch. It helped to have a partner in making decisions that would affect their business for years.

Luke worried about his occasional nighttime rendezvous with Rosalinda near the river. Each time they met he half expected to see her father step out of the shadows and shoot him. He loved Rosalinda, and she declared her love for him over and over.

With each meeting, it was becoming harder and harder for them to resist becoming lovers, but Luke knew he could not, would not, cross that line. He not only loved Rosalinda, but he also respected her. As much as he wanted her, he would not send her to a marriage tainted. He knew in the long run that would likely make her life more miserable.

Rosalinda had tried to enlist her mother's help to persuade her father to end the arranged marriage agreement, but her mother refused. She stood by her husband's decision even if she did not completely agree.

Luke couldn't understand Señora Ruiz's attitude. Surely, she dreamed about how her own life might have been much happier if she had been free to choose her husband. He couldn't help but wonder why she would stand by and watch her daughter suffer the same consequences. He also wondered why they had let their daughter be educated in the United States, instead of Mexico. Hadn't they considered that she would naturally pick up American ideas?

Rosalinda grew more miserable every day as her eighteenth birthday grew nearer and nearer. She told Luke the marriage would likely take place at Christmas.

As hard as the sweethearts tried, they could not think of a way out except to run off together. They both knew that would not only be dangerous but would alienate her from her family forever.

Luke could not bring himself to estrange Rosalinda from her family even if it meant losing her. He feared that in time she would grow to resent him if he permitted that to happen.

Naomi noticed Georgiana had been spending more time alone in her room. That seemed strange, as she had never been one to spend time alone. Normally, Georgiana wanted to be in the midst of whatever was going on around the ranch.

One morning she heard Georgiana retching as she passed her door, which was slightly ajar.

Naomi tapped on the door and pushed it open. She was shocked to see the pale-faced girl lying on the floor with her head bent over the washbasin. She clutched a rag that she was apparently using to wipe her ashen face.

"Oh, my, what's the matter?" Naomi blurted out.

Georgiana turned her sunken, dull blue eyes toward Naomi. She laid her head back on her arm and wiped her face again.

"Come in and close the door," she managed in a shaky voice.

"What is it? What's the matter?" Naomi asked again as she approached the rumpled bed and perched on its edge.

Georgiana did not immediately answer but took several deep breaths as though trying to steady herself.

A tear trickled down her white cheek and dripped onto her arm. "I'm in trouble," she whispered. "Real trouble."

Naomi gasped. She was afraid to ask exactly what Georgiana meant.

"I'm going—I'm going to have a baby," Georgiana murmured, as the tears began to flow more freely. "What am I going to do? When Gilbert finds out, he's going to kill me and him," she murmured. Georgiana burst into a full torrent of tears. Her body jerked with the onslaught of crying, and then she bent over the basin again.

Naomi put her hands over her mouth to hold back her gush of questions until she had time to think exactly what to say. At last, she gained her composure and calmly said, "Georgiana, you have to tell them, Gilbert and Marylee. They may be mad, but you'll need their help."

Georgiana shook her head violently as though trying to deny what was happening.

"No! Gilbert will—well, I'm not sure what he might do so don't say a word," she gave Naomi a pleading look.

"They're going to find out sooner or later. I think it would be better if you told them before they figure out what's the matter."

Georgiana sniffed and wiped her eyes with the damp rag. "I guess you're right, but," Georgiana's voice faded away.

"Have you told the baby's father?" Naomi asked, a bit shyly.

"Yes, but he doesn't want anything to do with me or the baby. He just wanted a good time," Georgiana confessed as tears reappeared.

"Well, you have to tell them. You've got to have help. Maybe you should tell Marylee first and see what she thinks should be done. Women understand these things better than men," Naomi tried to sound well-informed on the subject.

Georgiana lifted herself and sat on the bed beside Naomi. She stared into space for several moments and then looked at Naomi. "How do you know so much about having a baby?" she asked, a bit suspiciously.

Naomi blushed slightly. "I don't really, but it just seems like the thing to do. Surely, your family will stand by you."

"I don't know about that. After all, having a baby and not being married will disgrace my family and me. I doubt they'll be very understanding."

"Well, you still need their help," Naomi insisted.

In a way, she felt sorry for Georgiana. She hadn't grown up with her brothers and likely didn't feel very close to any of them. Georgiana was spoiled from growing up in boarding schools. Although she was well-educated, apparently, she was very lonely. Perhaps she had made a mistake trying to find someone she felt truly cared about her.

Naomi was even more grateful she had a brother like Luke. She knew she could depend on him, and he could depend on her, no matter what the circumstances. She also knew she wasn't likely to find herself in the kind of predicament Georgiana had created.

Chapter Twenty

A few days later, Luke rode in just in time to join the family for dinner.

That was the very evening Georgiana chose to make her announcement at dinner. Marylee was shocked. Gilbert was furious. Jim was silent, but his expression was one of disapproval. Floyd and Willie were still in town, likely having a good time.

Luke wasn't too shocked. During the past few months, he had seen her and Clint Swift meeting behind the barn and quickly disappearing into the pasture. He had said nothing. He didn't want to become entangled in family matters. Now he felt a bit guilty for not mentioning it to Jim. Maybe this could have been avoided, but deep down he had doubts about that too. Georgiana had proven to be more headstrong in having her own way than he had first realized.

Naomi felt uneasy. She felt somewhat trapped in the middle of a family uproar since she had been the first to find out besides whoever was the child's father.

Naomi and Luke exchanged looks. They quickly excused themselves from the table and walked out to the front porch. Loud, angry voices spilled out from inside. As close as they had become to the family, they still felt it was none of their affair.

"You tell me who did this!" Gilbert shouted at his sister. His face had become beet red with anger.

"What will you do if I tell you?" Georgiana asked in her usual sassy manner.

"I'll go get the son-of-a-bitch and make him marry you!"

"What if I don't want to marry him, and he doesn't want to marry me?"

"Both of you should have thought about that a while back. Now tell me his name!" Gilbert thundered.

"Georgiana, honey, you don't want to go through life with a blight on your good name," Marylee tried to reason.

"I could go away to have the baby and give it up for adoption."

"You'd give your own flesh and blood away to save yourself!" Jim stated almost in disbelief.

Georgiana stared at each of them. "Yes, I would. I don't want to be saddled with some squalling brat. Besides, it would be better off not knowing me or its father!"

Gilbert stood abruptly, knocking his chair backward. When he started around the table toward his sister, Jim intervened, uneasy about Gilbert's intent.

Jim spoke softly, "Georgiana, you need to think about what you are saying. Surely, you don't really mean what you just said," he implored.

Georgiana leveled her gaze and spoke clearly. "Yes, I do mean what I just said. I'm not ready to be a mother, and he certainly doesn't want to be a father."

Jim shook his head. He really didn't understand his only sister's attitude.

"Missy, you tell me who done this right now!" Gilbert demanded. His face had grown redder with anger.

"What will you do if I tell you?"

"I'll haul his butt back here, and you will marry long enough for you to have this baby!"

"Then what?"

Gilbert ran his hand through his hair and cursed under his breath. Before he could say more, Marylee spoke up.

"We'll take the baby and raise it like it was one of our own. You can leave and do whatever you please, but your child will be ours and remain with its family."

Gilbert stared at his wife but then nodded his head in agreement.

"Marylee's right, we'll take it and raise it just like our others. You won't be welcome here ever again. Do you understand me?"

"How will I live?"

Gilbert cleared his throat and looked at Jim.

"We will make a settlement for your share of the ranch. It will be a considerable amount. In fact, Gilbert and I have been working out the details to buy out our other brothers, and then the ranch will belong to the two of us. We are the only ones that seem to care about it anyway. Just understand, once the money is gone, there won't be any more," Jim emphasized.

Georgiana lifted her head and gave them her arrogant look. "What if I told you it's Luke's baby?"

Luke felt his body jerk in shock at Georgiana's words. "You'd be a damned liar," came Luke's livid reply from the front porch.

"Georgiana!" Gilbert yelled and drew back his hand as though to strike her.

She flinched but quickly recovered her composure. "It belongs to Clint Swift," she stated with a sly smile, knowing that would immensely displease her family.

"Clint Swift," Gilbert hissed. "I should have known you'd get mixed up with scum like Swift just to spite me!" Gilbert stomped out of the dining room, grabbing his hat off the hat rack beside the back door. They heard the door slam in his wake.

~

Gilbert rode south toward one of the wrangler camps. Normally he would not have put his horse through such a rigorous ride, but he wanted to reach the camp before dark. His ill temper rose as he rode. He blamed himself for this predicament. He should have known better than to hire somebody like Swift. Something about the man had spelled trouble from the start.

Gilbert had to admit Clint Swift was a good-looking man and had a swagger that seemed to appeal to women.

Although he didn't know his sister well, he should have seen she was more like their pa than their mother. A fellow like Swift was likely a real temptation to Georgiana, especially since he had forbidden her to see him.

When he spotted several tents in a small stand of trees, he called out before he even reached the camp.

"Clint Swift, Clint Swift, bring your sorry ass out here!"

Swift lifted the flap to one of the tents and stepped outside.

Gilbert did not bother to dismount. He didn't intend this to be a long conversation. Although he saw Swift still wore his gun, that didn't curb his temper. "Step on over here so the others don't hear what I have to say to you!" Gilbert demanded.

Swift walked slowly forward, never taking his eyes from Gilbert's face. As Clint looked up at the man still mounted on his big horse, he could clearly see the anger reflected in Gilbert's fiery gaze and face. Clint didn't particularly like having to look up to any man.

"Yeah, what is it you have to say?" Swift asked with a cocky air.

"I imagine you know why I'm here," Gilbert growled, as he looked down at Swift.

Swift spat a string of brown tobacco juice near Gilbert's horse. "Yeah, I reckon I do. Guess your sister done told you how we've been amusin' ourselves this summer."

"Yes, she did! You are going to marry her until after this baby is born! Then she'll give the baby to my wife and me. After that, the two of you can go to hell!"

"Is that so? Well, now, I think I need to be rewarded for that inconvenience. I ain't been plannin' on gettin' hitched any time soon."

"I guess your plans just got changed!" Gilbert snapped.

"I don't think so!" Clint sneered as he turned his back toward Gilbert and took a few steps.

"Swift!" Gilbert bellowed.

Clint whirled as a flash of fire exploded from his pistol.

Gilbert grabbed his chest, gurgled several times, and fell forward to the ground, landing with a loud thud. Gilbert's horse reared in panic from the sudden loud blast. His front hooves landed on Gilbert's back, pressing him into the hard dirt.

Before the horse could bolt, Clint grabbed the dangling reins, vaulted into the saddle, and put his spurs to the animal's flanks. He rode out of the camp at a breakneck pace.

Men came running from their tents and the shade of the trees.

They watched Clint Swift spur the horse as he headed west toward the Rio Grande. There was no doubt in their minds that Mexico was his destination. There he would be safe from the law and from the justice he deserved for killing a man in cold blood.

The men did not know what had taken place between the two men, but they knew their boss had been shot at point-blank range. They also knew Gilbert was a decent man, a fair man. As they raced toward the fallen man, they couldn't help but wonder why Swift would shoot him.

Two of the men rolled Gilbert to his back. His blank eyes stared toward Heaven. His face was contorted into an expression of surprise and pain. A red stain slowly spread across his chest. The bullet had hit his heart. He was dead.

Chapter Twenty-One

Marylee sobbed, paced the floor, and hugged her children close for hours after one of the men rode to headquarters to tell Jim about what had happened to his brother. Jim tried to break the news as gently as possible. But, how was that possible? A few hours before, Marylee had been a happily married woman with three children of her own and willing to take Georgiana's unwanted child and love it along with her own children. In the span of a few hours, everything had changed. Nothing would ever be the same. What would she do?

Georgiana wisely retreated to her room. She sat on the edge of her bed staring out the window into the darkness. Oh, what a fool she had been, she reflected. Tears trickled down her warm cheeks. Likely for the first time in her life Georgiana had feelings of remorse. It was her fault her brother had been killed. It was just as much her fault as Clint's that she was carrying an unwanted child. Now, who would take the baby? Who would love it like Marylee and Gilbert would have done? She must go away, far away, to have this child and give it to strangers. Maybe that was for the best after all, she decided.

In all honesty, she couldn't lay any more blame on Clint than she put on herself. He had never forced her against her will. She had known from the start Clint was a wanderer and took his pleasure wherever he found it. In fact, she had encouraged his ardent advances. Georgiana also wondered why it couldn't have been Luke instead of Clint that tempted her. She had liked Luke first, but he was not as forward as Clint. Luke was a decent man and would have married her without question. She hadn't expected to get caught. But for Clint to kill her brother was beyond her understanding. Yes, she knew she had truly been a fool.

Naomi hurried about the house trying to calm Marylee, look after the bewildered children, assist Jim in whatever way she could, and intermittently check on Georgiana.

It was late when the children finally settled down to sleep. Marylee and Jim sat in the main room talking quietly about the service for Gilbert. Georgiana still sat on the edge of her bed staring out at the darkness. Naomi felt exhausted but knew she could not go to bed until Marylee was settled for the night.

Naomi idly wondered where Luke had gone. Maybe he was seeing to the coffin being built for Gilbert. It was hard to believe the good-natured man had been killed by a no-good like Clint Swift.

Naomi could only remember a few times she had even seen Gilbert annoyed, much less mad. Apparently, he had been uncontrollably mad when Georgiana announced she was expecting a baby.

Georgiana had to be the most selfish person Naomi had ever met. She seemed to only think of herself. Naomi was grateful she had not snared Luke in her trap. She felt certain his life would have, beyond a doubt, been miserable.

Naomi caught a glimpse of Marylee entering her bedroom. She picked the lamp up off the kitchen table and started toward her own room.

"Naomi, do you know where Luke went?" Jim asked as she reached the doorway.

"I suppose he went to see to the coffin," she answered.

"I think I'll go check before I turn in. You go on to bed. Good night," Jim said as he brushed past her. Then he paused. He reached out and gently caressed the side of her face. "I don't know how we would manage without you, Naomi," he spoke softly.

"I'm glad to help however I can," she answered as she lifted her head to look at Jim.

Without speaking again, he leaned forward and brushed her lips with a gentle kiss. Naomi sensed his loneliness, his need for human companionship. She surprised herself when she stretched up on her tiptoes and returned his kiss with a lingering, fervent kiss. When they parted, they stood briefly looking into one another's eyes. Then they each hurried into the darkness in opposite directions.

Naomi's heart pounded as she walked briskly to her own bedroom. She did not hesitate at Georgiana's door for fear she couldn't speak, and she felt certain her face was flushed.

Naomi quietly closed her door and leaned against it, trying to calm herself before she undressed for bed.

A faint knock on her door made her heart race again. Could it be Jim coming to tell her why he had kissed her? Could it possibly be Jim was ready to say how he truly felt about her?

Naomi opened the door with great anticipation only to find Georgiana standing in the shadows.

"May I come in?" she asked, a bit unsure of her welcome.

Naomi hesitated briefly. She was tired and not in the mood to listen to Georgiana. Feelings of guilt prevailed. She stood aside to let her enter.

"I know it's late, but I need to ask a favor of you," Georgiana said as she sat on the edge of Naomi's bed.

"What favor?"

Georgiana hesitated, "I know I haven't always treated you very nice, but you are the only one I can ask for help."

Naomi did not speak but studied Georgiana carefully.

Georgiana rushed on, "I really am sorry for all of the trouble I've caused. Please, Naomi, talk to Jim and Marylee for me," she sounded more desperate as she spoke. "If you tell them how sorry I am, maybe they won't be so upset with me. They may even forgive me. You know they will listen to you. They like you," she paused, waiting for Naomi to answer.

Naomi remained standing beside the door as she listened and studied Georgiana as she spoke.

Somehow, she didn't believe Georgiana was as ashamed as she was trying to pretend. Naomi wasn't convinced Georgina was the kind of person to suddenly have a guilty conscience and truly regret her actions.

"No, Georgiana, I won't do it. It is not my place to become involved in family matters."

"But, but they will listen to you," Georgiana insisted.

Naomi opened the door, indicating it was time for Georgiana to leave.

"I won't do it. They are your family. You are the one who needs to talk to them, not me."

Georgiana gave Naomi one of her haughty looks. "I should have known better than to ask you for help. You've never liked me. I'm sure you're glad it isn't Luke's child. You never wanted him to like me either," she flung at Naomi as she flounced out of Naomi's room.

The funeral was a somber affair held at the family cemetery. The graves were on a slight rise near the pond just north of the homestead. Crude grave markers denoted the graves of various members of the Keller family, several ranch hands, one young woman, and two babies who had lived on the ranch.

Jim looked so somber, so lonely. Marylee cried softly as she held the baby, and the two older boys clung to their mother, still looking puzzled as to what had happened to their father. The other four brothers stood together looking sad but not as stricken as Jim. Georgiana stood between Willie and Floyd. She did not look at anyone. For once she had the good sense to keep her head lowered. Her appearance gave the impression she might be praying.

Naomi and Luke stood with the other mourners. Naomi felt certain the burden of running the ranch single-handedly already weighed heavily on Jim's mind. She felt a tear slip down her cheek as she thought about the sorrow of this entire situation.

More and more, lately, Naomi had caught herself glancing out the kitchen window late in the afternoon, watching for Jim to return to headquarters. She hoped each evening he would suggest they sit on the front veranda together after supper, but he had not. Now that the weather was turning cooler, she hoped he would remain in the living room for a while. On most evenings, before this tragedy, he and Gilbert had gone to their office for a while to discuss business. Then Jim would go to the bunkhouse to play cards or to his own room. Naomi was about to give up hope that Jim might actually be attracted to her. She knew in her heart she was definitely attracted to Jim.

After the service, most of those who attended the late morning service came to the house for a short visit with the family and to share the noon meal before returning to their own homes. Most of the neighbors brought food, but Naomi had also been busy since early morning preparing food for their guests. As she hurried about refilling glasses or cups, gathering dishes to be washed and used again, she often caught herself searching for Jim as he visited with neighbors and his own family. Her heart ached for him, for the sudden burden of running the ranch all on his own and having to deal with all of the problems Gilbert's death had heaped on him.

When the guests all departed Jim summoned his brothers, Marylee, and Georgiana to join him in the dining room. Naomi served more cups of steaming coffee as they gathered around the family dining table in a subdued mood. Naomi looked at those gathered and wondered if this might well be the last time these family members would sit together. She found that thought made her want to cry.

Naomi went in search of Luke to give the family the privacy they needed. To her surprise, Luke was nowhere to be found. She asked several of the ranch hands if they had seen him. They all shrugged and shook their heads. Naomi found it a bit strange that Luke would just ride off somewhere without saying a word. Maybe he told Jim where he was going, she decided.

After a long walk, Naomi sat on the front porch, waiting for the brothers to depart. As they filed out, each spoke politely but did not give any indication as to what had taken place in the family meeting.

A while later Naomi returned to the dining room to clear away the coffee cups. She paused in the doorway when she saw Jim remained at the huge table. He looked so alone sitting at the head of the long table surrounded by empty chairs. It looked as though his family had deserted him in his hour of need. Naomi walked quietly to his side and gently placed her hand on his shoulder.

"Would you like more coffee?" she asked softly.

Jim glanced up as he laid his hand on top of hers and gently squeezed her hand.

"Yes, thank you," he answered as he released her hand. "Bring one for you too."

Naomi returned with their coffee and took the chair to Jim's right. They sat in silence for several moments.

"Gilbert's death has brought a great deal of change to the Sycamore Creek Ranch," Jim said, as he gazed at Naomi.

"I—I'm sure it has," Naomi responded.

Jim let out a long breath. "Marylee wants to return to her own family. She says she can't bear to live here without Gilbert, and that's understandable. Georgiana will be going to Houston to have her baby and give it up for adoption," he said. He did not try to hide his sadness or his disappointment in his only sister's decision.

"All of my siblings have agreed to let me buy out their parts of the ranch. I'll have to borrow some money to do that, and things will be tight for a while. I don't see any other way to hold on to all of the land to keep the ranch solvent."

Naomi did not comment. She was a bit taken aback at this news. Such financial matters were far beyond her understanding. It just sounded like Jim would be more alone than ever.

Jim gave a slight laugh. "When Luke and I came back here to work, I certainly never dreamed things would turn out this way." Jim paused and gazed off in the distance. "I plan to make Luke my foreman. He likely won't be too happy to hear about that, but I need someone I can trust and depend on in that position."

Naomi was shocked. "What about Mr. Barnes? He's been foreman here a long time."

Jim turned his gaze back to Naomi. "I never cared much for Barnes. He's too much like my father to suit me. I don't trust him either."

"Oh, I see," Naomi answered. "I went to find Luke, but no one seems to know where he went. Did he say anything to you about leaving?"

Jim did not immediately answer. He looked down at his cup that was almost empty. "Don't ask me," he said in a somber mood. "All I can tell you is Luke will be back in a few days."

Naomi felt a shiver of fear run through her. What in the world was Luke doing? She instantly wondered if his absence could have anything to do with Clint Swift, or was it Rosalinda, or could it be something else? But what else could it be?

The days passed slowly. Naomi prayed every night and several times during the day for Luke's safe return. Three days, four days, five days passed. Over and over she wanted to plead with Jim to tell her where Luke had gone, but his words, "Don't ask me," kept coming back to her.

Late in the afternoon, on the sixth day, Naomi glanced out the kitchen window and, to her great relief, saw Luke and Jim standing near one of the barns talking. The two men gave a brief nod to one another and shook hands. After a few more words they turned and walked toward the house. As they grew nearer, Naomi could see Luke's growth of whiskers, and his clothes looked rumpled and dirty. He looked tired.

Naomi flew to the back door to greet her brother. She cautioned herself about what to say to Luke. Should she ask where he had been or just wait for him to tell her if he chose to confide in her about his absence?

Luke greeted Naomi with a brotherly hug but did not say anything about his six-day absence. Naomi felt a bit left out. She knew Luke was a grown man, but this made her feel their closeness was waning. Sadness came over her. She realized that she could not expect their lives to remain the same.

Lots of things had changed during the time she spent in Castroville and after she had come here. She knew Luke was deeply in love with Rosalinda, and wished she knew of some way to help Luke and Rosalinda work out a solution to their problem, but she didn't. It hurt her to see Luke unhappy.

She also knew her feelings for Jim were growing and wondered if Jim might possibly feel something in return. If he did, they might marry someday, and she would remain here the rest of her life. What about Luke? Would he stay here forever as foreman, or would he go back to Bandera at some point to build his horse training business?

Luke was surprised when Jim approached him about becoming the new foreman. He felt obligated to help Jim, his true friend. The thought of giving up being a river rider didn't set well, but he would do it for Jim. He couldn't explain his feelings about the contentment he felt when riding in solitude. Something about the isolation had gotten into his blood.

Luke had come to know every bend in the river and crook and turn of the trail. He could instantly tell if there had been any change since his last ride. Luke could now recognize the signs of the animals or humans crossing the river. The subtle changes in the river were instantly apparent. He relished the gurgling sounds the river made as it flowed over the rocky bottom of the shallows or its roar as it rushed through the narrow gorges. He had seen it moving slowly and even stagnant in places or fiercely flowing as it swallowed up the land and anything in its path. It cooled and refreshed him during the hot summer. Often it had yielded up a tasty fish to satisfy his hunger.

Luke remembered the surge of excitement he felt the first time he had caught sight of a brown bear splashing in the river. Unafraid, he sat for a long while just watching the majestic animal. Night after night he lay in his bunk at the river camp listening to the lonesome sound of the coyotes or wolves baying in the distance. He marveled at the flights of the birds as they soared above the river and watched the circling vultures as they prepared to descend on some helpless prey.

He had spent countless hours watching the majestic sunrises and sunsets along the meandering river. He marveled at the changing colors and shapes of the clouds, and the sky told him when to ride for cover or to expect a cooling rain in the summer.

Luke couldn't put his feelings into words. He just knew he was acutely aware of a certain serenity the solitude of riding the river gave him. It penetrated to his very core, his soul. He knew he would return to the river as often as time permitted. It was a place of ultimate peace, a quiet place to reflect, a place of rebirth.

Chapter Twenty-Two

J im, Luke, and Naomi sat at the kitchen table before time for the evening meal.

"Marylee and the children will be leaving in a few days. I'll drive them to the train and send a couple of wagons to take her belongings to Uvalde. Georgiana will leave on the same train and go on to Houston," Jim said in a subdued tone.

Naomi had not mentioned to anyone about Georgiana trying to get her to speak to the family on her behalf. Apparently, Georgiana had not tried to apologize for all of the heartache she had caused.

"It sure will be quiet around here without Marylee and the children," Naomi commented.

"Yes, I will miss them a lot," Jim answered. "Luke will be moving to the foreman's house tomorrow. Maybe you can help him get settled," he suggested to Naomi.

Naomi felt her face grow pink. "I think I better move to the foreman's house, too. It wouldn't be proper for me to live here with just the two of us in this house," she said as she blushed.

"Oh, I hadn't thought about that. It seems a bit silly since I'll be sleeping in one end of this big house and you on the opposite end, but

I know how people talk. Yes, I suppose that's the thing to do," Jim said as he looked at Luke.

"There's plenty of room in the foreman's house for the two of us and then some," Luke answered with a grin.

"Jim, will you want me to cook meals for you, or you and Luke?"

Jim looked more perplexed. "Well, I hadn't thought about that either. I think we might as well eat at the bunkhouse. No need in you getting up before dawn to cook for just the two of us."

Naomi sat quietly. After more thought she finally spoke again. "What exactly would you like for me to do to earn my salary? I won't need to be cleaning or washing and ironing but once a week."

"Well," Jim rubbed his chin as he gave her question careful consideration. "This is all so new, I'm not sure exactly what I do or don't need done. Just give me a few days to work things out. I'm sure I can think of something," he finally suggested.

"Jim, if you don't really need my help, I could get a job and room in town."

"I don't really want you off in town by yourself," Luke spoke up.

"I don't either," Jim agreed.

"Luke, if we are ever going to save enough money to go back to our own land, then I need to work. I don't want Jim paying me for nothing."

Jim and Luke exchanged a quick look.

Luke cleared his throat. "When Jim offered me the job as foreman, he also offered to give us one hundred and sixty acres if I would promise to stay for two years. We could sell the land at Bandera, keep saving money, and then I could set up my horse training business here."

Naomi gasped in shock. "Luke, are you sure that's what you really want to do?"

"It might prove to be the best plan. A man from the government came to talk to Gilbert and Jim last month about the government taking over the river riders. If that happens, all of those men are going to need good horses. We would be right here, right where the river riders are, and we'll be ready to supply all of the horses they need." Luke's excitement grew as he told Naomi about the possible changes.

Naomi's eyes sparkled as she caught Luke's excitement. "Oh, Luke, that would be great. How much do you think we'll get for the land at Bandera?"

"Jim's going to give me some time off in a few months. We'll take the train to Bandera and find out. How does that sound?"

"Wonderful, just wonderful!" Naomi answered with enthusiasm. "I do have a question. Why does the government want to take over the river riders?"

Jim leaned back in his chair and gazed thoughtfully as he reached for his cup of hot coffee. "The best I can understand it is, since we ship more and more livestock to all sorts of places, there needs to be better control over the quality of meat. It's to help prevent spreading diseased cattle. If that happens now, it is hard to know where the cattle were shipped from and diseased meat could make hundreds or even thousands of people sick. Apparently, some problems are already cropping up, and the government feels they can better control and enforce higher standards. There needs to be more control over protecting the ranches along the entire border from where the Devil's River empties into the Rio Grande all the way to the Gulf of Mexico. Some ranchers apparently aren't as careful about their livestock as we are," Jim speculated. "Unfortunately, some folks just look at the profit margin and don't really care what happens to others."

"Oh, my!" Naomi exclaimed. She turned her gaze to Luke. "All the way to the Gulf of Mexico," she repeated in dismay. "We could get rich selling horses to all of those riders, couldn't we?"

Luke laughed. "I don't think all of the riders would buy horses from us but a good many would. There will always be some that don't stay and new ones coming along. I do think we will be in a position to make a good living."

Naomi frowned slightly and turned her attention back to Jim.

"What about west of the Devil's River? Won't they need river riders out there too?"

"Not necessarily. The farther west you go the riverbanks become very steep in most places, and it is less likely livestock will cross over. Those ranchers can still easily manage the few places livestock might cross," Jim explained.

"Well, this is exciting news. What about your river camps? Will the new riders still use them?" Naomi asked.

"Yes, in fact, the government will actually buy the cabins and contents but not the land they sit on. I guess you could call this a cooperative effort between the ranchers and government." Jim leaned back in his chair as he took another sip of coffee. "I think it will all work out for the best in the long run. The government can pay the river riders a better wage than us ranchers. At the same time, that gives us more money and less to worry about in operating our ranches."

After Marylee and her children and Georgiana left, Naomi cleaned the entire house. She put clean linens on the bed in the room that had belonged to Gilbert and Marylee. Now it would become Jim's room. She supposed this room had always belonged to the head of the ranch, as it was larger than the other bedrooms.

The house seemed to echo from its emptiness. Gloomy shadows seemed to fill the house. There was no need to open the curtains or to light lamps with only one person to occupy the house. Naomi hated the hollow sound of her own footsteps.

The day after they all left Naomi cleaned every room, especially giving the kitchen a thorough cleaning. It made her feel sad to think she would no longer stand at the big cook stove preparing meals for the family and frequent guests. She carried the extra food to the bunkhouse for the cook to use. As she walked slowly toward the foreman's house, she felt downhearted. Luke really didn't even need her to cook for him and cleaning wouldn't take long. She couldn't help but wonder what she could do to fill her time.

A few days later, in the late afternoon, Naomi took a walk toward the pond. It was pleasant out, but she knew the late October air would cool quickly at sunset. On her return, she noticed a few piles of leaves and dirt on the big front porch of the main house. She got her broom and began to vigorously sweep away the debris. She hummed softly, happy to have something to do.

"Naomi, what are you doing?" she heard Jim ask from the open front door.

She whirled, a bit startled, as she had not heard him open the door.

"I'm sweeping the front porch. It was already dirty, and I don't want it looking like no one lives here," she answered, with a few final swipes with her broom.

"It feels like no one lives here," Jim answered. "Come on in and let's make a pot of coffee," he suggested, as he held the door for her to enter.

Naomi walked ahead of Jim to the big empty kitchen. "I think I did leave a bit of coffee here, but that is about all," she commented, as she reached for the smallest coffee pot.

Jim sat at the round kitchen table as he watched Naomi move about the kitchen. Naomi looked at home in this kitchen, he mused. He definitely needed someone to help him fill this big house. Naomi was the one he needed, wanted, loved, he told himself for the hundredth time or more. So why hadn't he made his feelings known to her? What was holding him back? he questioned. Jim knew the answer to his own question. He was afraid of Naomi's answer. She might say no and then what would he do? He could not imagine loving another woman enough to want to spend the rest of his life with her.

Naomi sat next to Jim while the coffee perked.

"Jim, have you thought of some more chores for me to do to earn my keep?" she asked with a teasing grin, although her question was a serious one.

Jim reached out and took her hand. Now was as good a time as any, he told himself. He steeled his nerves and answered.

"Yes, Naomi, I have. In fact, I have given that prospect quite a lot of serious thought," then he paused and just looked at her.

"Well, what have you decided?" she asked with a nervous laugh when she saw the serious expression on his face. She hoped he hadn't decided she should go to town for a job after all. What else could he find for her to do at the ranch? Recently, it had been hard to find enough work to fill half of her days.

Jim cleared his throat and leaned closer to Naomi as he looked into her pretty eyes. Their clear aqua-blue color reminded him of the sky on a spring morning. Jim felt his heart pounding and could hear it drumming in his ears. Suddenly, the room seemed stuffy, and he longed for a breeze to cool his damp forehead.

"Naomi—Naomi, I have grown very fond of you. Actually," he paused as though trying to find the right words. "As a matter of fact, I am in love with you and feel it would be appropriate, well, I mean, I think we should get married." He stopped but then felt it necessary to rush on before she could answer. "I am rather certain my feelings may come as a shock to you, but I do hope you will consider becoming my wife. I realize you may need some time to think this over. That's fine, just fine." Jim felt certain he was rambling on and on, but he was afraid to stop talking.

Naomi stared into Jim's hopeful face and felt as though her lungs might burst from the lack of air. Then she smiled. "Oh, Jim, I am surprised at your feelings for me, but not at my own. I have loved you for quite some time but was afraid to let my feelings show." Naomi burst into delightful laughter. "Now haven't the two of us been silly and wasted a lot of time because we were too afraid to let our true feelings show?"

Jim laughed with her, laughed with relief, laughed with joy, laughed with love. "Oh, Naomi, am I correct to believe you will marry me?"

"Yes, Jim, yes!" she answered. Her bright eyes were twinkling and her sweet smile engulfed Jim's heart and soul.

They hesitated no longer. Jim and Naomi rose and stepped forward into a tender embrace. Their lips met in a kiss of gentle love that soon turned to desire.

Jim ran his rough hand along Naomi's smooth cheek, brushing a stray strand of golden blonde hair away from her face, as he held her snugly against him. He kissed her eyes, her nose, her cheeks, and returned to passionately capture her supple mouth.

Naomi felt breathless. The sudden passion she felt, and realized Jim also felt, came as a pleasant surprise. She had often thought he might be too gentle, too careful with her. Now she knew there was a hidden side to him she had not expected, but it pleased her.

Finally, Jim held her at arm's length. "I guess I better go ask Luke for permission to marry his sister," Jim said with a chuckle.

"He may be glad to be rid of me," Naomi teased.

"I want us to marry soon. Real soon! This house is too empty. I dread coming in it even to sleep," Jim said, as he looked around the kitchen that now looked so empty. There were no pots sitting on the big cook stove, no bowls and platters on the long countertop, no dishes waiting to be washed and put away. Its desolate look reflected his own feelings.

Deserted was how Jim had been feeling since Gilbert was killed and the rest of his family had gone away. He had never felt so alone, even when he had left years ago and roamed from job to job with no roots, no ties to anything or anyone. The quiet solitude he now faced made him finally come to terms with his feelings for Naomi.

Now they would fill this old house with love and children. There would be no more lonely nights spent wondering if he was too old for Naomi, wondering if she could possibly love him.

"I would like enough time to make myself a pretty new dress."

Jim playfully tweaked her nose. "How about I buy you any dress you'd like for our wedding?"

Naomi frowned slightly. "I don't think that's how things are done."

"Just don't take too long to make that dress," Jim warned.

"I won't. Now, let's go tell Luke," Naomi said. She took Jim's hand and tugged him toward the door.

Chapter Twenty-Three

S hortly before Naomi and Jim married, she and Luke discussed
the fact that neither had ever told anyone about their family or
the circumstances that led up to them being on their own. They
agreed that, when the time was right, each was free to tell as much or
as little about their past as they chose.

Two weeks after Jim proposed, he and Naomi were married in the
main room of the big house that would now become their home.
Friends and neighbors crowded into the house to witness the happy
occasion. The newlyweds could hardly take their eyes off one another.
They danced, smiled, laughed, kissed, and began to wonder how much
longer their guests would linger.

Señor and Señora Ruiz, Rosalinda, and Antonio Flores also
attended the ceremony.

Luke had not seen Rosalinda for several weeks. She had warned
him Antonio was coming to make plans for their wedding.

The last time they had met beside the river, Luke had held her
while she cried in despair. They shared their feelings of hopelessness.
When they parted Luke forced himself to kiss her with tender love, not
the burning desire he fought against.

Luke felt miserable. When he saw the somber expression on Rosalinda's face, he felt certain she must have been feeling much the same as he. It hurt to look at her sitting next to Antonio. He wasn't quite as old as Luke had expected, but he was considerably older than Rosalinda. He wasn't a bad-looking fellow, but then, he wasn't too impressive either.

Rosalinda's stunning beauty was enhanced by the dark green velvet dress she wore enhanced with sparkling sequins. Her long dark hair was piled high on her head in soft curls and secured with a matching green, sequined, velvet band. Her large brown eyes did not sparkle as usual. Her gloomy expression seemed to penetrate Luke's heart clear to his core.

Luke could not ward off the burning memories of running his fingers through her long, silky tresses, caressing her lovely body, and tasting her yielding lips. He wanted to grab her and run and run, until they were far away from the border, far away from the man seated beside her, and far away from her family or any threat that would keep them apart.

Luke could stand their separation no longer. He squared his shoulders and boldly crossed the room to where Rosalinda sat.

"Miss Ruiz, may I have this dance," he asked with a slight bow to Rosalinda and nod of his head to Antonio.

Antonio stood and extended his hand to Luke.

"I am Antonio Flores," he said as he glanced at Rosalinda.

She rose slowly, smiled sweetly at Antonio and then at Luke. "Antonio, this is Luke O'Donnelly. He is the new foreman of this ranch. Luke, this is Antonio Flores. He has traveled in his new motorcar all the way from Mexico City for a visit."

Luke instantly felt encouraged since she did not introduce Antonio as her fiancé.

Antonio graciously gestured for Rosalinda to join Luke for a dance. As soon as they were out of earshot Luke whispered. "You didn't introduce him as your fiancé. Has there been a change of plans?" he asked hopefully.

"No, I am afraid not," she whispered. "I just can't bring myself to think of him in that manner. Papa is very unhappy with me for treating Antonio so cool."

"You told me he was an old man. He's not all that old."

"He's fourteen years older than me. He has been a grown man for as long as I can remember," she said a bit defensively.

"If people make these arranged marriages when their children are so young, why wasn't he promised to someone nearer his age?"

"He was, but she died about a year before I was born. My father saw an opportunity to elevate his position and make better political alliances by offering me as Antonio's future wife. I think Antonio was really devastated when his young fiancée died. This arrangement gave him plenty of time to grieve and get over her loss."

"Oh, Rosalinda, let's not talk about him anymore. Let's have this dance, a dance to last us a lifetime," Luke whispered as he tightened his hold. He instantly regretted his words when he saw her eyes mist with tears.

When the music ended, Luke reluctantly escorted Rosalinda back to her parents and Antonio. He gave her slim hand one final squeeze that sent a silent message of his love.

Rosalinda had to fight back the tears that threatened to spill over. She knew she must not make a spectacle of herself and embarrass her family or Antonio.

The trip back to the hacienda by motorcar seemed never-ending. On the ride home the cold night air had chilled everyone to the bone. Her parents soon retired for the evening, leaving Rosalinda and Antonio seated on the sofa near the huge fireplace.

They sat quietly, neither speaking. Rosalinda wondered if this was an indication of her life ahead, silent, empty, nothing! She felt the tears coming and could not hold them at bay any longer. She heard her sobs break loose and could not stop them either.

Still, Antonio sat staring into the flickering flames, silent!

She rose to rush from the room to find a place away from him, away from everyone, where she could weep and weep until all of her tears were used up.

Luke sat at the kitchen table in the foreman's house sipping the strong coffee he had brewed. He must remember to ask Naomi how much coffee to put in the pot. He had to admit he missed her cooking and her company. Now he understood better how Jim had felt. This house seemed too big and empty for just one person. Most evenings he lingered at the bunkhouse as long as possible to avoid the silence he knew waited for him.

The afternoon sun was sinking far to the west, highlighting streaks of orange and pink across the darkening sky. Shadows were already filling the house. Luke lit a lamp and reached across the table to pick up a ranching magazine he had borrowed from Jim. He glanced out the window just as a rider bounded into the yard. Luke squinted into the setting sun in an attempt to identify the person.

Luke stood and hurried to the door as soon as he recognized Rosalinda as she dismounted. Her feet hit the ground running. As he stood in the open doorway, she flew into him, grabbing him around the neck, planting kisses on his face, ending with his mouth. Between kisses, she spoke his name, as though she were reassuring herself he was real.

Luke managed to grab her shoulders, holding her away from him as he searched her face for an answer to her unusual behavior.

"What in the world?" was as far as he got.

"Luke, Luke! Antonio ended the marriage contract!" she almost shouted. "I'm free to marry you!" She kissed him again and laughed with the joy of telling Luke her good news.

"What? What made him change his mind?" Luke felt overwhelmed with joy, relief, and amazement.

Luke wanted to draw her inside but knew that wouldn't be proper as there were plenty of eyes watching what was going on. Instead, he led her to the nearby porch swing. "Now tell me what's happened," Luke said, as he put his arm around her drawing her close.

Rosalinda told him every detail of what had taken place.

"When we got home from Naomi and Jim's wedding, Antonio and I were left alone. It was awful. We just sat there not knowing what to say to one another. I burst into tears and was about to run away.

Antonio finally said,

'Rosalinda, don't leave.'

I stood beside the fireplace, but I did not return to my seat.

Then he said to me, 'I received your letter the day before I left Mexico City. When I first read it, I was angry, although your pleas to be released were touching. On the long drive here, I had plenty of time to give your request much thought. I came to realize my fury at your request was because I had always considered you another possession and that one of my possessions was being threatened. I had not completely made up my mind until I saw you and Luke dancing together tonight. It was obvious that you love him, and he loves you. Now I have made my decision. I will release you from this marriage contract. I realize if I do not let you go, you will indeed only be a possession and our life together will be miserable. You are free, Rosalinda. Go marry your gringo.'

I slowly turned and really looked at Antonio for the first time since his arrival. 'You will release me!' was all I could manage in complete dismay.

Antonio patted the sofa as an indication for me to sit beside him.

He said, 'It is not as big of a sacrifice as you may think. You see, I too have found another to love. She knew of this arranged marriage from the start of our relationship and is willing to be my mistress. But, I, like you, prefer to be married to the one I truly love.'

'Oh, Antonio, I am truly happy for you. I can't wait to tell Luke,' I burst out overjoyed. I'm sure I blushed slightly when I gave Antonio a hug and kissed him on his cheek to show him that, beyond any doubt, I appreciated his willingness to forego the marriage contract.

Antonio continued, 'You better wait until after I have talked to your father. I am going to tell him it is my idea to end the contract and will generously compensate him, so he does not lose the respect this marriage would have brought. I will also make a strong political alliance with him. There are numerous details to work out before you run off to announce your freedom.' Then he patted my hand and smiled at me like a true friend.

Then Antonio said, 'You are a brave young woman to have done what you did, and I respect your courage.'

Papa was quite upset with me at first. He thought my coolness towards Antonio had caused him to change his mind. Antonio assured him it wasn't me, but him, that wanted to end the marriage contract. He never told Papa I had written him a letter asking to be released. I don't know what Antonio gave Papa, but I am sure it was a sizable amount. Our family is not quite as high up the ladder as we might have been, but we are high enough. Papa still has his dignity and fatter pockets."

Rosalinda laughed with delight when she saw the look on Luke's face.

"You took a real chance when you wrote to Antonio. If he hadn't been a reasonable man, he could have made you and your family's life hell," Luke pointed out as he hugged her tighter.

"I thought about that possibility, but that was all I knew to do. I had to take that chance for us."

Luke was amazed at Rosalinda's courage. He would have to remember that in the future, he mused.

"I'm glad you did," he whispered. "Now will your father consent to us getting married?" Luke asked anxiously.

"Oh, yes, I believe Antonio told him he realized we were very much in love, and that was another reason for ending the marriage contract as well as his own situation. Papa knows I won't have things any other way. You still have to make the gesture of asking for his permission. Then we will be married in the church in Mexico and have another wedding here," she laughed. "You will be very, very married," she teased as their lips met in a lingering kiss.

First Luke had several talks with the priest in Del Rio and converted to Catholicism so they could be married in the Catholic Church. Since he had rarely attended any church, the thought of becoming Catholic didn't bother Luke. It would make Rosalinda happy, and hopefully, he would be more accepted by her family.

The old majestic cathedral in Mexico was a stunning setting for Luke and Rosalinda's wedding. The high, arched ceiling with rich, dark, wooden beams lent a feeling of grandeur. Tall, stained-glass windows lined the sides of the large sanctuary. The dark tile floors gleamed in the soft glow of lamp and candlelight.

Rosalinda wore an exquisite wedding dress made of fine silk over-laid with delicate lace. Tiny pearls added a dainty beauty to the pure white dress and lace veil that enhanced Rosalinda's dark beauty. Her mother, and grandmother before her, had worn the lovely ensemble.

Luke looked just as handsome in his new, fashionable, black suit.

Naomi held Jim's hand during the long ceremony and wished she could understand the words the priest spoke in Latin.

After the ceremony, they traveled to the Ruizes' hacienda for a huge wedding dinner and celebration that lasted almost until dawn. Jim had warned Naomi that no one knew how to throw a party like the Mexican people.

Two days later Luke and Rosalinda were united in marriage again, in a civil ceremony at the county courthouse in Del Rio. Luke remembered her teasing words that he would become very, very married.

Rosalinda's family bestowed on her a sizable dowry, which included a dozen fine horses, furniture, linens, jewelry, and money. After a year of constant badgering, Luke put his pride aside and was persuaded to let his persistent wife build their home on the hundred and sixty acres he had received from Jim as part of their deal.

Rosalinda oversaw the construction of a large U-shaped house with large airy rooms, partly furnished with elaborate pieces of furniture from her dowry. The other less formal furnishings were custom-made by a fine craftsman in Del Rio.

Luke kept his promise to Jim and stayed for two years as foreman of the Sycamore Creek Ranch.

A few months after they were each married, just Luke and Naomi rode the train to Bandera. They hired a buggy and drove out to their land for one last look at what they had once pinned their dreams on for a better life. As they stood together gazing around their lush land, it seemed such a long time ago they had come here with such high hopes that had been dashed almost before they got started.

"You know, Naomi, I have often blamed myself for this not working out," Luke said, sounding a bit sad.

"Why would you do that? You had no way of knowing someone would set everything on fire while we were at the Markhams' dance."

"No, that's true. I think it's for what I did to John, and how I got the five hundred dollars from him," Luke answered.

"Oh, Luke, John got what he deserved and that had nothing to do with this, so don't even think about such a thing," Naomi said, dismissively.

Luke smiled at his sister. "You never see my faults, do you?"

Naomi gave her brother an admiring glance. "Why would I look for any faults in you? You have taken very good care of me, and you are all I have to count on from our family," she answered as she hugged her brother.

Naomi let out a long sigh. "Luke, do you ever wonder about our brother and sisters?"

"Yes, sometimes," he answered softly.

"Now that we are both married and settled, do you think I could write to Ruth without causing trouble?" she asked, hopeful Luke would agree.

Luke mulled over her question before answering. "I suppose that would be all right," he finally answered.

Naomi still sensed reluctance in Luke for her to contact their family. He had changed over the past few years, mellowed. Yet, the thought of renewing contact with Ruth's no-good husband might still be a concern.

She studied her brother's profile for several minutes. "I'll think on it a while longer before I write to Ruth," she finally said.

Luke looked at her and smiled. Then he nodded his head in agreement.

Luke and Naomi split the money from the land sale, which was more than they had expected. They divided the money they had saved according to how much each one had contributed.

Jim insisted Naomi put her share of the money in the bank for a rainy day, if they ever had one. Naomi took comfort in knowing she had the money if she and Jim or Luke ever needed it.

Luke had invested his savings in barns, corrals, fences, and more horses to add to the ones Rosalinda had received. It didn't take long to start reaping the rewards of his years of saving and planning.

When Luke and Rosalinda moved into their new home, they left Jim and Naomi content with the arrival of their first son. The big house no longer seemed empty. Now it echoed with happy gurgles or disgruntled cries from their new arrival.

Rosalinda was expecting their first child in a few months. Luke felt certain their big house would soon be filled with similar sounds.

The Department of Agriculture had taken complete control of the tick eradication program along the Rio Grande. Large numbers of ranch hands signed on with the government program. Better pay, better hours with a good future was their promise.

There was some grumbling when the men learned they had to furnish their own horses, but it was good business for Luke. His reputation as a fine horse trainer soon spread. At times he found it difficult to keep up with the demands from the river riders and surrounding ranchers. Luke took great satisfaction in knowing all of his years of hard work were paying off.

Now Luke often trained his horses by following the same trail he had ridden as a river rider. He used the quiet solitude to mull over any current problems, and at times his thoughts reflected on the past. Occasionally, he would pause and gaze at the winding river as it stretched out as far as he could see. It reminded him of the twists and turns his life had taken and where that path had led him.

Luke had never told anyone except Jim about his trip to Mexico after Gilbert was killed. He knew Naomi was hurt when he hadn't confided in her, but some things were better left unsaid.

What he had done was because of his loyalty to Jim and out of respect for Gilbert. If it had only been Georgiana to be hurt, Luke would never have gone after Swift. Luke had realized Clint Swift could spend the rest of his wretched life in Mexico and never receive the punishment he deserved for shooting Gilbert in cold blood. Swift had thoughtlessly taken a good man from his wife and children. Luke knew Jim couldn't handle a gun like he could. It wasn't in Jim's nature to challenge Swift head-on. Jim was not only his friend but had become the brother he had never known and likely never would.

When Luke confronted Clint Swift, he watched Clint's hand move toward his gun and draw. The instant Luke pulled the trigger, seconds ahead of Swift, the faces of John Martin and Harold Newton flashed before his eyes. He felt no pity as he watched the worthless man stagger backward and fall to the ground. Luke saw the look of fear in his eyes, watched the crimson stain spread across his chest, listened to him gurgle, gasp for air, and die. He couldn't help but wonder if what Clint Swift had done to Gilbert crossed his mind, as he lay dying in much the same way he had ended Gilbert's life. Luke's pent-up hatred for John Martin, Clint Swift, Harold Newton, and other lowlifes like them ebbed away. In the span of mere seconds, Luke felt a release from his long years of pent-up hate and anger. Until this moment he would have never thought it possible to be free of those bitter feelings filled with disgust and hate.

Luke holstered his gun and walked calmly toward his horse, convinced he would never kill another man.

As the months passed, Luke had come to terms with what he had done and thanked God for the peace he now felt. In his heart, he knew that, at some point in the future, he would return to the river, a place of solace. He would become a river rider again.

Afterword

The premise for this fiction book is based on verbal and written information furnished by Mr. Billy Gene Moses, who retired in 2009 as Assistant Director for the U. S. Department of Agriculture Inspectors along the Texas and Mexico border. The inspectors are often referred to as tick riders or river riders.

Billy said he started to cowboy when he was in middle school. He graduated from high school in 1952 and attended college for a while but decided that was not for him. He worked on ranches for several years and served in the U. S. Army from March of 1955 until 1957. He went to work as a Tick Inspector but returned to the army in 1961 to 1962.

Billy laughed as he told about working in a movie starring Charlton Heston that was filmed at Alamo Village near Brackettville, Texas. He recalled being paid $15.00 a day to ride his horse as an extra in the movie, but if he fell off his horse, he got paid $35.00 a day. He recalled that while it lasted, that turned out to be better pay than working on a ranch for $75.00 a week.

After leaving the army in 1962, Billy returned to work for the

USDA. When he retired, he had 67 inspectors (river riders) under his supervision.

The program was started over one hundred years ago to prevent the spread of tick disease and anthrax. The early cowboys learned to scratch the stock for ticks and recognize the signs displayed by sick livestock. In the early years, the program was handled on and off by state inspectors.

The area the river riders cover runs about five hundred miles, from Amistad Dam, near Del Rio, Texas, to the Gulf of Mexico. The inspectors still travel by horseback, as motorized vehicles cannot always reach remote areas they have to inspect. Today there is still a dedicated group of river riders working to protect the United States against the spread of diseases brought across the Rio Grande River by infected livestock from Mexico.

Sadly, Mr. Moses passed away in December 2019. I have always felt it was a true privilege to get to know Mr. Moses. I gained valuable information from his willingness to share some of his personal experiences and materials. He was a fine gentleman and is deeply missed.

Acknowledgments

I want to recognize and thank my son, Brian McGonagill, for his interest and unwavering support of my writing. Brian, you are invaluable.

The Twelve Mile School

HEARTS OF TEXAS, BOOK 3

"Miss Hammon, Miss Hammon! Riders are comin'," Slim yelled as he came running into the classroom. He was breathing hard and his eyes were huge with anticipation as he pointed toward the south. "It might be hi — hi — him!" he stuttered in animated expectancy, thinking about who might be riding toward the school.

Ester quickly rose and hurried to the window to look at the approaching riders. She strained her eyes to see how many riders were coming toward the school. She could make out a dozen or more riders coming fast, she speculated, as she squinted her eyes again in an attempt to see more details.

She couldn't see any particulars of their dress at this distance, but so many riders looked very suspicious. Ester blinked her hazel eyes to clear her vision. The cloud of dirt their horses were kicking up drifted toward the clear morning sky.

Ester was a tall woman, five foot eight inches in her stocking feet. She wore her straight dark blonde hair pulled back and tied at the nape of her neck. Her features were rather plain with thin eyebrows, a straight nose, and small hazel eyes. Her one point of beauty was her full lips that turned up at the corners, making her look as though she were constantly about to smile. Ester normally possessed a pleasant demeanor, but she could be firm or even defiant if necessary!

An uneasy feeling of foreboding filled Ester as she keenly watched the oncoming riders. "Go ring the bell and give the signal," she told Slim in as calm a voice as she could muster. She didn't want him to become more alarmed and scare the other children.

Ester could feel her entire insides begin to quiver, and her palms began to sweat. She started closing the windows and securing shutters. Ester had to remind herself again to remain calm so the children would not panic.

Slim did not hesitate as he grabbed the bell rope and gave it a fierce yank to set the bell in motion.

He shouted at the top of his voice, "PANCHO VILLA COMIN', PANCHO VILLA COMIN'!" The girls dropped their jump ropes, and marbles were left on the ground as the children came running at full speed into the safety of the school. As they arrived, the older students helped Ester close the remaining windows and shutters.

Six-year-old Susie Hoffman began to cry, her chin quivering as tears streaked her dusty cheeks. "Don't cry, Susie," Ester soothed, as she pulled the child into her arms. "Here, crawl under this desk next to Lilly and hold her hand. Don't come out until I tell you it's safe," Ester said, still managing to maintain her calm manner.

Ester felt her stomach begin to knot as she watched the frantic activity around her. She quickly counted the number of students and found one missing. She counted again as she knew everyone was present. Then she realized who was missing. "Where is Walter?" she shouted above the clamor. "In the outhouse," several answered in unison.

"Oh, dear me," Ester mumbled as she ran to the back window. She yanked back the shutters and raised the window. "Walter!" she yelled. "Stay in the outhouse; riders are almost here; don't come out now; just stay there. Do you hear me, Walter?" "Yes-um, I hear you," came Walter's muffled response.

Ester slammed the window shut and secured the shutters.

Someday when she knew Walter better, she needed to ask him why he spent so much time in the privy, Ester contemplated, worried he might have some stomach disorder.

She hurried to the door and lifted the loaded Winchester from the rack. Twelve-year-old Willie Hoffman and eleven-year-old Slim Fitzpatrick lifted two other guns and positioned themselves on either side of the front windows near the gun portholes. The third porthole, where Ester stood, was to the left of the huge front door. They were small side-to-side rectangular openings with hinged doors that could be opened from the inside. This gave Ester and the two boys a fairly good view of the road in front of the school. There were several more portholes around the other walls in the event someone tried riding around the building.

Available in Paperback and eBook from Your Favorite Bookstore or Online Retailer

About the Author

Judy McGonagill is a native Texan and loves the rich history of the Lone Star State. Judy grew up in a small town where church and school were the focus of the community. She has been married to her beloved husband for many years and has two adult sons. She is a retired teacher with an interest in history and enjoys writing historical novels.

www.ingramcontent.com/pod-product-compliance
Lightning Source LLC
Chambersburg PA
CBHW020551020726
47494CB00006B/2013